BOOKS BY

Rick R. Reed
=====================

Obsessed

Penance

A Face Without a Heart

Twisted: Tales of Obsession and Terror

IM

In the Blood

Deadly Vision

Rick R. Reed

Quest Books

Nederland, Texas

ISBN 1-932300-96-1
978-1-932300-96-3

First Printing 2008

9 8 7 6 5 4 3 2 1

Cover design by Donna Pawlowski

Published by:

Regal Crest Enterprises, LLC
4700 Hwy 365, Suite A, PMB 210
Port Arthur, Texas 7764

Find us on the World Wide Web at
http://www.regalcrest.biz

Printed in the United States of America

Acknowledgments

Thanks to my publisher, Cathy LeNoir, my cover designer, Donna Pawlowski, for her always-beautiful cover designs; my editor Sylverre, and to Rob Buco for providing the back cover image.

In memory of my mother, Theresa Annette Reed
1928 – 2007

"I scent the track of crimes done long ago.
Have I missed the mark, or, like a true archer, do I strike my quarry?
Or am I prophet of lies, a door-to-door babbler?"

~Cassandra, in Aeschylus' *Agamemnon*

Prologue

"FIRST OF ALL, there are rules." She sits back in her chair, green eyes regarding the young couple. "Before we go any further, you have to agree to them."

The pair is desperate. The woman nods, eyes rimmed in red, moist. The man says, in a husky whisper, "Yes. Yes. If you can help us find him, we'll agree to anything." He rubs his hands on his khaki pants and she notices they are already stained dark with sweat. She feels a glimmer of sympathy, but then checks it; she's learned that it's best not to get too involved. There are things she might discover that will make their pain hers, and she's had enough of that.

"The rules." She falls silent, waiting for them to look at her. The man's gaze darts, the woman seems fascinated by the nap of the carpet, but she will not speak again until she receives this tacit agreement in the meeting of their eyes. "The rules are simple. First, I will not get involved with the police. No matter what. You're free to consult them after you speak with me. You're free to work with them, but I will not. Use what I tell you, but don't ask me to tell them. Second, I can make you no promises. If we're lucky, I'll get some impressions. But that's all they are. Impressions. Do you understand?"

The couple nods. The man whispers, "Sure."

"I don't get anything definitive. I may be able to help, and then again, I may not. I just want you to understand that going in."

"But you've been able to help..."

She holds up her hand.

"I know what I've done. And for every success, there are two failures. At least. You hear more about the successes than the failures. I get impressions. I don't know where they come from. I don't know why they come. But understand, sometimes they don't come at all. And other times, they lead nowhere.

"The third condition is that I take no money for what I do. So please, no matter what the result, do not offer me money." She's had problems with credibility in the past because of this.

The couple nods again and she can see they're getting impatient. She wants to help them, but fears so much what she might discover that she feels something very much like a rat gnawing at the inside of her stomach.

"Have you brought me something? Something of your son's?"

The woman digs in her purse, sniffling. A tear drops from her eye and falls to the black leather of her purse. She brings out a mitten, bright red, knitted, and a little dirty; her hand shakes, holding it, and when she speaks, her voice wavers. Still, she speaks as clearly as she can, holding back the sobs that are lurking just beneath her quavering voice. "They found this in the back yard when he disappeared."

The seer nods and takes the mitten. She doesn't really need it, having already seen what they have come to her for. But she hopes holding something from the missing five-year-old will add more detail to the portrait she saw in a dream just last night. She turns the mitten over in her hands and closes her eyes.

The room is silent, the ticking of the wall clock the only sound as its minute hand counts off the seconds.

Behind her eyelids, there is a swirl of colors, red predominant among them. Her throat is dry and she tries to work up some saliva.

She sees a house with a stone chimney. A thin plume of smoke emerges from the chimney. The house is old, two stories, a dingy white with the paint peeling back to reveal rotting wood. The windows downstairs are covered with plastic, the kind of stuff you'd get from the dry cleaners. Upstairs, one of the windows is boarded over, the other cracked.

"I see an old house," she whispers, knowing that this clue is useless unless she can provide some real geographic markers.

"The house is on a hill, about halfway up." She sees the tree line above and below the house, the way the backyard rises steeply into the woods. This is a house that's not far away. She gets something, then: a detail that may help them.

"The house sits back from a cinder road, black cinders, like coal."

She breathes deep, turning the mitten over, forgetting, for the moment, where she is, and the people in the room with her.

"The yard's messy. The grass wasn't cut in the summer and it grows high and yellow. There's all sorts of stuff in the grass, an old lawn chair, rusty, with dirty green and white webbing that's ripped and shredding." Damn, she thinks, why all the detail about a lawn chair instead of something meaningful?

She tries to relax, putting herself in this cold place, standing on the road in front of the house. And she gets something she thinks might be useful.

"The house looks down on Summitville," she says, naming the place where all of them live, a little Ohio River town that's as far west in Pennsylvania as one can go before crossing the border into Ohio. "I can see the curve of the river and the bridge to New Hope."

In her mind's eye, she turns, swears she can feel the cold snap of the wind on her cheeks, smell the snow that's in the gray, low-hanging clouds, pressing in, ready to break open.

Is the boy in the house? Somehow, she doesn't think so. Somehow, she knows the house is nothing more than a marker. These facts come to her minus logic, but she trusts them, knowing implicitly that they're right.

They always have been.

She closes her eyes more tightly and looks down the road. It ends in a copse of woods not more than a hundred yards or so from the house. There's a stand of pines, maybe some maples, and beyond them, a grassy field.

The grass is trampled down in one spot. She moves closer, and sees the boy, face down in the snow.

She snaps her eyes open, the bile rising so strong she grips her desk for a moment, trying to center herself, wishing she hadn't seen what she had. She lets the reality of the room filter back in.

"You'll find your boy near that house. A house on a hill just up from where the bridge crosses from Summitville into New Hope. There's a cinder road that leads up to this house."

She feels her skin going pale and clammy. She can't tell them. She can't mete out that cruelty. Or would it be kind? She can't call it, but she doesn't want to be the one to tell them their little boy is dead.

"Is he okay?"

She shrugs. "I can't tell you that."

"But..." the father says.

She holds up her hand. "One more rule: when I'm finished, I'm finished." She looks at them, biting her lip, ignoring the ball in her throat. "Now go see if you can find your boy." She wishes she could give them more; wishes she had the strength to tell them all her vision has revealed. But that vision is heartless and she is not.

Part One

Chapter
One

SHE WAS ONLY thirteen. It wasn't fair she now lay, bound, waiting for death. Before, there had been struggling: clawing and fighting, scratching their faces, pulling at their hair, batting at whatever part she could reach. Her breath had come in choking spasms, adrenaline pumping, burning, heightening the hysteria so much she thought her air would be blocked. Then had come the dread that made her lose most of her fight, when her terror-addled brain had begun to accept that her fate was to die here, in this tiny, hot room, with the only witnesses to her demise the sparkling eyes of her killers and the maddening, crooked whirl of a ceiling fan long past its prime and wobbling, doing nothing more than blowing the overheated, moist air around the room. The dread had risen up, a nausea twisting her gut and making her afraid she would vomit. And then had come the numbness, a dull tingling throughout her body that precluded movement, stripping her of coherent thought.

They stood above her, her killers. Faces she had trusted, faces she had seen before, around her neighborhood. The man she and her friends had had a crush on. He used to drive by her little house on Ohio Street in his old red Mustang, looking the picture of youth, confidence, masculinity. His hair was dark, cut bristle-brush short, his face always clean-shaven, always alert, aware. Looking at things, or for things.

At her young age, the interest of a man in his twenties was inconceivable, although it had been something she had hoped for since the first day she had seen him, back at the onset of summer, when the sun had turned white-hot, burning up the grass and making illusory waves rise from the hot, cracked sidewalks. She'd watched him through those waves, a vision of heat—especially his mouth. Thin lips bordered rows of perfect white teeth and when he had smiled at her, only hours ago, she had lit up; a tingling had started in her toes and had worked its way up, until the color rose to her cheeks.

He had pulled to the curb and sat there, car idling. She sat in the front yard, sorting through Barbie clothes: ball gowns and swimming suits, miniskirts and stretch pants. He didn't say anything, not right away. She had looked at him once, then looked away, certain his interest could never be in her. Suddenly, she felt ridiculous with her metal trunk, her Barbie dolls, and all the outfits she had once been so proud to collect. Swiftly, she returned the clothes to their case and slammed it shut.

She leaned back, resting on her palms, and lifted her face to the sun. Its heat beat down relentlessly, making the skin on her face feel tight.

She felt his eyes on her still. She opened her own eyes a crack and regarded him peripherally. He really *was* looking at her! The adorable little smile that caused a dimple to rise in his right cheek deepened in the sun's play of shadow and light. She leaned back more, left hand reaching out to surreptitiously move the Barbie trunk further away. In this posture, here on the withered and brown grass, she felt that her breasts, little more than two tiny bumps an unkind boy at school had once referred to as her anthills, looked larger. She could be eighteen, couldn't she? With the right make-up and her hair pulled up...

But now her long blonde hair was pulled back in a ponytail, clipped with a pink plastic barrette. She wore a pair of cut-off shorts and an oversized South Park T-shirt belonging to her older brother. He would have killed her had he known she was wearing it. But he was away at the Y's summer camp and would never know the difference.

The idling of the car was like an animal purring.

And then the sun disappeared and she sat in darkness. Beneath her closed lids, she sensed someone standing over her.

Why hadn't she heard the slam of the car door? Her eyelids fluttered, but she did not open them. It would be just like her mother to come outside now and stand above her, hands on hips, and ask her what she thought she was doing.

"Lucy?"

Finally, she opened her eyes and blinked at the brightness of the August day. He was smiling, dressed in pressed black slacks and a collarless white shirt buttoned to his neck. So unlike the other guys in Summitville.

"How did you know my name?"

"Oh, I make it my business to know the names of all the pretty young ladies around here."

Lucy felt the heat rise to her face once more. She grinned and could not think of a single word to say.

"Playing Barbie?"

She shoved the case further away, until it was completely out of her grasp. The case lay in the white heat, glinting, looking, she hoped, as if it had nothing to do with her.

"What? Oh...no, no. These are my little sister's. She always makes such a mess of things, and I was just organizing for her."

"What a good sister."

"Yeah, well..."

The two said nothing for a while and Lucy began to grow

uncomfortable under his gaze. She shifted her long, tanned legs in front of her, crossing them at the ankle.

"I was driving by and saw you sitting there and I had to tell you," he hunkered down beside her, "what a lovely sight you are. It made me stop, just to have a better look."

She laughed and thought she sounded way too much like the thirteen-year-old she was. "Thank you," she whispered, wondering where her voice had gone.

"No, thank *you*, for being here, for making the heat of this day a little more pleasant."

Oh, stop! she wanted to cry out, but whispered again, "Thank you."

He leaned closer, enough for her to feel his breath near her ear. In spite of the day's heat, his nearness caused gooseflesh to rise on her arms, her spine to tingle.

"Listen." He glanced around the empty street with eyes like none she had ever seen: green, ringed with thick black lashes. And in his gaze was a conspiracy that included only the two of them. "My car has air conditioning. I know this is out of the blue and all, but I wondered if you'd like to go for a ride with me."

Lucy glanced back at her house. She wished suddenly she lived in a bigger house, in a better neighborhood. Here on this modest residential street close to the river, her small white clapboard house was surrounded by other houses very much like it, some of them sporting tar paper that masqueraded as brick. She pictured her mother inside, on a vinyl-covered kitchen chair, watching *All My Children* on a thirteen-inch portable TV on the Formica-topped kitchen table. Her mother, she knew, would never approve of what was transpiring here, right in her front yard.

He stood suddenly. "Okay, okay, I get the message."

"Wait." She sat up straighter. A pickup rumbled by and left in its wake a smell of exhaust and a rush of hot air.

He turned. "What? Need to get your mom's permission?"

"Of course not!" Her voice came out higher than she would have liked, the whiny protest of a child. She stood. "I'd like to come with you. But I can't stay out too long." She was about to say, "My mom will be worried," but realized how immature that would sound. "I've got some people I have to meet in a little while."

He smiled. And the smile erased any nervousness she had about going with him. After all, she had seen him around the neighborhood dozens of times. He wasn't exactly a stranger, not really.

"That's fine, Lucy. I'll have you back within an hour. I promise. I certainly wouldn't want to get off on the wrong foot with you." He winked and she followed him to the waiting car.

Lucy tripped getting into the car. Her head bumped against the chrome surrounding the upper doorframe and her hand slid across the black vinyl seat. The laugh that followed came out high and flighty: a little bird. Lucy reddened once more, embarrassed by her klutziness.

He was grinning, already behind the steering wheel. "Don't worry about it. We are all prey to tiny lapses in coordination."

He drummed his fingers on the steering wheel while Lucy settled beside him, doing her best to recover her composure; with elaborate care, she positioned herself on the seat and crossed her legs. She admired her legs and hoped he did too: long and tan, smooth, the legs of a woman.

It was then she felt, more than noticed, the presence of someone else in the car. Lucy turned and saw her for the first time. In the back sat a young woman. Her hair, like Lucy's, was blonde, but more of a brassy platinum shade. She wore a pair of dark glasses with cat-woman frames, bright red lipstick, and a silk scarf tied around her neck. Her simple white shift contrasted sharply with her peach-colored skin. Lucy thought she was about the most glamorous thing she had ever seen in Summitville.

He noticed her looking. "This is my girlfriend, Myra. Myra, say hello to Lucy."

"Hello, Lucy."

Did Lucy detect a very slight British accent in the gravelly voice? Whatever it was, this woman seemed so self-possessed and confident, Lucy's dismay that this man had a girlfriend was almost overridden. Lucy was fascinated.

Lucy turned back to the man. "I don't think you told me your name."

He laughed and Lucy forgot about Myra. His laugh was musical, setting her heart to thumping. She wondered what it would be like to slide closer, to rest her head on his shoulder.

"It's Ian." He slid a pair of Ray-Bans over his green eyes and shifted the car into drive. They sped away from the curb.

Lucy watched as her little white house grew smaller in the side-view mirror.

It wasn't long before they were pulling up in front of a trailer on the outskirts of town. Lucy was disappointed; the dwelling didn't seem to fit Ian's character at all. She had expected something more romantic, a houseboat moored on the Ohio River, a high-rise apartment in nearby Pittsburgh, a mansion, a log cabin, anything but a trailer.

And it wasn't even a nice one. Set up on cinderblocks, the trailer was a big box wrapped in harvest gold and dingy white aluminum; a piece of the skirting had torn loose at one end, and there was rust around the corners.

Ian shut the car off and draped his arm across the back of Lucy's seat. "It isn't much, love, but it's all I've got. Care to come inside or should we take you home?"

"Oh, just take her home, Ian. She'll be late for supper," Myra said from the back seat, where she hid behind a cloud of cigarette smoke.

"I'd love to come inside. This is where you live, right?"

Ian laughed. "Yes, for now. Are you sure you have time?"

Lucy glanced down at her watch, embarrassed suddenly by the pink vinyl strap and the Hello Kitty face on the dial. She would have to get a new watch soon, no matter what. Mom would probably be wondering, right about now, where she had gone off to. "I have a little time. Let's go in. I want to see."

Lucy followed the two of them toward the trailer. Ahead of her, there was a copse of maple trees on a bluff. The Ohio River, looking brown and stagnant in the milky white light, curved as it made its way south.

Inside, the sudden change from the day's withering brightness to the dark interior blinded Lucy and she felt her first moment of panic. Neither of them said anything and she suddenly felt helpless. For the first time that day, she questioned their interest in her and thought herself foolish for not having wondered why a young couple in their twenties would want to bring her home.

But she *did* look older, didn't she?

Of course she did. Ian confirmed it. "We're going to have a glass of wine, Lucy. Would you care for one?"

A flush of pleasure rushed through her. They *did* think she was older, a peer. Perhaps they were just trying to make friends. Before the onset of the summer, she couldn't recall having seen either of them before. But what would Mom say if she came home with liquor on her breath? She groped in her pocket, thankful for the piece of Bazooka there.

"Well, maybe I could have just a small one."

"Excellent!" Ian clapped his hands together and went toward the kitchenette behind him. He took a jug of white wine from the refrigerator and poured three glasses.

After they were settled in the living room and Lucy's eyes had adjusted to the dim lighting, she said, "This is much nicer than I thought."

Ian and Myra exchanged glances, laughing, and Lucy wondered why. The place was run-down: the carpeting, a beige and brown tweed, was threadbare, and the furniture was a hodgepodge of mismatched pieces, all of it looking secondhand. The scarred coffee table held an odd assortment of items: a book called *Crime and Punishment*, a ceramic skull, and two black votive candles set on tin jar lids.

But the dimness and stale air bothered her more than anything else. Why were all the curtains drawn? "It's kind of dark in here, isn't it?"

That remark they found amusing as well; their laughter began to make her uncomfortable. She scratched her arm.

Ian said, "Lucy, haven't you noticed? It's hot outside. It keeps things a little cooler if I keep the drapes drawn."

Of course.

After they had finished their wine — well, after Ian and Myra had finished theirs, Lucy thought it tasted horrible — Ian disappeared for a moment. When he came back, he was carrying a video camera. It was one of those tiny ones you could almost palm in your hand, and the red light on it was blinking.

What was going on?

"Smile for the camera, Lucy."

Lucy tried to smile, but things were getting too strange. She managed to turn up the corners of her lips in a grin. Suddenly, Myra was on the couch next to her, too close, really: Lucy smelled her perfume. It was too sweet, with a bitter undertone. It smelled like she had rubbed incense on herself. The scent of the perfume combined with cigarettes and wine caused Lucy to lean back, away from Myra. Suddenly, Myra didn't seem as glamorous as she had in the car.

Myra put her arm around her and mugged for the camera. "Come on, Lucy, smile!"

Lucy bit her lip, thinking of the Barbie trunk she had left on her front lawn. Kelsey Timmons, just down the street, had coveted Lucy's collection for years now; she wouldn't be above taking the whole trunk home, given the opportunity. "I think I'd like to go home now." Lucy tried to look anywhere but into the lens of the camera. She wished he would turn it off.

"Nonsense!" Ian exclaimed.

"You just got here, dear," Myra whispered to her. Her lips were too red and Lucy suddenly felt sick.

"Please, I need to go home now."

"Just a few more minutes." Ian hunkered down in front of the two of them, moving the camera slowly up and down their bodies.

Lucy lifted the wine to her lips just to have something to quell her mouth's terrible dryness. She began to perspire, dampening at her armpits, her hairline. She whimpered, "You said no more than an hour."

"Such a pretty girl," Myra whispered, lifting Lucy's ponytail and turning it in her hand. "Oh, to have such tresses. What I wouldn't give to have hair this color." She giggled. "Naturally, I mean."

"Jealous?" Ian stood and aimed the camera down at the two of them.

Lucy shot up, heat and fear coalescing to make her sick. The walls of the trailer closed in. "I don't feel so good. Can we go now?"

Ian set the camera down for a moment and gave her his most winning smile. "The answer to that question, my sweet, is no."

AND NOW, HERE she lay on a mattress in the back of the trailer, arms and legs splayed apart, wrists and ankles bound by clothesline. The bindings were so tight she could feel a needle-like tingling in her fingers and toes; the rope chafed against her, cutting into her skin.

"Smile for the camera, Lucy!" Ian said, cheerful, as if this were a birthday party or holiday celebration rather than what it really was: an abduction. Lucy tried to turn her head away from the camera, but Ian followed her. "C'mon! I see that grin coming..."

"No." Lucy whimpered, tears stinging her eyes, trickling down her face and into her ears, tickling. She could hear the whirr of the camera lens as Ian zoomed in for a close-up of her tear-stained face.

"Please...I just want to go home."

"Why? The fun's just beginning." Ian nodded to Myra, who knelt beside the bed and began tugging at Lucy's shorts. Ian moved around the room with the camera, getting different angles.

Myra looked at Ian. "We should have gotten her undressed before."

"Scissors are in the kitchen drawer. You know where."

Myra left and came back in moments with a pair of kitchen shears. She knelt once more beside Lucy, snipping through her brother's treasured T-shirt. Kevin would kill her. Myra then cut her shorts off. And her underwear.

Lucy squirmed, helpless under the relentless eye of the camera. Everything was exposed. Everything. This wasn't how it was supposed to be.

And he kept moving around with that camera. What was he going to do with the tape? Lucy struggled against the bindings, the rope cutting deeper and more painfully into her wrists and ankles with every movement. She was panting. "I need to tell you something?"

Ian lowered the camera for a moment to run his fingers along Lucy's naked body. "A splendid sacrifice," he whispered, his breath coming in short gasps now as well. "A splendid sacrifice for the Beast."

"Yes." Myra reached over and cupped one of Lucy's small breasts, thumb and forefinger moving around her nipple, pinching.

"Please! I have to tell you something."

"For God's sake, what is it?"

Her breath was coming faster now, faster, and she couldn't seem to gulp in enough air. "I can't breathe. Please."

Ian and Myra regarded one another, and in Lucy's wild gaze, they seemed to be snickering. What was funny about this?

"Please, you have to let me go. I can't breathe."

Myra said, "The Beast is watching."

"He's waiting."

Lucy gasped. "I have to go now. My mom..."

Ian picked up the camera and recorded while Myra ran her hands over Lucy's body, harder and harder, the strokes hurting, chafing against her skin. "Please stop, please. You're hurting me. Why are you doing this?"

"The Beast is hungry." Ian's voice was dead, a monotone.

"My mom and me, we have someplace we have to go. She'll be looking for me."

Myra said, "She'll be looking for a long, long time."

Lucy screamed.

"Shut her up!" Ian barked.

"Who's going to hear her, all the way out here?"

"Just shut her up, Myra! The Beast will not be pleased."

Myra disappeared. When she came back, she had a black bandanna and a roll of duct tape in her hands.

"No, please. I'll be quiet. You have to listen to me. Mom! Mom! Please, you have to let me go. I swear on the Bible I won't tell anyone what happened. Please." The tears were hot, salty; they stung her eyes.

"Sorry, dear," Myra said, "The Beast does not approve of screaming."

"I won't scream. I promise. My mom..."

But Lucy never got the chance to finish her sentence. Myra stuffed the balled-up bandanna in her mouth and deftly put two strips of duct tape across her mouth. Lucy kicked as best she could with the bindings on her. She was going to suffocate and no one knew where she was. She saw her mother suddenly, standing in the yard and calling her name, telling her supper was ready. Her little brother, Todd, stood on the porch, sucking his thumb.

Lucy turned, trying to hide her face from the camera. Myra slapped her. "You're making this very difficult, you know." Her face was sweaty and her hair had come undone; wisps of it hung down in her face. "The more you struggle, the longer this will take."

And then Lucy was trembling. The shaking came of its own accord, but grew in intensity, rising with her fear, her body writhing on the bed.

Myra held her down, straddling her. "Get the pictures, damn it!"

Ian kept moving, back and forth, getting closer, then further away. How would her eyes look on the tape? Did they reflect her terror?

"To the Beast, we make this humble offering," Ian said.

Then Myra was sliding a pillow out from under Lucy's head.

And then she raised the pillow up.

And then Lucy watched as the pillow grew larger and larger, until all that existed was the pillow, darkness, and no air.

No air.

Chapter
Two

THE CLOUDS WERE the first thing making Cass nervous. They were angry, bruised, hulking gray shapes pressing down on the hills.

"Oh, there's one hell of a storm coming, that's for sure," she whispered as she chopped the burdock stalks into sticks for the Sicilian fritters called cardoons. Already, the wind was kicking up, becoming cold. The last few days had been unrelenting: temperatures in the upper nineties and humidity so thick you could drown in it. Miserable. She had lain at night in front of a box fan as it whirred and blew the hot air around, offering no relief. It was like lying inside a convection oven.

She beat eggs, added some grated Romano and salt and pepper and set the batter next to the burdock stalks. She wiped her hands on a dishtowel hanging on a rack under the sink.

The second thing making Cass nervous was that she couldn't see Max. Max, at seven, was prone to distraction and wandering away. Usually, such distraction wasn't of much concern, because Summitville wasn't like Pittsburgh, about forty-five minutes west, with its crime and traffic. Summitville perched on the banks of the Ohio River, overlooking the hills of the northern panhandle of West Virginia. It was mostly known as a town where nothing ever happened. Sometimes, the inactivity seemed like a drawback, but at other times, like when you had a seven-year-old boy, living in a dull, backwater town, where the worst crime you could remember was some kids breaking into Bricker's drug store last summer, was a real benefit.

So, why did Cass suddenly feel something wasn't right? Why did the fact that Max was no longer in the backyard make her queasy?

Cass and Max didn't live in some sort of exclusive area; their little house was surrounded by others much the same: older houses covered in peeling paint, rusting aluminum siding or asphalt tile that was supposed to look like brick, but never did. Cass had grown up in this little hollow down by the Ohio River and knew most of her neighbors. Just as they had watched her playing from their porch swings and gliders, many of the same people watched Max, even though their hair had turned gray and their children had grown up and moved away, especially when the steel mill closed down. The promise of any prosperity had closed down with it.

Maybe it was just the wind that made her feel so cold. The temperature had dropped at least fifteen degrees in the past half hour. This drop, coupled with the slate-blue clouds perched on the southern horizon, did much to raise the gooseflesh on her forearms. The chill might have been welcome if Max was at the kitchen table, playing with his Hot Wheels.

But he was not. And Cass, a single mother on the younger side of thirty, knew that at least a portion of the goose bumps on her thin arms were from a distinct, yet inexplicable, dread and not the cold breeze, the dark clouds, and the imminent storm making its way into Summitville.

The Swiss chard waiting to be cleaned could wait, as could the tomatoes from her garden, still unsliced. Cass did not like Max being out where she couldn't see him as a storm bore down. She didn't like it at all.

She slid into a pair of rubber thongs she kept by the kitchen door. "Bum!" she cried out, and a tan and black dog about the size of a boxer, with bright brown eyes, bounded into the kitchen, toenails clicking on the Linoleum. "Wanna go outside, boy? Wanna help me find Max?" Bum had been left behind two years ago by Stephanie, Cass's "friend and roommate" as her mother liked to put it. Stephanie couldn't stand the stifling life of a lesbian in a small town and had set out for the bright lights, tall buildings—and women—of Pittsburgh. Once she packed up her Nissan pickup, Cass never saw her again, and never found love again.

But enough about Steph! Cass didn't know why she ever bothered to think of the woman, who had never been much for motherhood...or even dog ownership, for that matter. "C'mon, Bum!"

Outside, the wind was getting fierce. Papers and small pieces of gravel skittered across the road in front of the house. Cars passing by had turned on their headlights, piercing the odd, darkening afternoon light. The maple trees lining the road bent in the wind, like fingers splayed backward. The sky had a funny, greenish tinge to it and Cass had seen that weird green color enough times to know what it portended.

Cass made her way down First Avenue, looking from side to side and pausing occasionally to rub a piece of grit out of her eye. "Max!" she cried out tentatively. "Max!" a little louder when there was no response.

A drop of water landed on her arm, icy. The rows of houses lining the yellow-bricked street had empty porches, everyone gone inside. The lights switched on inside the houses made them look like sanctuaries and Cass wished she could be in her own sanctuary, with her own son, smells of the Sicilian peasant food she had grown up on filling her little house. Cass supposed her neighbors had all retreated into their living rooms, where they could turn on the Weather Channel or listen to the radio, to validate what was happening before their eyes.

Everyone, that was, except for Lula Stewart, bless her. Lula, who had lost her husband the winter before, still sat on her glider, wispy dyed-black hair being lifted by the wind.

"He went thataway," Lula called, pointing to where First Avenue dead-ended at the woods.

"Great," Cass whispered to herself, then said to Lula, "Thanks. I'm going to wring his little neck for him."

"Be nice, Cass. He's only seven."

"I know, I know." Cass headed for the darkness of the trees at the end of the street; as she picked up her pace, so did the wind and the droplets of water, coming heavier every second.

The sky flashed with white light. Cass gasped as a crack of thunder ripped through the air, reverberating through the ground and leaving in its wake the smell of ozone. "God, that was close." Why didn't Max have the sense to come in out of the rain?

The rain poured down so hard it almost blinded her. In seconds, her clothes were drenched, her T-shirt and cut-offs clinging to her like a second skin. The sky blackened into premature night, brightened only by the lightning which rent the sky in two. The thunder's crash made Cass shriek with each boom. The volume and the bright light had a direct line to her heart, which began to pound faster.

"Max!" she screamed above the wind that was now lifting twigs and whole clumps of leaves from the trees overhead. An orange drink carton hit Cass in the back of the head.

"Max!" she cried, despairing, and watched as Bum ran back toward the house, tail between his legs. "Traitor," she whispered.

The woods were even darker than the street had been. Cass held her hands out in front of her to avoid crashing into trees. Already, her thongs were making a sucking sound as she pulled her feet out of the mud.

Cass sluiced water from her face, flung her black hair back, and tried to see. In the brief bluish flash of lightning, the woods looked empty. She wished she had seen Max cowering under a tree, running toward her, running *away* from her, anything but this dreadful emptiness, abandoning her to the woods and the storm.

"Max!" she cried again, trying to keep her voice on an even keel, so he wouldn't think she was angry, so he wouldn't hear her despair and terror. "Max, if you can hear me, yell. I'm not mad." And she wasn't, not at her little boy anyway, whom she pictured trembling under a tree or huddled under a neighbor's porch, shivering from fear and cold. But she *was* angry at herself, for not keeping better tabs on the weather and the whereabouts of a seven-year-old. What was wrong with her? Maybe her mother was right, maybe Cass was too young (and alone) to take on the responsibility of rearing another human being. "Max!" she cried again, competing for dominance with the wind, the thunder, the driving rain.

But all that answered her was the roar of the storm and the sound of detritus whistling through the air and smacking against the trees. Cass was beginning to think her quest was in vain, that Max was probably already at home, sitting at the kitchen table and wondering where she was.

It happened so quickly Cass only experienced the event through her instincts, like an animal.

The flash was so bright, Cass shut her eyes and gasped.

The air filled with the smell of ozone. Hair stood up on the back of her neck.

The rumble of the thunder deafened, so loud and close it drowned out her scream. And the crack of the tree branch above her was like the crack of a whip.

The branch coming down on her head brought her to her knees. She wasn't even aware of the crushing pain to her head.

Chapter
Three

"NANA? IS MOM over there?"

Sarah D'Angelo closed her eyes and clutched the crucifix on her neck. She made a "tsk" sound she hoped Max hadn't heard. Would her daughter never change? Never accept responsibility? Here was Cass's seven-year-old bastard (*now be kind*, Sarah thought, *be kind*) calling to see where his mother was. In the middle of an awful thunderstorm, no less.

"No, Max, your mother isn't here." Sarah never knew what to say to the boy. He wasn't like other kids. He spoke way too clearly, even when he was two, three years old, and his vocabulary seemed too mature for his age. "When was the last time you saw her?"

"She was making supper and I was in the yard. I went down the street to see if Theresa could come out and play and maybe her mom would let her eat with us." Max took a breath. "Theresa wasn't home and when I got back here, the storm had started and Mom wasn't home."

Sarah twisted the phone cord around her finger, wondering what she should do. Her husband, Sam, in the living room watching *Jeopardy!*, would suggest they go over to Cass's immediately, if only for the sake of the boy. But Sam didn't know Cass like she did; he'd always been too soft on the girl. Imagine, up and leaving a seven-year-old boy to fend for himself with no word of where she'd gone. Sarah peered through her black horn-rims out the kitchen window. It looked like night out there, and it sounded like they lived closer to the railroad than they actually did.

"Nana? What should I do?"

Sarah sighed. She guessed she would have to abandon her own dinner of *pasta fagioli* and walk over to Cass's. In the process, she would get drenched and supper would be late. It would serve Cass right not to — what was the word they were using these days? — not to *enable* her.

Sarah looked to the Dutch oven on the stove, where the beans and red sauce were bubbling, steam rising up from them, and decided she would *not* be used like this. Sam could walk over. Let him get wet. She had dinner to make.

"Nana?"

"Yes, Max. I'm going to send Pop over. He'll be there in just a few minutes."

Sarah hung up the phone without saying goodbye, or even checking to see if the boy had heard her, then felt guilty. Max was, after all, only seven, and probably scared out of his mind.

SAM D'ANGELO LOVED *Jeopardy!* He had watched the game show for years, since back when it wasn't electronic and its host was Art Fleming. He liked playing along (especially when the category was geography of some sort) and imagined that some day, he would get out to California, where he could be a contestant himself.

Alex Trebek had just announced the category for Final Jeopardy! and Sam leaned forward. He would bet a lot on "European Rivers," if he had been playing.

"Sam?"

Sam sighed and ran his fingers through his thick, close-cropped gray hair. He could sense his wife standing in the archway between the dining room and living room, her sizable shadow falling over his shoulder. "What is it, *bella*?"

"Cass's not home."

"And?"

"Well, it's just that Max called and he doesn't know where she is."

"What?" Sam turned in the recliner to regard his wife. "Max doesn't know where she is? In this downpour? Where could she be?"

Sarah rolled her eyes. "That's what we all want to know, Sam."

Sam stood, abandoning "European Rivers." "I guess I better get over there and see what the hell's going on." He glanced out the picture window. It looked like the wind, thunder and lightning had died down and the rain had settled into a steady downpour. It would be good for the lawn.

He glanced at his wife as he headed for the closet and his slicker. She had twisted her mouth into a straight line, indicating her disapproval.

"Cut it out," he said. "Max probably wandered off and she's out there, trying to find him."

Sarah returned to the kitchen, calling over her shoulder. "If she isn't home, bring Max over here. He can eat with us tonight."

As he headed toward the back door, Sam thought he'd never given much credit to inexplicable "feelings." Things like premonitions were best reserved for TV shows and movies, not for real life. But he couldn't escape the fact that he felt cold, in spite of the fact that Sarah's yellow kitchen was warm. The oven was on for the biscuits she was baking and on the stove, the beans, tomatoes, macaroni and ham were bubbling in the Dutch oven.

So why did he feel cold? Why was there this cloying nausea in his stomach as if he'd gotten hold of something rotten?

The screen door slammed shut behind him. Even though his daughter and grandson lived only a block over, Sam ran the short distance to their little house, panting. He couldn't explain it and wouldn't have wanted to try if someone had asked, but he felt in his gut there was something terribly wrong.

His fears were confirmed as he entered the back door of his daughter's rented house. Max was sitting quietly at the table, small face creased with worry. The boy wasn't doing anything, just sitting there, hands folded in front of him and tears welling up in his eyes.

"I don't know where she is," Max whispered, trying with all of his seven-year-old will to put a little breath and bravery behind his words.

Sam saw the plate of burdock on the counter and the bowl of Swiss chard next to it. It was odd that Cass would just leave in the middle of making supper. He knew Sarah would have accused Cass of being irresponsible, of going off on a whim, but Sam had seen his daughter mature a lot over the years, as she grew into a responsible mother.

"It's my fault," Max whispered, staring down at the table.

Sam squatted down next to him. "Now, what do you wanna go and say a thing like that for?"

"Because I wandered off without telling her where I was going. She was probably out looking for me." Max sniffed and searched his grandpa's eyes for disapproval. "She prob'ly got lost in the storm."

Sam, smiling, pushed Max's blonde hair away from his forehead and let it fall back into place. "Don't be goofy. Your mother's lived around here all her life. I doubt she's lost. But you might be right about her being out looking for you." Sam tried to frown at the boy, to show his disapproval, but didn't have the heart, especially when Max looked so upset. "Most likely, she's on one of the neighbor's porches, gabbin'...and waiting for the rain to die down."

Why did Sam feel like he was lying? Why did he feel this urgency tugging at him to get out there and look for Cass? Why did it seem so imperative, as if too much time had already been wasted?

"What do you say we go out and look for her?"

Max hopped down from the kitchen chair and Sam could see he was relieved to have something proactive to do. He started toward the door.

"Whoa, there, son. Don't you have a poncho or something? Don't want you to catch your death."

Max left the room and came back with a yellow slicker pulled over his shorts and T-shirt. Sam took his hand and the two set off into the rain.

Max was the first to see her. He let out a yelp, a sound almost identical to the sound a dog makes when someone steps on its foot.

And then he was running.

Sam saw his daughter lying at the entrance to the wood and his heart lurched. For a moment, it felt like someone had knocked the wind out of him and he couldn't move, couldn't speak, couldn't stop the boy from running toward his mother, who lay, still as death, on a bed of mud mixed with pine needles. Her skin was waxy, ashen. A large tree branch lay near her head.

The worst thing about this picture wasn't Cass's stillness or the pallor of her skin, but the huge, bloody gash in her forehead. It was like a dent, raw meat showing through the broken skin. Sam was certain his daughter's face would have been hidden by a mask of blood had it not been for the downpour sluicing its magenta alarm away from her face, which looked almost as if Cass were in repose, as if she were sleeping.

Sam hurried after the boy and grabbed his shoulder just as they reached her. He tried to turn the boy away, not wanting this gruesome vision to be stamped into his brain.

Oh God, Sam wondered, his mouth gone dry, heart thudding, what if Cass was dead?

Max was whimpering as Sam held him back, fingers clutching the boy's frail shoulder. Sam wasn't sure how to proceed. Cass looked dead, lying there, so still. He couldn't lose his daughter, not on a summer day. Not when he had just been watching *Jeopardy!* and thinking about the *pasta fagioli* his wife was in the kitchen making. Cass's palms were turned up and blackened with mud, as if she had tried to catch herself when she fell and her hands slid through the moist earth. At first, Sam wondered if her palms were burnt, if she had been struck by lightning and the electric circuit had escaped through her hands. He was relieved when, stooping, the blackness came off easily with his touch.

He was also relieved to feel the pulse of his daughter's blood through her wrist. Thank God she wasn't dead. At least, not yet...

And then he noticed the tremor coursing through his daughter's body every few seconds. Cass needed help. Traumas to the head required quick and certain medical attention.

None of this seemed real.

He tightened his grip on Max's shoulder, who was straining against him like a dog on a leash when it spies a squirrel. He couldn't let the boy go.

Could she survive until they got help? Would she suffer permanent harm? Brain damage?

She looked so pale.

Sam felt helpless, watching the tiny rivulets of water break and course across her face. He felt a knot in his throat and wanted to do nothing more than sink to his knees and cry out. He loved this daughter fiercely and if she was gone, he didn't know how he would stand it.

Something had to be done.

He squatted down next to Max. "Listen, boy: your mom's been hurt. It might be serious...we need to get her some help right away." Why was it so hard for him to breathe? "You need to be a big fella for me. Can you do that?"

Max stared at him, wide-eyed, and nodded.

"I need you to run over to the Wyatts and ask them to call 911 and get an ambulance down here right away."

Max stared at him. "Is Mommy dead?"

Max sounded so plaintive, so young, that Sam was afraid he would burst into tears, but he knew couldn't do that. Maybe later, but not now. Not when he had to be the strong one. Not when time was in such short supply. He smacked Max on the butt. "Of course not, Max. She's just hurt. Now scoot, we need to get some help."

Max dashed off without a word, heading toward the Wyatt's green-shingled house. Sam bit his lower lip, gnawing at it until he got the surprise of a squirt of his own blood in his mouth. It tasted metallic, and Sam pushed at the tiny cut on his lower lip with his tongue. "Get hold of yourself, old man."

The ambulance would be coming soon, and with its flashing red lights and sirens, the neighbors would come out too.

And Sarah.

Sam could picture her running down First Avenue, wiping her hands on her apron, her face creased with worry, knowing that the commotion was for Cass, knowing, as a mother would, that something very bad had happened to her child.

Sam sucked in a great, quivering breath and thought he could already hear a siren in the distance. Perhaps he did. The hospital was only five minutes away.

And here came Max, running on little toothpick legs, blonde hair blowing back in the wind.

And the Wyatts, an older couple he and Sarah had known since they had moved to the little neighborhood down here by the Ohio River back in '63...they were trying to keep up with Max.

And behind them, Sarah, running, stumbling. Even in the rain, Sam could see she was crying, tears born of a terrible, yet still inexplicable, knowledge that something was very wrong.

Sam turned back to his daughter's twitching form and knelt on the ground beside her, tenderly touching her neck where a weak pulse beat. "Thank you," he whispered, "thank you."

Chapter
Four

HER AWAKENING CAME by degrees. First, the sense of an unfamiliar bed beneath her, linens starchy and stiff against her bare back. When her eyelids began to flutter, there were glimpses: metal rails on either side of her, a tray topped with a box of Kleenex, a vase of daisies, dials and lights, and a long metal pole with a fluid-filled plastic bag hanging from it. She noticed the tube going into a big vein on the back of her hand and, for just a moment, had to resist an urge to yank the tube from her vein.

Then she was back asleep, moving from semi-consciousness to sleep swiftly, with almost no change at all.

Walking down a dark corridor: narrow, colorless walls pressing in around her. If she raises her arms, she can touch both sides of the corridor as she moves along, toward a pulsating bluish light and the cry of a child.

The cry is familiar. It's Max. Comprehension comes full force: he is not lost, but needs her. She moves faster, faster, but it's weird: his crying does not get louder, nor does she seem to get any closer to the light she supposes signals the end of the corridor. It's as if, when she moves forward, the hall stretches.

"Max! Max, honey can you hear me?"

"Mama. Come and get me."

A shriek.

And suddenly, she was awake again. The sheet beneath her was drenched with sweat. Her hair stuck to her head and little beads of perspiration ran down her forehead and tickled the back of her neck.

There was pain, dull, constant, and thudding behind her eyes. Tentatively, she reached up, feeling a mass of gauze at her forehead. Even the slightest pressure on the bandage made Cass wince, sending bright tendrils of pain into her head.

A nurse stared down at her. When their eyes met, the nurse smiled. "Can you hear me?"

Cass moved her tongue around in her mouth, but she couldn't get it to wrap around any words. She nodded, staring plaintively up at the nurse's moon face, ringed with dark blonde hair. She recognized her as a girl she'd known in junior high school. Debbie something.

The nurse's hand on her forehead was cool, dry. "You don't need to say anything right now. I'm going to go get the doctor."

And Cass slept once more.

A rainswept landscape, thunder and lightning. So cold. Her clothes cling to her, hair plastered to her head, dripping down her neck, tickling.

Ahead of her a hill and at its top, Max.

She tries to run to him but every step she takes seems to make the hill recede farther into the distance.

And then she was awake once more. A different nurse, or perhaps an aide, stared down at her. This one was an older woman whose skin had seen far too much sun. Even now, it had a rich bronze hue and was the texture of distressed leather. Her hair was frosted, bubble cut. Her brown eyes seemed larger under the thick lenses she wore.

"Honey? Can you hear me?"

"Yeah." It hurt her chest to speak. "Where's Max?"

"Who, honey?" The woman's voice was raspy, telling a history of too many cigarettes. Cass suddenly had a vision of the woman at home, laying out in a floral print bikini too young for her, in the tiny backyard of a white aluminum-sided house. There was a little redwood table next to her yellow vinyl lounge and on top of it was a bottle of Budweiser, beaded with condensation, a black portable radio playing Shania Twain, and a ceramic ashtray, overflowing with Camel Light butts.

"Max, my son."

The woman bit into her lip, and then she smiled. "I'm not sure, *right now*, hon, but he's okay. I've seen him in here with his grandma." Her voice was gravelly, deep as a man's.

Cass glanced out the window. The day was cloudy. She must have been on a high floor because all she could see was a milky white sky and the tree-covered hills of West Virginia. "Why am I in the hospital?"

The aide busied herself for a moment, checking Cass's IV. She glanced out the window, then looked back to Cass. "You took a pretty nasty blow to the head. Looks like a tree branch caught you right in the forehead. Concussion, I guess. You've been out for quite a while, honey."

"What are you talking about?" Cass felt panicky. Her heart started to race. The woman's words were so simple. Concussion? How was she having glimpses into this woman's personal life and yet had no recollection of her own? "You're kidding me, right?"

"No, sweetheart. It happened. Yesterday afternoon. You made the paper." The aide, whose badge said her name was Wilda Carr, smiled at Cass when she told her this, as if Cass had accomplished some sort of feat. She fussed with Cass's blanket, pulling it up tighter around her chin.

Yesterday afternoon? Where had the intervening time gone? Cass felt too tired to wonder. Suddenly, all she wanted to do was sleep. Her eyelids felt heavy, burning, and it seemed like it would take all of her effort to just lift her hand to her mouth to stifle a yawn.

But what awaited her on the other side of consciousness?

And where was Max?

Cass forced herself to get up on her elbows. "Wilda, I really need to know about my little boy. Can I call my mom?"

Wilda wasn't sure what to say, and Cass knew it. Wilda wanted to get home, because tonight she was planning on meeting up with a guy named Lorenzo, who was all of twenty-six and supposed to be dating her daughter.

How? Why am I thinking these things?

Wilda smiled—falsely, Cass was sure. "Let me see if I can find the doctor, hon. Then we can see about makin' that phone call."

And even though Cass was certain Wilda had not spoken out loud, she could hear the woman's raspy voice as she left the room. "Damn her. Why couldn't she have waited until my shift ended?"

"YOU WERE LUCKY you weren't killed." The doctor brushed away a strand of hair from Cass's forehead. "That oak branch was heavy. We were worried there'd be serious damage. When they brought you in, the ER folks weren't sure you were going to make it." The doctor, a man who couldn't have been much older than Cass herself, smiled down at her. "But here you are. Twenty-four hours and some change later and you seem in pretty good shape. Blood pressure's low, your heart rate is good, and other than a nasty gash on your forehead, you don't look too shabby. We'll want to run a few tests—EEG, brain scan—just to make sure everything's functioning okay up here." The doctor tapped his forehead. "But I'm not foreseeing any problems. I mean, you're looking more bright-eyed every minute." He smiled at her. "I guess you should count your blessings it was the tree the lightning struck and not you."

The doctor's words, which should have been reassuring, weren't. They caused a kind of queasy panic to rise up in Cass. She couldn't recall much of the previous day at all. Certainly not being outside when a tree branch, freed by lightning from its connection to a trunk, had fallen on her *head*. *How in the hell...* Even when she used to drink (more than her share, at times) she had never experienced a blank space as some of her friends did, unable to remember how they got home or how they wound up in bed with a strange woman.

But that's what she had. A blank space. The last thing Cass could remember was making supper in the kitchen.

And looking for Max...

"My son. Do you know..."

"Max is fine. Your mom and dad brought him in last night. Smart little boy."

Cass closed her eyes with relief. There was something nagging her about Max. Something awry. But it seemed like everything was okay with him. She shook her head. "You know, I can't remember any of this. I mean, wouldn't you think that when a person gets hurt like I did, they'd remember? I mean, how exciting." Cass laughed. "And we get so little excitement here in Summitville."

The doctor shook his head, unsure how to take Cass, and then allowed himself a laugh. "Yeah, I think you're going to recover just fine." The doctor put his hand to Cass's shoulder and gave it a squeeze. *He lives alone. He's only been in Summitville since the spring and he knows hardly anyone. He spends most of his time watching CNN and sports on TV...when he's not at the hospital.* Cass glanced up at the doctor's dark-complexioned face. He met her gaze, smiled. "I'm Carlos Soto, by the way." He took one of Cass's hands in his own, squeezed. "I've been looking after you since they brought you into emergency yesterday."

Gingerly, Cass felt the gauze mounded on her forehead, the adhesive tape. Underneath the throbbing pain there was a tightness. Stitches? "How long will I have this?"

"A couple more days. I'll write you a prescription for pain. The stitches can come out in about a week. I'm sorry to say you're going to have a nasty scar. You might want to think about getting some plastic surgery down the road."

"Or getting some bangs."

Carlos Soto chuckled. "That would be the economical alternative."

"And that's the kind of alternative I'm always in the market for."

"What kind of work do you do?"

"I'm a waitress."

Carlos nodded. "Then you'll need to be getting back on your feet pronto."

Cass looked up into the face of the doctor and felt something akin to warmth. There was a kind of strength to his dark features that Cass liked and, for no good reason except what she would call intuition, immediately trusted. His dark hair was cut short, shaved on the sides and sticking up on top; it gave him a childish look that made Cass wonder if it took away some of his authority with older patients. His face was round, and he had eyes so dark Cass could hardly distinguish the pupils from the irises. "You're not from here, are you?"

"What gave me away?"

Cass thought of saying she just knew, but realized how stupid that would sound. She didn't even understand it herself. "We don't get many Hispanic people in Summitville. Pretty much German or English, bland salt-of-the-earth types."

"And I'm a Mexican spitfire."

Cass blushed, "Well, no, I didn't mean..."

"It's okay. I'm kidding. My family's originally from Cuba, but I grew up in Chicago." Carlos glanced down at his watch. "Listen, I have rounds to make, but I'll check in on you in the morning. Okay? We should probably be able to release you then. Anything I can get you?"

"I'd love to see Max."

"I'm sure he'll be in soon." Carlos tapped his watch. "Visiting hours'll start in about an hour. Anything else?"

"How 'bout a paper? I hear I'm a celebrity."

"Oh, I think I can have one of the aides bring you a *Review*. I'm pretty sure you're on the front page: 'Local Woman Survives Head Trauma in Storm.' I guess that's big news for Summitville."

Cass shrugged. "It's big news to me, anyway."

Cass watched as the doctor left her room. She felt a funny mixture of anticipation and consternation. She wished she hadn't asked for the newspaper. She couldn't quite understand why, but there was an element of dread in its imminent arrival.

And that was bad. "Stop it, now," she whispered. Maybe she just realized it wouldn't be the world's most pleasant experience reading about how she had been taken down in the first round by the branch of an oak tree.

But that wasn't it. Cass turned to look out the window at the milky sky and waited for the newspaper, knowing it was about to bring her something a lot more jarring than news of her own accident.

But she had no idea where the knowledge came from and why it was causing her stomach to churn.

THE SUMMITVILLE PAPER was nothing much. It never had been—reporting on the lives of some 15,000 citizens filled usually no more than twenty or thirty pages. The national news occupied the front page and maybe continued on to the second. The remainder was taken up by advertising, editorials about such things as high school activities and earth-shattering decisions like whether local merchants should continue to stay open late on Thursday nights, and reporting who had gotten married, divorced, arrested, been involved in automobile accidents, or admitted to the emergency room of Summitville City Hospital. There was a comics page and a crossword puzzle, sometimes a syndicated movie review. If someone wanted something meatier, they purchased the Pittsburgh paper.

But still, Cass was more than a little intrigued when a nurse's aide brought her that morning's edition. It had obviously already been read, clumsily folded, the crossword puzzle attempted. But Cass could count on one hand the number of times she had been celebrated enough to make its pages: her birth, when she had been on the homecoming court in high school (a *Carrie*-like fluke...Cass had already been deep into her first crush on another girl and hadn't even known why she had accepted Tommy Nevins' invitation), when she had given birth to Max, and when she had sprained her ankle and had been admitted to the emergency room.

And here she was on the front page. There was no picture, but the headline was identification enough. Cass had assumed that when people got hit so hard in the head it knocked them unconscious for hours, they eventually died. But, obviously, that wasn't true, because here she was, feeling better, actually, with every passing moment. The article gave credit to quick action by the Summitville Fire Department in saving the "local woman's" life. "We were on the scene immediately," paramedic John Fore was quoted as saying, "and were able to restore the woman's breathing within a couple of minutes." Cass smiled, thank God for that. She went on to read how she had been rushed to the hospital and was now in stable condition.

Cass was just about to put the paper aside when another article caught her eye. "Teenager Reported Missing," by Dani Westwood. It wasn't so much the headline that got her attention, but the picture of the young girl beneath it. Pretty. Long blonde hair. And disturbingly familiar.

Even though Summitville was a small town, the girl's name, Lucy Plant, didn't ring any bells. Perhaps Cass had waited on her at the Elite, the diner where she worked. But still, no specific recollection came back. Cass couldn't visualize the girl sitting at the counter, nor at one of the booths.

And yet she looked so familiar, as if she were someone Cass was friends with, or even a relative.

Cass scanned the story. The girl had been reported missing by her mother yesterday afternoon, just before the storm that had caused such a turn in Cass's own life.

There were no clues. The girl, at least according to her mother, could not possibly have been a runaway. "Lucy's a good girl," Karen Plant had told Summitville police officer Myron Briggs. "She wouldn't even go down the block to visit a friend without telling me first."

The last time anyone had seen Lucy Plant was when her mother looked outside the living room window. Lucy had been playing with her Barbie dolls on the front lawn.

Cass closed her eyes. She remembered, suddenly, the storm coming, and not knowing where Max was. She sympathized with the girl's mother and the panic she must have felt when she couldn't locate her daughter.

A ceiling fan. Beneath her closed lids, Cass saw a ceiling fan. She didn't know why. She didn't own one herself, and the one in her parents' living room was an entirely different model from this one, which was white, with a plain globe. Her parents' fan had four frosted-glass light fixtures and faux wood blades.

Cass kept her eyes closed, watching the ceiling fan whirl, its blades blurring and becoming singular: there was something wrong with the fan. It didn't work quite right.

Cass felt nauseated and opened her eyes. Her face was glazed with sweat. Her stomach churned and she was afraid she would vomit. Why was seeing a ceiling fan so disturbing? Or was this some sort of aftershock, an effect of her accident in the woods near her house?

Cass didn't think so.

She glanced down at the face of Lucy Plant and sucked in some air. "Oh my God," she whispered, "she's dead."

The smell of the Ohio River, fishy and damp, suddenly came to her, even though her hospital windows were hermetically sealed and the river was a good four or five blocks away. Why had she said Lucy was dead?

What did she know about it?

She closed her eyes again and saw a blinking light: red.

What did it mean?

Part of her wanted to close her eyes again, to see if more of the vision would come to her; part of her dreaded ever closing her eyes again. Where was this coming from? *It's just aftereffects, Cass,* she told herself. *You suffered a blow to your head, brain-jarring. That's all.*

She lay back on the pillows, letting the newspaper drop to the floor. When she closed her eyes again, she saw the blinking red light and a shadowy figure behind it: a woman's head. The image, for no objective reason, was horrifying.

Cass sat up in bed, heart pounding. "No," she said loudly, then whispered, "no."

She forced herself to breathe deeply. She looked down at Lucy Plant's calm, smiling face again: the straight blonde hair, the kind someone more romantically inclined would refer to as "flaxen." The wide eyes, too big for her little-girl face, but which would someday be beautiful. The dusting of freckles across the bridge of her nose. The chipped front tooth.

Cass felt her eyes brim with tears, a lump in her throat. "So innocent," she whispered, rocking back and forth in the bed, unaware that she was even moving. "So innocent. What a waste." She smelled the river again, and when she closed her eyes once more, she had another vision: the brown murky water of the Ohio River, its tree-lined shores and...and... Cass bit her lip so hard she tasted blood.

A freshly dug grave.

Cass opened her eyes and batted at her own face, as if she could physically remove the odd imagery. She didn't want to see these things. It was like a dream, a nightmare, but she wasn't sleeping.

The images were so vivid—the knowledge so certain.

Lucy Plant wasn't coming back.

Her gaze fell upon a line of type in the news story about the girl's disappearance. Her mother was making a plea. "Please, if anyone knows anything about my daughter...if anyone has seen her, please, please, let us know. All we want is to know that she's safe. No. All that we want is for her to be home again, where she belongs. Her little brother misses her. I miss her. Her father...we all do. Please, if you know anything about our girl, come forward."

And Cass wondered what she should do. She visualized herself down at Summitville police headquarters, telling them she knew something about the girl's disappearance. "Yes, I had a vision. The girl is dead and she's buried near the river. I saw a ceiling fan and a blinking red light, like on a video camera."

She would be treated with understanding and pity. Scorn and laughter behind her back. The police would call some mental hospital in Pittsburgh.

But what could she do?

She did know something about Lucy Plant. She was sure of it. She wished she didn't, but there it was.

Cass flung the newspaper to the floor and forced herself to look out the window, where the tree-covered hills of West Virginia stared dumbly back at her, much as they stared dumbly at the shallow grave Cass was certain this poor young girl was buried in.

Footsteps. A child.

Cass sighed with relief. Max.

"I wanna see Mama!" he yelled.

And her mother was telling him to slow down.

It was the real world. Cass wondered if she'd ever be part of it again.

Chapter
Five

MYRA STOOD AT the bathroom sink, appraising her reflection. "Odd," she whispered to the platinum blonde waif gazing back at her. "So damn odd." The edges of the mirror were rimed with steam, so that her reflection had blurred edges, adding to the surreal aspect. It wasn't her. Myra wondered where the girl she had been had gone. Just a few months ago, she had been Penny Landsdale. She had lived across the river, in a small West Virginia town called New Hope, where she had been a senior at New Hope High. Penny looked nothing like Myra, she thought, opening a contact lens case. She slid the lenses onto her eyes, turning them from hazel to an almost electric green. The color was unnatural; Myra hated it, but Ian had bought the lenses for her and insisted she wear them. "Green is the color of the Beast," he had whispered in her ear as he pressed the small plastic case containing the lenses into her sweaty palms. "And the eyes are the window to the soul." He stared into her hazel eyes with his own green-lensed ones. "I want us to have the same window, so the Beast will know we're a pair." Myra hadn't understood him then and wasn't sure she did now. Still, Ian was handsome, with his dark, curly hair and chiseled features. Older. Not many boys had paid her much attention at school, not when she was Penny Landsdale. Not when she was twenty pounds overweight, with thick thighs and a big ass. Not with her acne and the gap between her front teeth. Not with that long, mousy brown hair that hung in split ends to the middle of her back, lank and thin.

But a man had paid attention to her. Twenty-four years old and handsome — Myra giggled — as the devil. She picked up a bottle of Cover Girl and began dotting her face with the peach-colored foundation. It hid the acne pretty well. Ian had taught her that. He had taught her a lot of things since school had let out last May and she had left her parents' home (over strenuous objections, but she wasn't about to be dragged down by those scenes right now). For example, he had taught her to cut all fats from her diet and to subsist on a diet of fruit and vegetables, both raw, and lots of water. The weight had melted off, and her love for this handsome stranger who had appeared almost out of nowhere, like some Prince Charming, had helped her keep it off. Now, when she looked at her naked reflection in the mirror, she saw the lines of her ribs below her small breasts. Her hips had shrunk, her thighs had gone from tree trunks to willow limbs. For the first time in her life, she was skinny.

And beautiful, she thought, smoothing the foundation into her skin, blending it below her jawline. Ian had cut her hair in the kitchen of his trailer, cut it short and bleached it platinum. The result had been startling. Myra had almost not known herself when Ian finished and finally allowed her to look in a mirror. She had giggled, a nervous high-pitched sound, equal mixture of glee and wonder. Her blonde hair, the crimson lips, the black lashes framing the green eyes and her newly thin body transformed Penny Landsdale into Myra Hindley—a name with which Ian had christened her. Where did he come up with such things?

She switched off the bathroom light and headed toward the bedroom, where Ian had laid an outfit on the bed for her: black leather skirt and a leopard print blouse that he had said she was to tie beneath her bust. Next week, he said, they would look into having her navel pierced.

God, she loved Ian. He was the only one who had ever managed to look beneath her exterior and see her for the sexy young woman she was. She had him to thank--and thank him she would.

But the Beast, as Ian referred to him, must also be thanked. According to Ian, the Beast was the source of her beauty. It was the Beast guiding his hand in her transformation.

Beast. Ian. Whatever. Myra knew only that she was happy and she would do whatever it took to hang on to that happiness.

No questions asked.

She paused in the bedroom doorway, hearing the bass roar of the Mustang's engine as it pulled up to the trailer. She closed her eyes, whispering, "Thank you." Allowing herself one final once-over in the mirror, Mrya tied the knot in the leopard print blouse so her navel showed above the black leather, and headed out into the twilight.

Their trailer wasn't much, Myra thought as the door swung shut behind her, but what a view they had. There was nothing else here on this hilltop other than woods. The hill behind the trailer banked sharply down, and below them, the village of Summitville, where warm yellow lights were just beginning to wink on in the frame houses. The small town was bordered by the greenish-brown curve of the Ohio River. Myra stared at its churning waters for just a second and felt an odd sensation in the pit of her stomach: nausea.

No, she wouldn't think about that.

She turned to the car, where Ian was just emerging. Tall, skin pale against his black clothes. He smiled and her nausea melted away.

She came to him, silent as a cat, a barely perceptible grin playing about her lips.

He cocked his head. "Are you wearing panties?"

She shook her head.

The next thing she knew Ian had flung her across the hood of the car, its dying engine hot beneath her; he'd crammed two fingers inside her, was kissing her roughly, holding her head by her hair. It hurt, and Myra whimpered, but as she felt the warm wetness growing inside her, sliding down, it felt better and she found her cries turning to gasps.

Ian unbuckled his pants.

"For the Beast," he whispered, pushing her legs back and, finally, biting her tongue so hard she tasted the metallic tang of her blood.

Later, after Myra had cleaned the blood from her thighs and the corner of her mouth, she sat with Ian in the living room. It was a cramped space, its furniture third-hand and threadbare, the kind of stuff one found piled in alleys behind homes that were, at best, considered modest. But with the curtains drawn and the coffee table transformed into a makeshift altar, replete with a dozen candles of varying sizes, shapes and scents, the room took on a different dimension.

Ian sat close, his arm a comforting weight across her shoulders. The room was silent save for the sound of a low-hanging branch hitting against the back of the trailer. The tree back there was a dead maple, its trunk stooped like the back of an old man.

This was their quiet time. This was the time when Ian did not speak to Myra of his financial woes, of how they were going to bring money in because he had quit his job as a caster at the pottery in the valley below them. Ian considered himself above working at the pottery, filling molds with the liquid clay called slip, moving down rows of molds, filling, filling all day long. No end to the monotony. No end to his complaining, Myra thought, no end to the long discourses on how the Beast had better things in mind for him and how they must trust in the Beast to take care of them. Would the Beast come up with the rent payment which was due next week? Would he deliver it to them in a blood-red envelope, left secretly outside their door while they slept inside, Myra's fitful slumbers interrupted by nightmares of being buried alive?

Ian, as if he had read her thoughts, her doubts, said, "We should pray to the Beast."

The two of them knelt before the coffee table, and each gazed into the flickering light of the candles. Why did Myra feel like laughing? There would be no mirth in the laughter.

Ian intoned, "Green-eyed Beast, master of all that is evil, we pray to you, offering up our bodies and souls in exchange for your sustenance." Myra, not knowing what else to do, bowed her head. Was it right to ape the practices she had learned as a child attending the First Lutheran church with her parents? Did the Beast require her to bow her head or would the Beast expect her to hold it high, in defiance of Christian traditions? (Christian mythology, Ian would have called it.) She glanced at Ian out of the corner of her eye and saw his head lowered, so assumed she was doing the right thing.

"In the name of all that is evil, we pray for guidance."

Myra bit her lip. She squeezed Ian's hand and tried, really tried, to believe that what they were doing was right and Ian knew best. After all, he was the one who studied the books: texts by authors with names like Alistair Crowley and Anton LaVey. He was older than she and, of course, far more worldly and mature.

Ian lifted his head and slid back onto the couch. After a second, Myra joined him.

He turned her head to his and stared at her. For the first time, Myra wondered what lurked behind those eyes. There was a deadness to them that belied the handsome face and strong jaw.

"The Beast has spoken. It's time for another sacrifice."

SHERYL MCKENNA WAS sixteen. "Sixteen going on thirty," her mother would tell her friends when they sat smoking in the kitchen, drinking coffee and complaining about the teenage children they had in common. Her mother hadn't understood her since she had reached puberty three or four years ago. And her stepfather, well, perhaps he had understood too well...

But there was no time to think of that now. Now was a quarter 'til eleven on a Thursday night and Sheryl was due to meet Mike in forty-five minutes. She looked at herself in the mirror, knowing Mike would like what he saw. Sheryl had inherited her late father's black hair, so dark it possessed almost a bluish sheen, straight and silky and hanging to the middle of her back. It was her best feature, a stamp of her father's Irish heritage. He had died when Sheryl was five. Her blue eyes ranked a close second, contrasting wonderfully, sexily, with her dark hair. Pale blue eyes that were ringed in black lashes that needed no mascara, even though Sheryl reached now for the Maybelline and began brushing at those same lashes, lengthening and thickening. It was important she look especially good for Mike tonight. Sheryl was a girl with plans.

The rest of her bore traces of her mother, a one-time alcoholic who had lately found religion. Sheryl knew that her mother, Janet, had been far wilder than Sheryl would have ever dreamed of being. She had heard the stories. Summitville was a small town and its secrets could never be buried very deeply. Janet McKenna was the kind of girl that boys snickered at when she walked by them at Summitville High. But their snickers were absent when they showed up late at night outside her house, tap, tap, tapping on her window, exhorting her to come out and play. Janet was a girl who just couldn't say no. Even now, her mother endured winks and stares from men on the downtown streets, at the grocery store, in the Laundromat. All of them, Sheryl assumed, had been "suitors" at one time or another.

But Sheryl retained, at sixteen, the youthful beauty to which her mother had long ago bid a reluctant farewell. The button nose, the full breasts, the small waist, the hips that flared out seductively, perhaps too big for a modeling career, but definitely attractive to boys...and men. Like Mike. Mike was twenty-five, a fireman with the Summitville Fire Department and all man: buzz-cut blonde hair, a moustache and blue eyes that rivaled her own, framed with the same thick black lashes. And his body...good Lord! The most serious weightlifters at Summitville High couldn't compete with Mike's hard body, which had almost no fat, and was blessed with perfect definition.

Sheryl lined her lips with a dark red that was almost brown, then filled in the rest with a paler red, a color called "Cherries in the Snow." She dusted her cheekbones with a little blush and looked at herself. She was beautiful. Never mind that all she wore on this warm night was a black camisole and ripped jeans. She slipped on the ring Mike had given her shortly after they had met early in the summer: a tiny, perfect sapphire set in sterling silver. Mike said it reminded him of her eyes.

Sheryl walked to the window. Gently removing the screen and box fan, she placed them silently on the floor. Tonight would be a big night. An important night. A night that would change Sheryl's life forever. Mike would be crazy not to take her up on her offer.

She swung a leg over the window sill, then slid down the side of the house, wriggling her toes for purchase in the moist earth. Once on the ground, she reached up, felt around, and located the screen so she could put it back in the window, loosely enough to get back in later, when the first pink rays of dawn peeked over the hilltops. This return was a scene Sheryl had repeated many times since she had first met Mike last summer, when she had been out with a bunch of kids from school, drinking beer and smoking weed on the banks of the Ohio. She had never been caught.

Well, she thought, as she started away from the house, lighting a Marlboro Light with a pink disposable lighter, she had, in a way, been caught, but not by her parents. It had been two months since Sheryl had any use for the tampons stashed beneath the sink in the bathroom.

At first, there had been worry, a kind of sick anxiety when a week, then two, had passed with no period. Mike had used condoms off and on, but despised them so much Sheryl hated forcing him. He had always pulled out, squirting his seed on Sheryl's flat belly.

Apparently, he hadn't always pulled out soon enough.

Sheryl moved down the cinder road in front of her house that led toward the banks of the river, keeping close to the trees so as not to be spotted by a neighbor who might tattle. The river, not far from the little one-story she shared with her mother and Rick, had a definite smell: fishy, but Sheryl liked it. There was something clean about its smell, and its waters, in the darkness, had always fascinated her ever since she was a little girl and would ride in the backseat of her mother's car, along Route 7, coming home from visiting relatives in Wellsville, Ohio. Sheryl would watch the moon on the water, watch as it seemed to follow them all the way back home to Summitville.

After tonight, Sheryl thought, turning down a path bordered by oak and pine trees that led her down to the water's edge, she might not need to sneak around anymore. After tonight, she might find herself making all sorts of changes: leaving home and setting up housekeeping with Mike, getting ready for their baby.

It was going to be great.

She paused for a moment, on top of a rise. Below her, the river flowed heavily; she listened to the water as it made its trip toward the Mississippi (she *had* paid attention in Geography, contrary to what her mother thought). And just upstream a ways, Mike's car, a dark blue Honda Civic, was parked, headlights extinguished, on a flat barren piece of land that jutted out into the river.

This was their spot. Sheryl made her way down the little rise, gripping tree roots for support. Reaching the bottom, she brushed her hands off, clapping them together to free them of dirt, and started toward the car.

Mike waited inside, his CD player on low. Strains of Led Zeppelin drifted out. Mike loved the "classic" stuff, which Sheryl had known nothing about until she met him. Her mother liked old music, too, but favored disco from the Seventies, when, Sheryl supposed, her mother was getting screwed in dance hall parking lots up and down the Ohio River between Summitville and Pittsburgh. This was the *II* album, the song "What Is and What Should Never Be."

Sheryl opened the door and slid in wordlessly beside him. Mike glanced over, giving her one of his lopsided grins, mouth turned up at one corner. He smelled of cigarettes and beer, a little after-shave. Old Spice. They didn't say anything and Sheryl leaned back against the seat as Mike took her in his arms, a little roughly, and began kissing her, forcing his tongue deep inside her mouth. He pushed her shirt up slowly, sliding it up over her bare skin.

It didn't take long. It never did. As the two of them silently pulled their clothes back on, Sheryl decided that this moment, when he was satisfied and so surely in love with her, would be the best time to bring up her news.

She shrugged her shirt back on and left her jeans in a bunch on the floor. She stroked his face, the stubble rough beneath her fingers.

"I've got some news," she whispered.

Mike lit a cigarette and blew the smoke out the window. "What?"

"Guess."

"C'mon, Sheryl."

"Just guess."

"You've made it for cheerleading." Mike reached down and cracked open a Bud, drank greedily from the can, and belched.

Sheryl mock-slapped him. "It's nothing like that. I wouldn't want to do something like that anyway. Bunch of losers, little girls."

"Well, what is it, then?"

"I'm gonna have our baby," she said, making her voice come out sing-songy and whispery, kind of like that actress. What was her name? Jennifer Tilly.

Mike stiffened. She felt his muscles bunching. He stared out the window for a long time. Sheryl had imagined a big smile, a hug. This was not what she wanted. But still, she supposed the news must come as a shock. There would be time for celebrating later. After they had their own place...

"Shit." Mike stared out the windshield, not looking at her. "I thought we were being careful. I always pulled out or wore a rubber. Every fuckin' time." He frowned and Sheryl recoiled at the way his eyebrows creased together. "You sure it's mine?"

"What?" Suddenly, the whole scenario she had envisioned earlier that night as she got ready to meet him vanished like a wisp of smoke. "What do you mean?"

"I mean I always fuckin' pulled out, little girl. No come. No baby. Not from me, anyway."

Sheryl swallowed, trying to get a little spit around the lump that had formed in her throat. Her eyes filled with tears. "But you're the only one I've been with, Mike. I thought you knew that."

"You're sure?"

"Of course, I'm sure."

"What were you, some kind of virgin?"

Sheryl thought sickeningly then of her mother's husband, Rick, and his late-night visits to her room, which had begun when Sheryl was twelve and had yet to end. But this baby wasn't Rick's, couldn't be. Rick had had a vasectomy. Her mother had mentioned it several times and so had he, when he assured her that "no harm" could come from what the two of them had done. Sheryl shook her head. "No, I'm not a virgin." Then Sheryl lied: "But no one else has been with me since last winter." She tried to look him in the eye, but Mike stared straight ahead, at a starless, murky night thick with humidity. "The baby is yours. There's no doubt." Sheryl felt herself begin to tremble in spite of the heat and tried to move closer to Mike, but he shrugged her away.

"We gotta do something about this, then."

Sheryl blew out a sigh. Mike was good guy, deep down. "I knew you'd want to do the right thing."

"I can scrape up some money for an abortion. That won't be a problem."

Sheryl bit her lip to hold back the tears. "I don't want an abortion!" Her voice came out shriller and louder than she had intended. "I was thinking maybe we could get married." Clutching...desperately. "Or at least live together. Give our kid a mom and dad."

"Are you serious?"

"Yes! Yes! Of course I'm serious." She wanted to pound on him with her fists. What had she done? Made up some guy in her mind? She suddenly felt as though Mike was someone she didn't even know.

"Can't do it, babe."

"Why not, Mike? Don't you love me?" And the tears and the snot started coming now. She felt pathetic and stupid.

"Of course I love you, honey. But I can't..."

"What's the problem, then?"

Mike looked at her for a long time. Was that a stupid grin playing about his lips? What was going on? A line of sweat formed at her hairline, trickled down her back. She felt sick.

"I probably should have told you, babe. Should have been upfront from the start."

"What? What is it?" Gorge rising, Sheryl was afraid she already knew.

"I'm married."

She reached out to hit him, then checked herself.

She had to get out of the car. She pulled her clothes on, struggling, jumped outside, where the night air was heavy, and ran halfway down the river bank. Her dinner came up and she fell, retching on and on until she felt dry heaves.

Surely, Mike would come after her.

But all she heard was the bass thrum of his engine starting up and the decreasing hum of that same engine as it headed away, leaving her alone.

She sat on the bank for a long time. At first just to catch her breath, to try to quell the queasiness and the shock. Then she stared out at the water for a long time, letting the minutes slip by, feeling numb. The night was oppressive, too warm, and Sheryl longed for a cleansing rain; wished, almost, that it would come down so hard it would drown her. But the air hung heavy around her, a cloak, enveloping her in moist air. Gnats dived for her eyes. Night insects hummed in the trees. Sheryl felt nothing, not even the sandy earth beneath her hands that, without thinking, she dug into, fingering and discarding pebbles that had once been on the river's bottom.

The moon glinted off the water. For a while, Sheryl expected to hear Mike's car, the sound growing louder as he returned. But that sound never arrived, and Sheryl knew it never would.

The water, she noticed, didn't smell good at all. Brackish. Dead fish. A slight chemical undertone.

She put her head in her hands and wept. What was she to do now? She imagined getting up, brushing the mud off the back of her jeans and heading home, where, silently, she would pack a bag and then, at dawn, walk swiftly to Route 60 and stick out a thumb. Maybe someone trustworthy would pick her up and deposit her just a little to the east, in Pittsburgh. She could start a new life. Just her and her baby.

Yeah, right. What would she do for money? How would she secure a home for the two of them? Sheryl was certain there were endless numbers of employers in Pittsburgh just looking for a pregnant sixteen-year-old girl, a high-school dropout with no skills.

Oh yeah, it would be quite a new life.

She would have to tell her mother, endure her Christian wrath. It was ironic that the town sinner had become the town saint, converted by her so-called "born again" husband, who was raping his stepdaughter on a regular basis.

Why not just wade into the river and get it over with?

"You look like the saddest little girl in the world."

Sheryl jumped at the sound of the voice behind her. For a moment, she thought her mother had discovered her, sitting here, close to 2:00 a.m. on the banks of the river. But although the voice was feminine, it definitely was not her mother's. Too deep, too raspy, too young.

Sheryl turned and saw her standing there, a vision. A girl, really, not much older than she, with platinum blonde hair, wearing a leather skirt, some sort of animal-print shirt, bare feet, and holding a pair of heels in one hand, a cigarette in the other.

"What's the matter, honey?"

Sheryl stared. "Who the fuck are you?"

The girl laughed. "My name's Myra. Myra Hindley. No need to get snippy. I just saw you sitting there and thought you could use a friend." She snickered. "Or two."

Sheryl stood up. "What are you talking about?"

Myra came closer and the moon revealed Sheryl's first impression as correct. She wasn't much older than Sheryl's own sixteen years. There was something creepy about her, but Sheryl couldn't understand where that feeling was coming from. Maybe it was just the fact that someone was staring at her when she thought she was down here alone. Maybe she was just embarrassed that this girl had seen her crying.

Myra smiled. "Don't be weirded out. I just happened to be down here with my boyfriend." She laughed. "We were parking." She nodded toward upstream. "He's up there now. I just needed to take a little walk and I saw you sitting there, and, oh, I just felt sorry for you."

Sheryl wanted to cry again. Just someone else recognizing her pain touched her in an odd way. God, she did need a friend. Did need someone to turn to.

Myra moved back. "Look, I'm sorry if I interrupted or something. I should leave you alone. Get back to Ian. He'll be waiting. I just thought you might want to talk. I thought I saw you crying and, well, I've been there myself. A guy?"

Sheryl nodded.

"I knew it. Fortunately, I have my Ian now." She grinned. "He's one in a million."

Sheryl didn't know what to say. All she knew is that she *did* want to talk to someone. Maybe Myra being here now was sort of a gift. It would be easier, she reasoned, to tell her problems to someone she hardly knew .

"You wanna come back to the car, chat for a little with Ian and me? We've got some wine. No pressure."

"Yes," Sheryl said, trying to keep her voice even. "Yes, that'd be nice." She twisted Mike's ring around her finger, and Myra noticed her fidgeting. Reaching out, Myra took Sheryl's hand in hers. She held the ring up to the moonlight. "Pretty. From an admirer?"

"A former admirer," Sheryl said. "Let's go meet that one-in-a-million guy of yours."

And Sheryl followed Myra into the darkness.

Chapter
Six

CASS WAS TIRED as she sat in her kitchen. More than tired; exhausted. Uncertain if she had the strength to make it through the day. Even the thought of work made her ache from head to toe. She had been back at the diner now for three days, and had yet to get back into the groove of things. The orders seemed to come in faster than they used to. Her coordination was off. Her memory didn't work the same way it once had and she was forced to ask her customers who ordered what as she unsteadily brought their orders to the table, something she had always prided herself on never having had to do. Carlos Soto, her "new" doctor, had told her it would take her a while to completely recover, that the shock her system had taken was large and time was the only remedy for the damage it had wrought. The bangs she had carelessly cut across her forehead to hide the wound tickled it, making Cass want to reach up and scratch, something that would not be good. Unless she wanted to see if she could earn extra tips from her customers by having blood trickle down her face.

Very appetizing.

The trauma to her head had sapped her energy. The two weeks she had taken off from the diner, which she'd thought was plenty of time to get back to normal, hadn't been enough. For one thing, she couldn't sleep; her dreams were filled with phantom images that caused her to awaken sweating, twisted in her sheets, a garbled scream still hot on her lips. She had begun to fear going to sleep, terrified of the nightmares that awaited her. She had seriously considering calling up Casey Williams, an old friend from whom she knew she could purchase some pot, but she didn't want to go down that road again. When it got late enough and her body was aching for sleep, Cass would have a glass of red wine, and that might help her fall into a fitful doze.

And Max, the little dear, seemed to have no respect for what his mother had gone through. Right now, as she tried to work a crossword puzzle at the kitchen table, Max was in the living room, the TV volume turned to ear-splitting, the explosions, screams, and other sound effects accompanied by his giggles. Perhaps the cacophony would have been cute if Cass hadn't been so tired, if she could have found it within herself to go in and turn down the TV volume and tell her son that he had only fifteen minutes before bath and then bed. But getting up from the maple kitchen chair would have taken too much effort.

Four letters. Nick and Nora's pooch. Cass closed her eyes. The clue was a familiar one in crosswords, but she could think of nothing, inane TV dialogue blocking out any thoughts she might have for herself.

She put the Bic down, shoved the newspaper away, and stood. Breathing in deeply, she promised herself she wouldn't be angry with Max. It wasn't his fault she was neglecting him lately. Well, not really neglecting, but not paying as much attention as she could have. She took care of the basics: saw to it that he was clean, well-fed, looked after. But Cass had little energy for anything beyond the required child-rearing basics.

In the living room, Max lay on the floor, a throw pillow from the couch beneath his head, thumb in his mouth, eyes wide as images from the TV screen flickered over him. Cass doubted if he had even noticed his mother standing over him. She picked up the remote from the coffee table, aimed it at the TV, and watched as the screen went black.

"Scoot. It's time to get cleaned up and then bed."

"But, Mom..." Max whined. "That program only had about ten more minutes."

"And you've got only about ten more minutes to get a quick bath and into your PJs."

"Come on, Mom." Max reached for the remote.

Cass snatched it up. "No, Max. I mean it. Upstairs. Now."

Reluctantly, the little dark-haired boy roused himself from the floor, put the pillow back on the couch, and started upstairs.

"Make it quick. I'll be up in a couple minutes to tuck you in."

"Okay."

Cass returned to the kitchen, glanced down at the newspaper and whispered, "Asta." But she was too tired to bother with filling in the crossword puzzle clue. Instead, she switched on the radio and slumped in a kitchen chair, head in hands.

A song was just ending. One of those hip-hop numbers that she hated. Just as well there was no music. Did music even exist anymore? After an ad for a local car dealership, the news came on. Cass had started to tune the announcer's voice out, making of it white noise, a background drone, when something he said made her perk up and listen.

Listen with horror.

Another teenage girl had gone missing.

She read the next chapter of *The Wind in the Willows* on automatic pilot. The act of reading to Max was more a matter of eye/mouth coordination than of conscious thought. Cass was surprised when she came to the end of the chapter and could not remember even one word she had read to her son, who lay on his side, thumb in mouth and eyes closed.

Cass reached down and ran her fingers through his hair, trailing her fingertips across his cheeks, still baby-smooth and plump. She tugged his thumb out of his mouth and wondered when he would ever break this habit. "I sure do love you," she whispered to the sleeping boy, pulling the sheet up around his neck. Max smelled sweet, of the baby powder she had sprinkled on him after his bath, and the clean smell of little boy, something indefinable and uncorrupted.

The air coming in through the screen was a little cooler, foretelling the approach of autumn. It had been a hot, miserable summer in so many ways, Cass was grateful for the change.

For a while, she simply sat in the chair beside her son's bed, staring down at him in the dim light of his Mickey Mouse night-light. Cass had once decorated the room in a Disney theme, a time that now seemed many more years ago than it actually was. Partly, Cass recognized the fact that she just wanted to spend some quiet time with her son, who, during his waking hours, was a bundle of energy, impossible to pin down for more than fifteen or twenty minute intervals before he was off to something else. The doctor had once asked her if she wanted a prescription for Ritalin for Max, the drug that supposedly calmed down hyperactive kids. But Max was just a kid, Cass thought, his manic energy just part of his makeup. She had seen enough of drugs in her own days to realize she didn't want to start her son on them when he was a boy of seven. Briefly, she thought of Steph again, her devastating Irish-Italian good looks, her compact yet muscular frame that Cass had watched go from robust to skeletal as she became more and more enamored of cocaine than she was of her, or of anything else for that matter. She had read somewhere that Ritalin was very similar to cocaine in its chemical make-up. God forbid. So Cass sat back in the chair, listening to the sound of the dog, Bum, as he made his way up the stairs, which creaked in all the familiar places. She appreciated being able to just sit for a change and look at her son, recharging her maternal batteries, which had been running on a low current for the past week or two.

Bum came into the room, giving her a mournful look with his brown eyes, and hopped onto the foot of Max's bed, where he curled into a ball and, after a lick of his lips and a yawn, fell immediately to sleep. "Dog, you don't know how much I envy you," Cass whispered.

One part of Cass thought she should get up, brush her teeth and head for the comfort of her own bed, sheets cool from the night breeze. But the other part of her recognized the fact that she was dreading going into her own bedroom down the hall. News of Sheryl McKenna's disappearance lurked like a stranger behind the door, just behind her more pleasant thoughts of Max and the peaceful rise and fall of his chest, the warm air coming out of his mouth. She knew that once she got into bed, the door would close and the missing young girl would begin, in a way, to call to her. All it took was hearing her name and description on the radio, just that small connection and it was like igniting something in her brain.

And that call would make Cass feel helpless...and terrified. She feared the weird, dreamlike images that would rise up, forging a bond with the girl that Cass had not sought.

Why was this happening?

THE SOUND OF a car alarm outside Max's window awakened her. Cass had fallen asleep in the chair beside Max's bed. The alarm wound down, replaced by the sound of chirping cicadas and crickets, the distant rumble of thunder. Heat lightning flashed, muted blue-white swatches of color that illuminated the street in front of their little house.

Cass's neck hurt, and she reached up to massage it, trying to loosen the knotted muscles. She glanced up at the Donald Duck clock on the wall opposite; it was going on midnight.

In spite of the crick in her neck, Cass thought perhaps falling asleep in the chair next to Max's bed was a good thing. After all, her body was bone weary, and perhaps she could just drop her jeans and T-shirt on the floor next to her bed, crawl in under the sheets and fall back asleep.

And maybe she would dream of nothing.

Hell, maybe she'd even have a pleasant dream. Something sexy. Cass grinned as she padded, barefoot, down the hall to her room.

She slipped out of her clothes, folding them and putting them on the rocking chair in the corner, pulled the scrunchy out of her dark hair, and crawled under the sheet.

She closed her eyes.

SOMEONE WAS STANDING above her. Cass awakened to see a dark-haired girl staring down at her. She let out a little cry, not too loud, because she didn't want to awaken Max. The girl held a finger to her lips, leaning over so that the long, dark curtain of hair partially obscured a very pretty, very young face.

The girl motioned for Cass to follow her; Cass shook her head.

The girl reached down and took Cass's hand in her own. Her touch was ice-cold and Cass glanced down at the hand. Even in the dim light, she could see the sapphire ring on her finger.

Cass got up, following the girl, not bothering with clothes. Eventually, she stood naked in the gravel driveway of her house with the girl, who gestured toward the river. And even though the river was two blocks away, Cass could suddenly see its brownish curve, the hills of West Virginia along the opposite shore. Up high, at the top of one of the hills, was a red brick house that Cass had admired since she was a little girl. Fronted by white pillars, the old house occupied the only space on the hilltop, and Cass had often envied the solitude and the panoramic views the house must command.

Cass stood alone in the driveway, shivering. A light rain had begun, cold needles on her skin. And she knew she had sleepwalked...the touch and vision of the young girl had been a dream. She gasped as she looked down at herself, seeing her silvery-white nude body in the dark, and hoped none of her neighbors had insomnia and had witnessed her unintentional exposure.

She turned and trudged back inside, picking her way through the sparse gravel of her driveway. She could protect her feet, if nothing else.

As she went back up the stairs, avoiding the places she knew would creak, she thought of the dark-haired girl, how beautiful she was. And how cold.

The girl was Sheryl McKenna, the one whose disappearance had just been reported on the radio. Cass knew this with the same certainty as she knew her own name.

The bed waited for her. Reluctantly, Cass made her way back to it, and lay down. She closed her eyes and everything started. There was a reddish color behind her eyelids; Cass willed it to go away. She begged for sleep; simple, untroubled sleep that did not contain unwanted, mysterious images that seemed to have their own volition and a purpose Cass wasn't quite sure she yet understood.

The visions came rapid-fire, with no consistency or order. Cass ground her teeth, knowing she could stop the montage if she would just open her eyes, but unable to lift her eyelids. It was as though they were glued shut.

The sapphire ring she had seen earlier, still on the girl's finger. A scattering of earth covering the hand that lay limp against a tree root.

Sheryl McKenna's face, cold in repose, her blue eyes clouded and open, gazing at something only she could see.

A beetle skittering across the porcelain-white skin.

A shift, and Cass found herself in some sort of pornographic movie, only there was nothing titillating about this one. No lurid bump-and-grind musical score to accompany the sex taking place, the sex to which Cass was forced to bear witness. She heard only the sounds of the man's panting breath and the whimpers of the girl, occasionally interrupted by a gasp, a small cry that didn't begin to describe the pain Cass knew she was feeling. The girl lay beneath a dark-haired man in the back seat of a car, which was nothing more than a dark hulk in the night, details indecipherable. His back was slick with sweat and the girl's eyes were wide as the man thrust into her, hard, making her whimper and bite her lip with each thrust.

As if the volume was just switched on, like a mute button pressed to release the sound, Cass could hear music coming from the dashboard, odd electronic beats, something no radio station would ever play. It created a hellish background score to the rape taking place in the back seat.

Cass turned, and there it was in the darkness: the blinking red light and a shadowy figure, another woman, peering through the viewfinder of a video camera.

And then she was high on a hilltop, looking down over the Ohio River's rushing, muddy brown current. Skeletal branches reached out over the water like fingers of bone.

Cass started awake — sweat-slick, heart pounding, twisted up in her sheets like a mummy.

Tomorrow, she had to do something.

Chapter
Seven

SUMMITVILLE, PA HAD only one police station. It was housed in the basement of City Hall in what was still grandly called "downtown" even though the term referred to only about three or four city blocks that consisted mostly of bars, dollar stores, and boarded-up storefronts. As Cass parked her car near the squat limestone structure that housed the workings of the municipality of Summitville, she remembered when she was a little girl and the downtown was a bustling little area, with two movie theaters, a soda fountain, a JC Penney, and assorted clothing stores, along with a few restaurants and bars. But those were the glory days of western Pennsylvania's steel mills, and those days were long over.

Earlier, she had dropped Max off with her parents and had endured her mother's questions about her whereabouts while their grandson was with them. Now, as she listened to the engine tick down and the cooling fan of the Escort come on, she wished she had just told her that Mike, her boss at the diner, had called her in for an extra shift.

Her mother had never been much for children, even for Cass. She was a brittle woman who valued the Hummel and Precious Moment figurines that adorned almost every available surface in her two-story home on Pennsylvania Avenue more than human contact. Cass could never stand to spend very long at her parents' house, because she would become so stressed watching the tension in her mother's face as Max moved about their home, the fear just beneath her mother's olive skin that the little boy might break something. It was a shame because Cass loved her father, the heavy-set crew-cut man with the husky voice who had an almost endless capacity for tolerance and love. Someday, when she got him alone, and the two of them were enjoying some of the homemade wine he made every year, she would ask him what on earth had ever drawn him to her mother, who had been high-strung and worrisome even when Cass was a little girl.

"What do you need to go to the police station for, Cass?" her mother had asked her, slapping at the Formica-topped kitchen table with a tea towel to free it from any evidence of the breakfast she had just shared with her husband.

Cass stared at the gold-and-rust-patterned wallpaper as if she had

never seen it before, as if an answer was buried within its abstract
pattern. Max had already taken off for the living room, where he sat
next to his grandfather on the couch, watching Drew Carey and *The
Price is Right.* Cass could hear the upbeat music from the show in the
kitchen and wished that she, too, could be lost in the guessing games of
prices and the studio excitement of who next might be exhorted to
"Come on down!" Instead, she had to face her mother's interrogation,
her searching for some way to show disapproval of whatever it was her
daughter had decided to do *now*. Worse, she had to face the nervousness
in her gut as she tried to figure out what to say to her mother and the
police about the dreams, and—what would you call them?—*visions* she
had been having lately without sounding like a complete lunatic.

"I just think I have some information that could be useful to them,"
Cass said softly, opening the refrigerator and desperately searching its
shelves for an escape. She knew such a cryptic statement was opening
the door to all sorts of questions, questions for which she wasn't sure
she had suitable answers. The desperation almost made her want to give
up on the whole thing, but the faces of the two young girls still haunted
her.

The expected question came: "What kinda information would you
have? Information about what?" Her mother washed the breakfast
dishes, up to her elbows in steaming hot water, while giving her
daughter a look that, even under the thick lenses of her glasses,
indicated her disapproval of whatever Cass would say next.

"Nothing, Ma. It's kind of personal."

"This doesn't have anything to do with drugs, does it?"

Cass rolled her eyes. Ever since her mother had found a quarter-
ounce Baggie in her dresser drawer when Cass was seventeen, she'd
been certain her daughter was a drug addict. She wondered about
Max's safety, and pointed out to Cass articles in newspapers and
magazines about the "war on drugs" and how marijuana was a
"gateway drug."

"No, Ma, it has nothing to do with drugs." If only she could just
rush out the door, but normal people didn't rush out the door of their
parents' home in the middle of a conversation, even if that conversation
was doomed. "You heard about those two girls that disappeared in the
past few weeks?"

Her mother dried her hands and took off her apron. "Yeah. Who
hasn't? Probably runaways."

"Maybe not, Ma. Maybe I know something that might help the
cops."

"What would someone like you know?"

"I might have seen them before they disappeared. I just think the
police should know."

"Where—"

Cass cut off her mother's next query with an upturned hand. Her salvation came in the form of a small white lie. "Listen, I made an appointment. I don't get going, I'm gonna be late. We'll talk when I get back, okay?"

Begrudgingly, her mother accepted the lie. In her mother's world, one did not arrive late for appointments with official bodies like the police.

And now, as Cass exited her car, she hoped her interview with the police would go better than the one with her mother and there would be some way she could help. But how? How could she tell them what she knew without them making a phone call to alert the men in white coats?

Cass started up the stone steps of City Hall.

MARION HARTLEY WAS the Summitville police force's first, and only, female detective. She had started back in the 1960s, when she was an oddity, when she had been referred to officially as a policewoman, instead of the genderless nomenclature of today, where female cops, like their male counterparts, were simply police officers. Marion had endured teasing, practical jokes, and often the kind of behavior from some of her coworkers that would now win her a sexual harassment suit.

The daughter of a police detective in Pittsburgh, Marion's only dream had been to follow in her father's footsteps. And she might have had an easier time of it if she had remained in the much larger city of Pittsburgh, but she had followed an older woman, her first crush, here to Summitville back in '64. The woman, Terry, was what people unkindly referred to as a bulldyke. But Marion had loved her strength, the way she took charge and how she encouraged Marion in her dreams of law enforcement, not finding them unsuitable as her mother did, or even her own father, who harbored his own suspicions about Marion's relationship with her masculine "friend."

Now, Marion was alone. A thick-waisted woman with close-cropped gunmetal gray hair and a pair of black-rimmed oval glasses, she made working for the Summitville police force her life. Terry had passed away from breast cancer in '77, and Marion had never sought a replacement other than the scarred desk at which she now sat, and its mounds of paperwork and its black dial phone. Through sheer persistence, she had made detective, and she fully expected that one day she would run the show here in Summitville. She knew more about law enforcement than anyone in the building.

She wanted a cigarette, but smoking in her office had been banned a few years ago, the result of efforts by city council health nuts. She popped a piece of Dentyne into her mouth and imagined what it would be like to step outside and light up her Marlboro Medium and feel its comforting smoke fill her lungs.

But that would wait until she had seen the young woman they were sending in. Two figures appeared behind her frosted glass office door and Marion could see that one of them was a uniform and the other a slight woman with dark hair.

The door opened and the officer, a young kid with brush-cut blonde hair, gave Marion a roll of the eyes behind the head of the young woman. Marion knew what the look meant: another nut case. Whenever anything went beyond the pale of crime in Summitville, the nuts came in with their information. The two missing girls had already elicited a couple dozen phone calls, all claiming to have seen one or both of them at various locales between here and Pittsburgh.

But this young woman was the first to have bothered to make the trip in to actually speak to someone in person. She didn't *look* like a nut case, but Marion's years of experience told her appearances counted for little. The most normal-seeming people often harbored secrets at odds with their bland exteriors. This one was pretty, with a slight frame and the black hair, strong nose, and green eyes indicating a southern Italian heritage. She looked a little frightened, her gaze darting about Marion's cluttered office, looking anywhere but at the detective.

Officer Hyatt spoke. "Ma'am, this is Detective Hartley, she's one of our best. You can tell your story to her." He gave Marion a look that was almost a smirk and said, "Marion, this is Cass D'Angelo. Says she might know something about the missing girls."

Marion stood. As she shook Cass's hand, she noted that it was damp, clammy. "Why don't you have a seat, Ms. D'Angelo? You can close the door on your way out, Matt."

Marion found it was often best to let people begin. When they started first, it kind of put them on the spot and their true feelings were more likely to emerge. Marion picked up a Bic pen and began to chew on its plastic cap.

"Well," Cass D'Angelo swallowed, "this might be a little hard to believe, but I think it's important." She looked out the window at the day, which had turned sunny and bright. "See, you might have heard about me. A little while back, I was, um, caught in a storm...I just missed getting struck by lightning." Cass paused, looked down at her knees. "But I didn't miss getting struck by a tree branch, about the size of a small tree?" She pulled aside her bangs to show the detective her scar, still painfully red and bordered with purple, yellow, and green. She let her hair fall back over the wound. Cass grinned, then stopped. "It was on the front page of the papers."

Marion nodded. "Yeah, I do seem to remember something about that." She took the pen out of her mouth and leaned forward. "But I'm a little confused. What would that have to do with the missing girls?"

It was obvious Cass didn't want to go any further. To Marion, Cass looked like she wanted to do nothing more than run from her office. A line of sweat formed at Cass's hairline. Her mouth was dry.

"You know something about Sheryl McKenna and Lucy Plant?"

Marion sat up straighter.

"Well, maybe..." Cass's voice trailed off. "Maybe not. Believe me," she said, and gave the detective a lopsided grin. "I do know how, um, incredible what I'm going to say might sound."

The detective nodded.

Cass bit the inside of her lip and swallowed audibly. "I know this sounds ridiculous, but since my accident, I've had, well, for lack of a better word, visions. And some of those visions have had to do with the girls."

Marion smiled and tried to put on a sympathetic face, but it was an effort. "Well, what did you see?"

Cass let it all out: everything, from a vague description of the man and woman she had seen with the girls, to the blinking red light of the video camera, to the visions of the fresh dirt by the side of the river, even down to the detail about that fresh dirt being across the river from the red brick hilltop house in West Virginia. "I think there's some validity to what I saw."

"Why is that?"

"Because I knew what Sheryl McKenna looked like before I had ever seen a picture of her in the paper." Cass explained the dreams she had had the night before, and how her dreams meshed perfectly with what Sheryl McKenna actually looked like.

The detective asked, "Where do you work, Ms. D'Angelo?"

Cass cocked her head. "Down at the Elite Diner. Mike Bailey's place?"

"Oh, I know it," Marion said. "Great burgers and fries, but my old stomach won't tolerate that crap anymore."

"Why are you asking me about where I work?"

Marion leaned back in her chair, regarding the ceiling for a moment. "Well, it's just that sometimes we see people and don't remember that we have...but our brain files it away. I'm just saying that it's possible young McKenna was in the restaurant before, and when you saw her picture in the paper, it might have come together for you."

"Even if that was true, why on Earth would I dream of her the night before the story came out in the *Review*?"

"So you knew nothing about her disappearance when you went to bed last night?"

Cass blew out a sigh. "I heard about her disappearance on the radio."

The detective nodded, folding her blunt-nailed hands in front of her. "So maybe Ms. McKenna was in the diner with some girlfriends, you heard her name, and your brain filed it away. This kind of thing happens all the time."

"I'm sure," Cass said, staring down at the floor. "Couldn't you just check things out? I mean, take a look down by the river where I said?"

"Of course. I'll add your information to the other information we're building on these cases. Believe me, we check them all out." Marion waited for Cass to say something more. "Now, I do have a lot of work to do, Ms. D'Angelo, so if you don't mind."

Cass stood on trembling legs. "Please...check things out."

"Will do." Marion picked up the phone.

WHEN SHE REACHED her car, Cass turned and looked back at City Hall, remembering the police headquarters inside...and Marion Hartley. Both were grim, efficient, worn, no-nonsense. Would Hartley help her if Max had turned up missing? Would she pay any attention to her hunches (visions, dreams) *then*? More likely, she would file them away under "ravings of the mother" and continue plodding through an investigation the tried and true way, the way that might yield no results until Max turned up dead somewhere, in a shallow grave in the woods, maybe. Or down by the river...

Cass shook her head to clear it. The prospect of Max being missing, or worse, dead, brought hot tears to her eyes. She got back in the car and, with shaking hands, brought the key to the ignition.

She had to do something.

Later, after Max was tucked into bed and the little house was silent once more, the darkness pressing against the windows like something palpable, Cass sat alone in the living room. She had flipped through TV channels, but as usual, there was nothing she wanted to see. Besides, she didn't know if she could concentrate on a movie, and a sitcom would just be too absurd, in light of the thoughts that were going through her head, thoughts of getting in touch with the parents of the missing girls herself, bypassing the official route she had so unsuccessfully attempted earlier that day.

The phone rang, its chirp startling in the evening's quiet, and Cass jumped from the couch, hurrying to stop its ringing before it could wake Max. She wished for a moment that the late-night call would be from Detective Hartley, saying she had given it some serious thought, and that maybe she would be wise to at least hear Cass out a little more and to look into her feelings, just to see if they had any validity. After all, the detective would say, they had little else to go on, so they might as well try and see what Cass's ideas might bring them.

But as Cass made her way to the kitchen at the back of the house, she knew it wasn't Marion Hartley. And she knew not only because logic told her it wouldn't be so, but because, as with the visions, dreams and certainties she had experienced since the lightning strike, she simply *knew*.

The caller would be a man.

Cass snatched up the phone on the third ring, a little breathless. "Hello?" It seemed strange to be getting a phone call; Cass realized suddenly she had no one in her life. Certainly not a lover. And the friends she had had, party pals mostly, had faded away as Max began to take center stage in her life.

"Cassandra?"

The voice was deep and completely unrecognizable. "Yes? Who's this?"

"This is Dr. Soto. Carlos. From the hospital."

Cass visualized the handsome young resident who had cared for her down at Summitville Community. She recalled his black hair and eyes so dark the pupils were lost in them, the dark skin that felt slightly hot to the touch when he took her pulse or laid his long fingers across her forehead.

"Is something the matter?" Cass remembered the battery of tests she had been subjected to in the days following her incident. What if one of them showed something abnormal? But again, Cass's heart did not begin to race, she didn't begin to worry because, although she wasn't sure of the reason for his call, she knew that Carlos Soto was not calling for professional reasons.

"No, no, nothing's the matter. I just wanted to see how you were coming along."

Cass twisted the phone cord around her finger and let it twirl back to its original state. "Oh, I'm all right, I guess. A little more tired than I was before the, um, accident."

"That's to be expected."

She thought of telling him about the visions, the horrific nightmares about the missing girls, but would he too think she was crazy? No, this was something better kept to herself...shared carefully. Cass was tired. She looked out at the dark, moonless night and thought how she just wanted to hang up the phone and go to bed. "Is that all, then?"

"What?"

"Were you just calling to see how I was? I'm fine. I'm scheduled for a check-up with my regular doctor in a couple of weeks."

"Well, Cass, I was actually calling for another reason..."

"Oh?"

"Yeah, see, I'm new to Summitville and the area and I really don't know too many people." Carlos laughed, and Cass picked up on the nervousness in his voice. Once, she thought, she would have found his trepidation endearing, but now it only seemed vaguely irritating. She wished he would just get on with it. She knew what was coming.

"Me either, doctor. Working on my feet eight hours a day and running after a seven-year-old boy the rest of my waking hours leaves so little time for a social life."

He laughed again. *Doesn't he realize I'm not making a joke?*

"I was actually wondering if you could free up some of that busy time for me? Maybe you'd let me take you to dinner?"

He hardly knew her. Their relationship at the hospital had been little more than perfunctory: doctor-patient stuff. What did he see in her? Let alone she obviously didn't see much in him; she had done the man routine years before. It was supremely unsatisfying—though at least she now had Max.

"Wait a minute. You want to take me out? This is, like, a request for a date?"

"Well, it's not actually *like* a request for a date. It *is* one. I'd really be pleased if you could make some time for me."

And you could make some time with *me*, Cass thought. Her father was a retired welder, her mother had been a waxer in a pottery down the river in East Liverpool, Ohio. They were blue collar all the way, second generation Sicilian. And Cass was a waitress with a high school education. Doctors didn't ask waitresses out. At least that hadn't been Cass's experience.

"I...I don't know. Things are kind of busy right now."

"You have a boyfriend, right? Someone as pretty as you, I kind of knew..."

"No, I don't have a boyfriend. The last one I had knocked me up and then headed for Florida." Cass snorted. She didn't know why she was behaving so rudely to this man who just wanted to take her out.

He wants to get laid.

The idea hit her like a splash of cold water. It was as though there were an ugly little woman hanging out in the recesses of her brain, laying it all out, straight and no-nonsense. *And is that such a bad thing?* Cass wondered. *Maybe I want to get laid, too. But not with him.*

The voice made her sick. There was a rebellious part of her that wanted to tell the voice to go fuck itself, but again, there was that odd certainty.

"Why do we need to bother with dinner?" Cass asked, testing. "My boy goes to bed around 8:30, you could just drop by some night...show me what that Latin lover thing is all about." Cass laughed, but it was cold.

"We could do that..." Carlos stammered.

"No, no, Dr. Soto, we couldn't. Good night."

"Wait a minute. Wait a minute." Something in his voice prevented her from hanging up the phone. "What's wrong? Not the right type?"

"Not the right sex." Cass replaced the phone in its cradle, thinking of black hair, smooth olive skin, and the touch of strong, yet delicate hands on her breasts.

Chapter
Eight

"BUT WHAT IF my teacher doesn't like me?"

"Your teacher will like you."

"But what if the other kids don't remember me from first grade?"

"They'll remember you."

"What if it's too hard, Mom?"

"It won't be too hard. Everything you learned last year will come back and then you build on that. Trust me, in a way, school gets easier every year. *If* you pay attention. You'll see."

Cass took the empty cereal bowl away from in front of Max and went into the dining room to get the new red nylon backpack she had just bought for him at Target. She had loaded it up with fat pencils, the sixty-four-count box of Crayolas, three spiral-bound notebooks, safety scissors, a red plastic ruler, and a small bottle of Elmer's glue. If he needed anything else, Cass could pick it up later. *Anyway,* she thought grimly, *shouldn't my second sight help me make sure my son has the right stuff for his first day of second grade?*

Cass helped Max slide the backpack on and walked him to the kitchen door. She watched him walk down the driveway, knowing he wanted to look back, knowing his green eyes were moist, and knowing that, already, the masculine side of him was kicking in, for better or worse, and that he was being brave: fighting the urge to run back to his mother.

She fought back her own urge to run after him, to give him one more hug and kiss before he joined a group of kids heading up the street in front of their house.

After Max was gone, the house seemed unnaturally quiet, eerily empty, as if Max had taken more than just his physical being with him.

Cass sat for a long time in the kitchen, staring at the telephone, a cup of coffee going cold in front of her. She had already looked up the McKennas' number in the phone book and had scrawled it in the margin of yesterday's newspaper. The blue inked number faced her, as if it was waiting. Cass didn't have to be at the diner until three, so she had plenty of time to do what she felt needed to be done.

The day was a warm one, suffocating even early in the morning, with a dirty white sky and the angry buzz of insects filling the air, spilling in through the kitchen's screen door.

Cass stared out at the day for what seemed like hours, but was in fact only fifteen minutes or so. Like a scared actor forcing herself to take the stage, Cass lifted the wall phone from its cradle on the wall and pushed the buttons rapidly for the McKennas', preventing herself from backing out. She knew, if these were the days prior to technological advances like Caller ID and *69, she might have lost her nerve and hung up.

But someone did answer. A woman, the youth in her voice obvious, gave away her West Virginia "down the river" origins when she said hello with a slight drawl, the twang of a country western singer.

She had to say hello twice before Cass spoke. It was as though Cass needed the shove of that second hello, slightly annoyed, to get her going.

"Mrs. McKenna?"

"This is her. Who's this?"

"You don't know me. My name's Cass D'Angelo. I live not too far from you." Cass felt a trickle of sweat run down her back. "I was wondering if I could talk to you."

"That's what you're doin', isn't it? What's this about, anyway? I don't have time for any sales calls."

Cass laughed, but it came out closer to a squeak. "Oh, believe me, I'm not trying to sell anything here. I just wondered if I could stop by and see you for a little bit this morning."

"About what?" Suddenly, wariness crept into the woman's voice and just as suddenly, Cass knew that the thought that someone was calling about Sheryl was dawning on her. It was almost as if she spoke the words, spoke her trepidation that this odd woman was calling to make a ransom demand (although from where the money would come Sheryl McKenna's mother had no idea), or was calling to tell her that Sheryl was dead.

And Cass knew she should be honest, but wondered how much to say over the phone. This would all be easier if she could face the woman, look into her eyes, reassure her, mother to mother.

But what reassurance did she have? That bag was empty.

"I need to talk to you about Sheryl."

"What about her?" The West Virginia twang turned to ice.

Cass sighed. "It's so hard to explain over the phone. I think I might know something about her...about her...disappearance. Maybe not. I'd just like to talk to you in person."

"What could you possibly know?"

"Can I just come over? I can be there in fifteen minutes."

"Why don't you just tell me what you're calling about right now? Why can't you do that?"

"It's just easier to explain in person. Please, Mrs. McKenna."

She sighed. "Whatever. Fine. You know where I live?"

"Yes. Give me fifteen minutes."

And now, as Cass knocked on a weathered, green-painted door, again she questioned why she was doing this. Could she really help, or were her nightmares the result of the lightning strike? Some sort of mental after-effect that had nothing to do with reality?

She looked around the yard, trying not to think. Sheryl McKenna's home was a study in grim: the tiny wooden house had scabs of white paint that clung stubbornly to it, trying in vain to hide the black and rotting wood beneath. The yard was balding; only a few patches of dry grass, mixed with weeds, grew. A black and tan dog, looking like some sort of pit bull/German Shepherd mix, was chained to a tar-papered dog house; the animal stared at her with rheumy eyes. Cass was sure if she reached out a hand to pet it, that hand would be taken off.

The smell of the Ohio River, just a block away, was strong, brackish: fish with an undercurrent of mildew. For an instant, Cass detected something rotting, akin to the odor of spoiled meat, and wondered if it had simply been borne up by a wind from across the river, or if it was another of her premonitions, or whatever it was they were. She closed her eyes, saw a shovel making impact with dark, damp earth, and shuddered.

When Sheryl McKenna's mother opened the door, Cass felt as though she had already seen her. And maybe she had. Summitville was, after all, a small town. She could have passed the tired-looking woman on the street downtown, or served her in the diner. The woman stared at her with bright gray eyes, looking her over as though Cass were something she had discarded in the yard that had managed to make its way back to the porch. Mrs. McKenna was small, with no fat on her bones; she looked almost skeletal. Her skin was weathered, the result of too much sun, too much smoke. Her skin, combined with straw-like bleached blonde hair and hard eyes made her, Cass was sure, look older than her years. She held a cigarette in her hand, and the smell of tobacco smoke came out of the house like a wave when she opened the door.

"You Cass?"

"Yes. I'm Cass D'Angelo." Cass bit her lip, uncertain whether she should extend her hand or not. In the end she decided that the woman would just stare at her, so she didn't bother.

"I'm Janet McKenna. What do you want?" Her voice was dead.

"Can I come in?"

"Who is it, Jan?" A man's voice came from the back of the house and Cass, upon hearing it, immediately stiffened; she didn't know why. She felt cold.

Janet turned her head, took a drag on her cigarette, and called, "It's that Cass, the one who called." She turned back around. "I guess you may's well step in."

Cass followed her into a cluttered kitchen: stacks of dirty dishes in the sink, an old stove covered in grease and food stains, counters filled with newspapers, magazines, and overflowing ashtrays. The centerpiece of the room was a wood-grain laminate table with four mismatched chairs. A man with a crew cut and a beer gut glared at her from behind a caul of cigarette smoke.

"That's Rick," Janet said, sitting down.

Cass nodded and took a seat. She rubbed her forehead. She stared at the pack of Kools in front of her and, even though she had given the habit up seven years ago, she wanted one, wanted the calm the smoke would bring.

But she didn't dare ask.

"You said you knew something about Sheryl."

Cass bit her lower lip, hating the bile moving around in her stomach and making her feel nauseous. "Well, yeah. I think I might. But it could be nothing."

"What the fuck are you talking about?" Rick continued to stare at her, not looking her in the eyes, but somewhere lower. Cass felt soiled. It hit her then, like a flash on a movie screen: this man on top of a young girl. A young girl who peered over his writhing, sweaty back with dead eyes.

God, no, Cass thought.

"I...I..." How could she put this? "See, I kind of have these visions? I know it sounds silly, but—"

"Oh Lord." Janet McKenna regarded the ceiling.

"I don't know if it's worth anything at all. But I've seen Sheryl and I think I might have seen something that might help you find her."

"Get out."

"What?"

Janet McKenna stood, and the hand holding the almost-burnt-to-the-filter cigarette trembled. "I said get out."

"Okay." Cass stood, holding onto the table for support. "I just thought I might be able to help."

"Do you know how many lunatics have called, driven by, showed up at our doorstep since my daughter disappeared? Do you?"

"No," Cass whispered, backing toward the door.

"A lot. A whole lot. And not one of them could help us. Do you know why?"

"Why?" Cass's mouth was dry.

"Because none of them had been sent by the Lord. And you have the nerve to come in here with your devil's visions and try to tell me you can *help*? I don't need your kind of help. What do you call yourself anyway, some kind of psychic? Psychics come straight from Satan, missie. You don't fool me. Only through the power of Jesus Christ will my Sheryl come back to me."

Cass closed her eyes. When she opened them again, both the man and the woman were staring at her. "I just think you should listen to me for a minute. If you don't like what I have to say, forget it. But maybe it can help."

"I don't think so." Janet McKenna had begun to cry.

"Now you go on, get the hell out of here." Rick dragged angrily on his cigarette and blew the smoke at her.

"I know about you," Cass whispered, leaning toward the man. "I know all about you. Listen: I can see the truth. I know what you did."

When she said those words, Cass knew she was right and knew, for the first time, her visions had validity. He sucked in some breath, held it. His eyes grew larger. Cass saw the truth written on his face, the way it had gone ashen.

But Janet McKenna was picking up a food-encrusted plate from the sink and preparing to fling it at her. "You get out of my *house!*"

The plate broke just over her left shoulder, against the wall.

Cass turned and ran from the house.

Chapter
Nine

"THIS ISN'T WHAT I ordered!" the old woman called out, the irritation in her little old lady voice heightening her pitch, making her sound like a harpy. "Miss! Miss, I didn't order a grilled cheese. I ordered a..."

Cass hurried over to her table, hoping her boss, that prince among men, Mike Bailey, didn't hear the old lady's cries. "Ma'am, I'm very sorry." Cass picked up the plate. "Now, what was it you had?"

"I shouldn't have to tell you again, young lady. I already placed my order. You wrote it down." The old woman toyed with the paper napkin on the table, not giving Cass the benefit of eye contact. She said, in a much softer voice, "You figure it out."

Cass consulted her pad and went back to the kitchen. The old bitch's tuna melt was, fortunately, still waiting under the heat lamps. But who got the grilled cheese?

Cass hurried over to the woman and set the plate before her. "Listen, ma'am, I'm very sorry."

"Mmm-hmmm." The old woman lifted a slice of bread to peer at the tuna and American cheese underneath. "Don't worry. It'll come out of your tip."

"You do what you have to." Cass sighed and hurried away. She glanced up at the clock for what seemed like the fiftieth time tonight. It was ten o'clock, one more hour until the end of her shift. Cass's feet ached. Worse, she was still stinging from her visit to the McKennas'. How could they have been so cruel? She had only been trying to help.

The frustration simmered just beneath the surface of her consciousness, a consciousness she needed to devote to her work, however menial it seemed in comparison to what she knew. Sheryl McKenna, she was certain, had been buried on a hilltop, somewhere overlooking the river. She wished there was something she could have done before that fact became reality. And, God, how she wished she could have convinced Janet McKenna to listen. Cass was certain that just knowing what happened to her daughter would give the other woman some closure, a release. At least that's what would have been true for Cass had she been in the other woman's shoes.

This line of thinking led Cass to wonder how Max was doing. She had left him with her parents and knew that they indulged the boy too much, letting him stay up far past his bedtime, feeding him ice cream and candy — and making his next day at school a useless one.

Cass started over to the pay phone; the waitresses weren't allowed to use the regular phone in Mike's office.

"Where do you think you're going, miss?" Mike glared at her from his position behind the cash register.

"I have to call my parents, Mike. Max is with them; I just want to see if he's all right."

"Cass, you have two tables still waiting for you to take their orders."

"I know. I'll get right on it. Just let me make a quick call. Two minutes, tops."

"Yeah." Mike scratched his bald pate. "I hope your customers won't mind waiting while you take care of personal business."

Somehow, Cass managed to get through her shift without any more major errors. Somehow, she managed to get Max home, give him a glass of Alka-Seltzer and tuck him into bed.

"I want a story," Max whined.

"It's too late; you have to get up at seven o'clock for school in the morning." Cass glanced at the clock on his nightstand. "Seven will be here before you know it, and then I'll have to drag you out of bed, stick your head in the toilet to wake you up. And flush, flush, flush."

Max giggled and didn't press the story issue. Cass lay down beside him for a moment, taking some solace from the warmth of his little body beside her. She sighed, "Mommy's really tired." She turned to Max and tousled his blond hair. "I love you, Max."

The two lay quietly for a while, then Cass sat up. "You need to get to sleep, little man." But Max had already dropped off.

Cass went downstairs and into the kitchen, where she poured herself a glass of milk and stared out the screen door at the darkness. Cars whooshed by on the street in front of their house every couple of minutes. Otherwise, it was still. The air coming through the screen had a chill to it; fall wasn't far behind. She wondered if this night, after the trauma of the day, would be one in which she could find some sleep. Sleep uninterrupted by visions.

The phone ringing behind her startled her, sounding like an alarm in the still night. Cass raced to it and snatched the receiver from its cradle.

"Hello." Who could be calling now? It was almost midnight.

"Is this Cass?"

A man's voice, unfamiliar. She immediately wondered if she would pick something up from his voice, get a mental picture of the man. But there was nothing.

"Who wants to know?"

"I'm sorry. I should have introduced myself. My name's Ron Plant."

Cass's heart made a small leap. The name Plant meant something to her. It took a minute for her conscious mind to catch up with her thudding heart. Lucy Plant, the first girl who disappeared; that was where she had heard the name before.

"Oh, hello. Yes, this is Cass. Can I help you?"

"I'm sorry to be calling so late. But see, I just got a call myself from this woman, Janet McKenna? She said you talked to her today."

Oh God. Cass wondered where this was leading. Was this Ron Plant about to chastise her? Tell her she was nuts? The spawn of Satan? He didn't sound upset. His voice was calm, husky. It had a velvet quality that made Cass feel at ease, even if she didn't have a clue why he was calling her.

"Yes, I did speak with her earlier. What's this all about?"

Ron Plant paused. There was silence for a moment or two. "She called to warn me about you. See, I'm Lucy Plant's father? Our daughter disappeared a while ago."

"I know who you are. But why are you calling me? I'm sure I can't help you. Didn't Janet McKenna tell you that?"

"Janet McKenna, if you'll pardon the expression, sounds like a nut case. I thought you might be able to help my wife and me. Lucy disappearing has just about destroyed her and I'm ready to try anything that might help us find her."

"I can't help you." It seemed the air was being sucked out of the kitchen. Cass was having trouble breathing. *Please don't make me get into this. I never asked for it. I don't want it.*

"But Janet McKenna told me you've had some sort of psychic visions concerning her daughter."

"Yes." Cass wanted to cry. "That's true. But I don't know that they really mean anything. I...I've been sick."

"Whether they mean anything or not doesn't matter so much to me. We have nothing to go on right now, nothing. And what you might know is better than that. It has to be."

A long silence followed. Cass didn't know what to say. It seemed Ron Plant didn't, either; it seemed Ron Plant was waiting.

"I never said I knew anything about Lucy."

"I think you might. Do you?"

Cass swallowed, breathed in deeply. "Yes...I may have seen something. I don't know." Cass rubbed her forehead, trying to force away a dull throbbing that was beginning just behind her eyes, trying to force away the vision of a crookedly whirring ceiling fan. Cass couldn't account for the nausea and the dread this prosaic image provoked.

"Look, Cass, I've heard of cases where psychics have been able to help find missing people. It happens enough that sometimes police departments use them in their searches."

Except the one here in Summitville. "I don't know if I'm psychic, Mr. Plant." *But you do know...you do.* "What do you want from me?"

"Just to talk to you. To see if you can help. You're right, it may amount to nothing, but it's more of a shot than we have right now."

"I don't know."

"Please." Ron Walter's voice dropped to almost a whisper; Cass could hear the pain in his voice. "Please. Don't make me beg."

"Okay. I guess we can talk. But I can't promise you anything. When would be a good time?"

"Can you come over right now?"

"My little boy's in bed right now. I can't."

"How 'bout tomorrow? In the morning?"

"Yes. Tomorrow. In the morning." Cass got Ron Plant's address and hung up the phone.

It would be a long, sleepless night. She stepped out onto the back porch, sat down on the stoop, and wept.

Chapter
Ten

THE FIRST THING Cass noticed, as she headed down Ohio Street, was that the Plants weren't far from the McKennas. They lived in the same, run-down neighborhood, referred to rather grandly as "Little England" because of some vague historical connection. Perhaps early settlers had first come here, settling on the banks of the Ohio River and setting up the industrial potteries that had once given the area its prosperity, but that prosperity was now but a memory. Out of a couple dozen such enterprises in the tri-state area (Ohio, Pennsylvania and West Virginia), only three remained, a representative business for each of the three states. The area was the first to be flooded whenever the Ohio River got bloated, because the small neighborhood was at, or maybe even below, river level.

The second thing Cass noticed was that, though the Plants were obviously poor, they were not trashy like the McKennas. Their small white clapboard house was well-maintained, with a close-cropped green lawn fronting it, its white and green trim impeccable. The windows were clean, the shrubbery trimmed, and the lawn edged.

Cass pulled over to the curb in the front of the house, putting her Escort in Park and sighing as it chugged down to a stop. The car had nearly 140,000 miles on it and Cass didn't know what she would do if it decided to become one of the dearly departed. Out of the corner of her eye, she saw a blonde-haired girl with long legs, playing with Barbie dolls on the front lawn. The image was comforting, so normal, but as Cass turned her head to get a better look, she discovered, with a jolt to her heart, there was no one on the lawn.

Lucy Plant. Cass felt something sharp-edged and mean gnawing at the pit of her stomach. She briefly fingered her keys, still in the ignition, tempted to restart the car and pull away from the little, well-kept house. She wouldn't have to look back. She owed the Plants nothing. Perhaps, she rationalized, her visions would only add to their grief, raising hopes where none should blossom, and making even more of a mess of their lives.

But Cass couldn't do that. She had never been the kind of person to shrink from helping anyone, even if it was to her own detriment. She remembered briefly her years of trying to "help" Stephanie with her cocaine addiction and how long it had taken her to give up on a situation everyone she knew felt was hopeless. Cass was the only one who believed her "this time will be the last" promises. Cass put faith in her each time she dumped the straws, the screens, the mirrors, in the trash, tearfully telling her she was through with the stuff for good. She seemed so convincing, and perhaps she, too, hoped her resolve would be stronger this time than the last.

Cass shut out the memories, pulled the keys from the ignition, and tossed them into her purse. She took a few deep breaths, unsure how she should handle this new role. Glancing in the rearview mirror, she ran trembling hands through her dark hair and tried to quell the pounding in her chest and her quivering breaths. The woman looking back at her seemed older; the signs of age—a hollowness in her cheeks, a flatness in her green eyes, and even how her lips looked thinner— were all recent developments.

Someone looked out quickly from behind a curtain as Cass walked up the front sidewalk. This, Cass was sure, was no illusion.

She knocked on the door and listened. She swore she heard footsteps and then a staccato burst of urgent whispering. Again, Cass had the urge to turn and run back to the safety of her car. But empathy for other parents' suffering caused her to remain rooted to her spot on the concrete front stoop.

Ron Plant answered Cass's knock. He was a big, raw-boned man, with thick, dark blonde hair. His eyes were wide-spaced and large, so pale blue they were almost startling. His teeth were slightly crooked and his lips were thick. There was something solid about him that was immediately reassuring to Cass.

"Cass?" His voice had a velvet quality, deep but soft enough to make Cass lean slightly forward to make sure she heard him.

"Hi. You must be Ron. We spoke on the phone."

Ron Plant swallowed, and she saw that he was nervous. Cass wished again she hadn't come, wished again she hadn't been drawn reluctantly into this vortex of murderous premonition.

But...maybe she could help.

Ron stepped back, gripping the brass door knob tightly enough, Cass noticed, to whiten his knuckles. "Come on in," he said hoarsely. "I really appreciate you coming by."

Cass walked into the almost blinding darkness of the little house. It took her eyes a couple of minutes to adjust to the dimness after the brightness of the September day outside.

"Sorry about the dark. Karen likes it that way. Or she has, anyway...ever since Lucy, um, went away." Cass followed Ron into a small living room that was done in shades of brown and gold, maple wood, and "country" touches on the wall like straw wreaths with hand-painted wooden geese figures on them. There was a fireplace along one wall, and Cass saw that it wasn't a working one: someone had placed an arrangement of pillar candles in the hearth.

Cass perched on the edge of a brown vinyl recliner and the two said
nothing for a minute. Cass looked around at the knickknacks on the
occasional tables, Precious Moment figurines, ceramic testaments to
times gone by. There were schoolgirls dressed in long dresses, little
boys on tractors, an old-time country church. She noticed the framed
school pictures on top of the console TV. A tow-headed boy in one, a
pre-teen boy with darker hair in a second, and a freckled girl with long
blonde hair in the third. (*Lucy, oh Lucy!*) In between these, there was a
family portrait taken years ago, when the children were still small.
Karen sat proudly with her three children, husband behind her. She was
a small, rotund woman, with brown eyes and short, light brown hair.
Cass felt something stir within her, a recognition of someone who lived
through her children.

"That's Karen and the kids," Ron said, noticing Cass's gaze. "That
was taken a few years ago." Ron stopped for a moment, looking away.
"She's nuts about those kids." He pulled back the sheer curtains
covering the picture window to peer outside. "So am I," he said softly,
speaking more to the glass than to her.

He finally turned back and went to the photo of Lucy on the TV. He
held it out to Cass. "This is our Lucy." Cass didn't want to take the
photo, was afraid of what touching it might inspire in her, what visions
and terrors, but she had no choice.

The brass-framed photo sent a jolt through her. Cass felt an almost
electric surge pass through her and it made her sit back suddenly. Her
hand jerked and she dropped the photo on the floor, cracking its glass.
Lucy's face appeared, for just an instant, in her mind's eye: ashen, milky
open eyes staring up at nothing, a contorted mouth in a final scream or
perhaps gasping for air. And then a shovelful of dirt obscured the
image.

"Oh, I'm sorry." Cass stooped to pick up the photo. "Tsk. Look...I
broke it. I'll buy you a new frame."

Ron knelt beside her. "It's okay. The picture still looks okay." Ron
set the photo back on the TV. A large diagonal crack ran across Lucy
Plant's smiling face.

Cass's heart was thudding and she was afraid that, in a moment,
she would find it hard to breathe. "Do you think I could have a glass of
water?"

"Sure thing." Ron hurried out of the room and Cass heard him in
the kitchen, running water from the tap. She took a few deep breaths,
trying to calm herself. What was she going to say to these people?

When Ron came back with the water, he grinned sheepishly.
"Sorry, we're all out of ice. But I ran it for a while to get it nice and
cold." He sat down across from Cass while she drank, staring at his
hands, which he had folded in his lap.

Cass took a while, drinking the water slowly, trying not to think, staving off the inevitable. She didn't want to discuss Lucy, didn't want to tell this kind man that she thought his daughter had been killed, that her last moments were filled with terror and pain. Why had she been chosen to bring this message?

"Where do you work, um, Mr. Plant?"

Ron looked up from his hands and smiled. "Please. Mr. Plant's my dad. Call me Ron."

"Okay, Ron."

"St. Clair Ceramics. Down the river a bit?"

"Oh yeah, I know it. One of my girlfriends used to work there, in the color room. She was a dipper. Do you know what that is? She would dip the ware in different colors before it was fired..."

"I know what it is. I work there, remember?"

Cass laughed. "Stupid of me. What do you do there?"

"Caster. I work with the liquid clay; we call it slip. I fill the mold, time it, and out comes a piece of pottery. A jug or a decanter. Vases. Stuff like that." Ron stretched. "Been there fifteen years, ever since I graduated high school. How 'bout you?"

"The Elite diner. Waitress." Cass smiled. "It pays the bills. Barely."

"Great fries."

The two fell silent, neither looking at the other. Cass went back to studying Karen Plant's knickknack collection and Ron to the study of his big, calloused hands. Making conversation when Lucy Plant was out there somewhere, missing, bordered on inanity. But Cass needed Ron to bring up the subject of his daughter first. If she did so, it seemed too cruel to her, almost as if she was eager to deliver her hopeless portents.

"Would you like to meet Karen?" Ron said finally.

"Sure. If you think she's, um, up to it." Cass looked around. "Where is she?"

"She's upstairs."

Karen Plant was no longer the woman in the Sears family portrait downstairs. Gone were the laugh lines around her eyes, the alertness in those same dark brown irises. Karen Plant lay in bed, her skin so sallow it almost blended in with the cream pillow supporting her sagging head. Her hair hung straight and dirty, partly obscuring her face. She stared at a TV set on a stand in a corner of the room, its volume so low it was barely audible. When Ron and Cass entered the bedroom, her eyes registered only the barest flicker.

How was this woman managing to get by? How were the brothers Lucy had left behind coping?

Ron knelt beside the bed and took one of his wife's plump, but tiny hands in his own, engulfing it. "Cold," he whispered, then spoke in a louder voice. "Karen, honey, this is Cass D'Angelo. She's stopped by to visit. Don't you want to say hello?"

Karen moved her head slowly to Cass, who stood in the doorway, shifting her weight from one foot to the other. It was as if the woman saw her for the first time. She lifted colorless lips in a glimmer of a smile, then resumed staring at the TV screen.

Ron looked helplessly at Cass. "Karen's taken this really hard."

"I understand." Oh God, why did she have to bear witness to this? Cass moved a little farther into the room. "Hello, Karen." Cass didn't know what to do with herself.

But Karen wasn't speaking. Whatever was on the flickering TV screen required all of her interest.

"I should be going," Cass said in a barely audible voice. There was just too much here: too much despair, too much hopelessness, too much loss. She didn't know if she could bear it much more. She turned and hurried down the blue-carpeted stairs.

Outside, she stood gasping, wanting to cry, wanting to bring Lucy back to the Plants, whole and smiling, the victim of some youthful misunderstanding. But even though she had no provable evidence to back it up, she was certain such a homecoming was no longer a possibility.

She was about to dash for the safety of her little Escort when the door opened behind her. She could feel Ron Plant standing behind her, blue eyes pleading.

"You know something. I've heard about people like you. Psychics. I've seen on TV where they've helped people find...lost...loved ones."

Cass turned to look at him, took in his reddened face and moist eyes.

"I don't know."

"I think you do."

Cass walked back toward the house, feeling pulled by a force beyond her control. She stood in front of Ron Plant, staring down at the sidewalk, where a horde of ants busied itself with the sticky residue on a discarded Popsicle stick. She breathed in, raised her eyes to the man, and rallied herself.

"She's somewhere down by the river. When I see her, the bridge to West Virginia is in the background, due south I would guess."

Ron took one of Cass's hands in his own, engulfing it and squeezing so tight, it was painful. But Cass did nothing to withdraw her hand from his grasp.

"Will you help me look for her?" His eyes were wet and Cass knew he had nowhere else to turn.

Cass bit her lower lip, bit so hard she tasted the copper of her own blood, then gingerly explored the tear with her tongue. The words she wanted to say were, "I don't want to."

But what she said was, "Of course."

Chapter
Eleven

CASS STARED OUT the window of Ron Plant's car, a late-model American. Maybe a Grand Am? Cass didn't know cars. The radio played softly, tuned to one of those "smooth jazz" stations out of Pittsburgh. Dulled brass instruments tried, without much success, to bring to life Duke Ellington's "Take the A Train." The piece was an abomination, Cass thought, something that would have the late Duke spinning in his grave.

Cass wanted to think of anything but the man beside her. The two had not spoken since she had gotten in the car. Cass had gone home from the Plants' long enough to greet Max when he came home from school and to give him a quick supper of white trash pasta (Kraft Macaroni and Cheese blended with a can of tuna and a box of frozen peas) and chocolate milk. Cass's stomach had not allowed her to eat anything. She downed a cup of black coffee, for fortification, she supposed. But all the caffeine did was up the jangling of her nerves. After Max had finished eating, she took him over to her parents.

"Date tonight?" her mother asked. "You could have let us know a little sooner."

Because she didn't want to get into the real reason for dropping Max off with them, Cass let her mother believe what she wanted, even if it included the belief that Cass would be out drinking and slutting around. It was easier than trying to explain to the old woman that she would be off with Ron Plant, the father of a missing girl, helping him find his daughter. The latter would entail far more questions than a simple night out at the Green Mill.

The moon was full, a big silver orb setting on the hills towering above the Ohio River. Its pale light gave everything a silver glow and Cass was grateful. At least they would be able to see as they searched. Gratitude, however, might quickly be usurped by horror, if Cass's intuition about Lucy Plant was right.

But Cass didn't want to think about that. In fact, Cass didn't want to think about anything. She continued to stare out the window, trying to keep the visions that danced just below consciousness at bay. Visions of a small pale hand on a background of rich, black river soil, the pink nails besotted with grime.

Ron pointed the car toward the river. "This way, right?" His voice came out just above a whisper, shaky.

"Right." Cass tried to think of Max and other, more conventional, worries. The Ohio curved along the town of Summitville and even though Max had been warned, over and over, to keep away from its muddy banks, Cass was certain her admonitions wouldn't keep him away. Parental warnings had failed to blind generations of boys from the river's allure. As a child, Cass herself had explored its banks, searching for discarded treasure among the rusting metal cans, abandoned tires, and other detritus that the river expelled, even wading into its brackish waters when the weather turned hot. And she was still here.

And yet, Cass couldn't calm herself with thoughts of her own survival. Almost every summer, the river claimed another life, usually a young boy who ventured out into the water and found himself flailing against the strong currents away from the shore, currents that carried him toward an unexpected, yet certain, oblivion. And there were always the older women whose husbands had vanished, either through death or desertion, who would wash up, free from loss...free from everything.

Such cheerful thoughts! Cass reprimanded herself.

And then thought of the alternative. *Lucy. Will we find you tonight?*

Ron steered the car down a bumpy road filled with potholes, and headed toward the river. In the distance, cooling towers from Summitville Power, one of the nation's first nuclear power plants, rose up against the night sky, tiny lights on the towers blinking in the darkness. The towers, sentinels against the silvery night, gave an almost surreal feel to their venture. Wafts of steam came off the tops of the two towers, to be snatched up by the wind. Cass thought of how a girl back in grade school had thought the towers manufactured clouds. She wished she could be back there, among such innocent thoughts.

"This the right way?" he asked. His mouth was set in a line, his stare intent on the bouncing twin lights illuminating the road in front of him.

"Yeah, this is what I've, um, seen. See the New Hope Bridge? It's south of here. Just like in..." Cass's voice trailed off. Just like in what? Her dreams? Her visions? It all sounded so full of hocus-pocus. This was not the kind of person Cass had ever imagined herself being. She cleared her throat and simply said, "I think this is the right way."

The road grew narrower, bumpier and dirtier as they neared the water's edge, until finally it petered out altogether. Ahead of them lay a large, grassy field and beyond that, a copse of trees already beginning to shed their leaves with the approach of cooler weather.

Ron switched off the ignition and turned to Cass. She didn't need to look at him to know his large blue eyes were pleading with her to shoulder the burden, to lift from him this cloak of doubt and anguish, even if it meant getting the worst possible answer to his questions.

Ron swallowed hard. Cass knew what he was thinking: if Lucy was in this field, there was no way they would find her safe.

Cass longed for some optimistic words to give him, some reassurance. She wished there existed some optimism for herself. She hoped to find Lucy Plant cold and shivering, hiding behind some trees, a runaway too scared of parental wrath to come home, but grateful to fall into the arms of her father.

Even with the windows rolled up, Cass got a sudden whiff of dark earth, its smell telling a tale of something recently buried. There, she knew, near the water's churning edge, where the soil would be easy to dig, that's where they would find Lucy.

And finding Lucy that way, Cass thought with horror, was the last thing she wanted tonight.

She wanted to be wrong.

Wordlessly, the two got out of the car. The air had a slight chill. Cass wrapped her arms around herself..

"It's going to be okay," Ron said to her. "It's going to be okay, isn't it?"

Cass said nothing as the two of them stepped over a chain that supposedly barred anyone from entering the field.

The ground beneath them squished with each step they took, and as they progressed, their feet sank deeper into the mud, causing them to have to pull their feet out sometimes, with a loud sucking noise. An odor of fish wafted up from the river.

"She's not here," Cass said. "This is pointless. You should be home...in case the police call, in case Karen needs something."

"Is that what you really think?"

Ron stopped and turned to her, his blonde hair lifted by a gust that smelled of something rotten. "If that's what you really think, let's go back to the car."

Cass swallowed hard, bit her lip. For a long time, she stared out at the black water of the Ohio, its surface splashed with the silver of the moon. It would be so easy to just go back to the car, in fact. Wouldn't it? She could return, guilt-wracked but ignorant — pick up Max, take him to her own little home, put him to bed, drink some wine, and try to put this behind her. *Yes...that would be so easy*, Cass thought. *So simple.* She turned back to Ron. "No." She took in some air, exhaling slowly. "Give me a second."

Cass had never tried to make a vision come before. The visions themselves were unwanted, intruders to her psyche that she would have excised from her brain if she could have. Gladly. But she wanted to help, even if helping meant ending this family's suffering only by replacing it with a new kind of grief. At least there would be the comfort (if you could call it that) of knowing. She closed her eyes, breathing in the cool, damp air, and made herself go limp, opening herself up, in a way, to whatever her newly found vision might bring her.

For a while, there was nothing. Just random thoughts, then a hope, and a dread, that this bizarre gift had left her as mysteriously as it had come.

And then a flash: a wash of red, dark, like blood, across the inside of her eyelids. "Near the water," Cass whispered. "She's near the water." She didn't open her eyes, not wanting to see the pain on Ron Plant's face, and wanting to be more certain of where they might find...something. She saw herself walking closer to the pebbled, sandy shore, a place where the grassy surface of the field dropped off to meet a littered beach. In her mind, she made herself look up, peering across the dark water to the opposite shore, West Virginia.

And across the shore was a house, its yellow lights like a beacon in the darkness. The moon gave just enough light to supply details: a one-story ranch constructed of light brick. Run down. The drainpipe broken and falling off the side of the roof. There was a doghouse, and outside it, a mutt was chained. Dark, big, with pointed ears. A Shepherd mix.

Cass attuned her senses and, far off, but still close enough, she heard the barking of a dog. Its bass woofs were barely audible and coming from somewhere downriver.

She took Ron Plant's cold, callused hand in her own. "This way," she said, leading him along the shoreline. She wanted to cry, but she held back the pain, swallowed hard against the ball forming in her throat. "This way."

It wasn't long before the two of them came to what she had seen. The brick ranch was the only house occupying this part of the West Virginia shore. The barking of the dog had led them ever closer, almost as if the animal were a guide. Cass stopped and looked at Ron then, her eyes bright with tears in the darkness. She didn't need to say anything.

Before them, the grass had been trampled.

They trudged forward, on through the darkness and the damp, silent. Cass stumbled and fell to the ground. She grunted as the air was knocked out of her. "What the hell?" she groaned, when she had found enough breath to put behind her words. But she knew. She knew.

The two looked down to see a mound of fresh dirt. Some tin cans had been pulled over it, along with some drying weeds, but the dirt looked freshly dug; nothing could hide that. All around them, weeds and various grasses grew unchecked. But there was this spot, a rough rectangle in shape, about as long as Cass was tall.

Cass dropped to her knees in the mud and began digging.

Ron grabbed her shoulder. "Maybe we should go back and get the cops."

"I can't!" Cass shrieked. "I can't wait that long. I have to know." She threw up clumps of wet dirt behind her as her hands went deeper and deeper into the moist soil.

Ron couldn't wait either. He knelt beside her and began to dig, clawing through the moist earth.

They dug for about a half hour before Cass's hand hit on something. She recoiled, wanting to vomit, yanking her muddy hand back from what she had just touched.

It felt like cold flesh.

"Cass, stop." Ron pulled her hands out of the dirt. She turned to him, her lower lip quivering.

"What is it?"

"I hit something."

"What?"

"I don't know," Cass said, lying. She knew all too well what she had felt: flesh and bone. "Please, let's go call the cops. I think we need to."

"I won't stop. I can't." Ron buried his hands in the earth once more, near Cass's. She knew what he would find and didn't want him to experience the icy touch she had just felt. She pushed him away, hard. She was gasping. Turning from him, she dug some more. Maybe what she had felt wasn't really human flesh...

Only seconds passed before she stopped as if stunned and screamed.

"It felt like hair! It felt like hair!" She closed her eyes, trying to hold down the acid bile rising up to splash against the back of her throat.

She heard Ron behind her, wheezing, gasping. She thought it would be only moments before he began to wail. She bent over and dug more.

The moon appeared from behind a cloud and revealed a silvery whiteness in the dirt.

It was a human hand. A small, heart-shaped ring glinted on the third finger.

Ron whispered, "It's Lucy."

He brushed away more dirt. Long blonde hair emerged, and a face that made him turn, finally, and retch into the weeds.

The face of a young girl, decomposing and half-eaten, stared up from sockets devoid of eyes. Lucy Plant. Even though insects and decomposition horribly disfigured the face, Cass would have recognized the blonde hair anywhere. She remembered, with a jolt, Lucy's school photograph: a smiling young girl, on the brink of womanhood, with the same long blonde hair. Hair that was now streaked with mud.

Cass shut her eyes. She reached out to touch Lucy's cheek, looking blue-white even in the darkness, already mottled with mold. She snatched back her hand, biting her lower lip so hard she tasted blood. "Oh God, why?"

Chapter
Twelve

THERE WAS LITTLE Dani could do to escape this shit-hole of a town. Summitville, Pennsylvania. God, in her wildest of wild dreams (and she'd had more than her share of those), she'd never thought she'd find herself in such a place. Foothills of the Appalachians. A little town, population 15,000, clinging desperately to the banks of the Ohio River and an economy, once buoyed up by steel mills and industrial potteries, in rapid decline. The people downriver just a bit were called hoopies (with vague origins in the Mingo Indian language, Indians that had once occupied this fertile land, now home to nothing more than the smell of decay and better times gone before). *How in the hell?*

She knew. Oh, she knew. Some ten years ago, in her home in the West Midlands of England, she had met a woman who had been traveling through, on vacation, visiting Cannock. A fair-haired woman with blue eyes, blonde hair, and a body made for porno movies, but with a spirit made for the nunnery.

They had met on Cannock Chase, a large, unspoiled area of trees and meadows, creeks, the whole of it covered in pale purple heather. The perfect meeting, like something out of a Jane Austen novel, updated for the 20th century.

And it was all over for Dani. At thirty, the anarchist and cynic had fallen hopelessly in love. All the silly love songs she had poked fun of took on new resonance. Fucking morphed into making love. Two weeks was all it took. Two weeks of traipsing around her little island of a country, showing Sharon everything from Stonehenge to the Glastonbury Tor, to the Roman baths in Bath, to the pebbled beaches of Brighton, to the houses of Parliament and the bright lights of the West End of London.

Ten years ago, it had taken only two weeks for Dani to find herself on a British Airways plane, bound for New York City, then Pittsburgh, then riding next to Sharon in a beat-to-shit Datsun Sentra to Summitville.

It took only ten months for Sharon to disappear. Her disappearance mysteriously coincided with the appearance of Dani's love of mind-altering substances, the most innocent of which was single malt Scotch and the most nefarious of which was crystal methamphetamine, which could keep her going for days. Sharon never understood why Dani couldn't sleep...and why she no longer had any interest in making love to her.

And so Sharon had fled, run back to parents in Warren, Ohio, leaving Dani alone, an alien in a country with no funds to get home and an appetite for destruction.

Dani had always been able to write, and over several varieties of malt in a local bar one hazy, half-remembered night, Dani had "interviewed" with the editor of the *Evening Review*, Summitville's only newspaper. The man and the rail-thin woman with graying hair, who shared a taste for mind-numbing and endless chatter, found reciprocal needs in the other. Sean Green needed a reporter. Dani needed a job.

And so her journalistic career was born. Intending at first only to make enough money to get back to England, Dani, at least in the first few years, never achieved her goal. The funds went up her nose, down her throat, up in smoke.

As she grew older, the substances lost some of their allure and Dani was able, with no small amount of difficult starts and stops, to put them behind her. And she found herself yet another character in this fucked-up post-modern version of Sherwood Anderson's *Winesburg, Ohio*. She became another character on the periphery and a byline people recognized. She was a familiar face at domestic disturbances, courtrooms, and jail cells. Danielle Westwood became a resident of Summitville, and eventually a citizen of a country she had never intended to visit.

Was Dani settled? Was Dani happy? In a word: no. But the pull of life's orbit was too strong for her to resist, and like so many middle-aged and thick-through-the-middle women, she had lost the route out of a life that only chance, and certainly not she, had chosen.

So on nights like this one, Dani sought oblivion. Gone were the jangling highs of crystal meth, but the Scotch had hung around, an old amber lover, warm at night though ruthless in the morning, eating away at Dani's liver but rescuing her from having to think too hard about the mess she had made of her life — a life spent alone in a shabby, one-bedroom apartment in Summitville's in-critical-condition downtown, where her downstairs neighbors were an interchangeable family of hoopies from down the river in West Virginia.

And she had her music. Dani favored bands of her youth: the Ramones, the Kinks, Cockney Rebel, early Bowie. She could down half a fifth, listen to the music at ear-splitting volume, and fall asleep with all the lights on, thinking that this life wasn't so bad after all. Until the next morning.

She was about to fall into just such a stupor when her phone rang. Dani sat up, heart pounding for all it was worth. The music had ceased about an hour ago and the phone was like an alarm. "Bloody fuck," she whispered to herself, rubbing her salt-and-pepper hair with one hand and reaching for the cordless with the other.

" 'Lo?" Why hadn't she just ripped the thing out of the wall, let it ring, let the machine pick up...make one of myriad choices people chose when they didn't want to be bothered by the twentieth century's most obtrusive instrument?

Because Dani, in spite of it all, was an eternal optimist, and every time that telephone jangled, it just might be good news, a savior come to call, to whisk her away from a life she certainly had no control over anymore, and that she had no means to escape.

It was Sean Green on the other end, former drinking buddy, editor, only friend, and pain in the ass.

Dani lit a Marlboro and looked at the blue display on her DVD player. A little after eleven. The call couldn't be good news. Not at this hour. Green had found himself a wife somewhere along the way and the days of hours-long drunken late night calls were long past.

"Dani. You awake, buddy?"

Once Dani would have bristled at being called anyone's "buddy." Now she barely gave it a second thought. "Barely. This better be good."

Sean sucked in some air, making a noise that sounded half between a gasp and a chuckle. *What the hell?* "It is good, at least in the way you mean it. But it's bad, bad news."

"Listening to your police scanner again?"

"Right." There was a long pause then. Dani's stomach lurched. She knew something bad was about to be said. Something really awful.

"You've been writing about those missing girls?"

"Yeah, yeah." *Oh shit, no...*

"Well, they found one of them. Down by the river. Lucy Plant. I think you need to get down there."

Dani saw the photo of the little blonde girl in her mind's eye—sweet, uncorrupted—and shook her head, drawing in deeply on her cigarette. "Christ, no. She's dead, right?"

"Afraid so."

Dani shook her head, amazed at how quickly trauma, and despair, could clear it. "Murdered?"

"Looks that way, Dani. Listen, go down, get the details, write it up. I'll hold tomorrow's edition until you get the story in. Think you can turn it around in a couple of hours? You up for a big byline?"

"Don't try to tempt me with fame, mate. It's too late for that. I'll get my skinny ass down there, but for the girl's sake, not mine."

"Whatever. This is front page, and once it hits, you're going to be elbowing for a place at the table with the big boys from Pittsburgh and the like."

"Right. I'm on my way." A cold shower and a clean set of clothes, assembled in less than ten minutes, would transform her from lush to ace reporter. At least that was the ruse that had been working this past decade. "Who found her?"

Another pause. "The girl's dad."

"Christ."

"And an unidentified woman. Don't have all the details."

"I'm off, then." Dani hung up the phone, stubbed out her cigarette, and headed for the bathroom.

THE NIGHT HAD turned cold. Cass wrapped her arms around herself, thinking the chill creeping into her bones was so much more than meteorological. It seemed that no matter how much she hugged herself, she could find no warmth. Ron Plant stood near her, face gone blank, ashen in the moon's silver light. Even without the pale illumination, Cass was certain that Ron Plant still would have looked white. After trying to talk to him a few times, to offer some useless words of comfort, she had given up. The man had turned to stone. No tears. No furrowing of the eyebrows. No screaming to the heavens. Nothing. Ron Plant's zombie-like demeanor was more disturbing than any expression of grief could have been.

Cass wished there was something she could do for him. An attempt at a hug did nothing; it was like hugging a statue. She did all she could think of, wrapped her pink sweater around his broad shoulders. It looked ridiculous hanging there, doll clothes on a giant, but Cass knew a little about shock and knew that a person headed into that numb condition needed warmth. She had given him all she possibly could.

Which is why she was left shivering and unable to think what she should do. There was that selfish voice inside her, the one she so often wished she could quell, but it always spoke the undeniable truth. And that voice, try as she might to ignore it, told Cass to give Ron Plant a squeeze on his shoulder, tell him to keep the sweater, and that she would find some way home without him. The police would be there soon; the coroner. She longed to hold Max in her arms, to feel his solid, small warmth against her, the reassurance of his soapy-smelling hair, and the satin of his skin, still like a baby's. She wanted to bury her nose in his hair, make him uncomfortable by holding him too tightly, and revel in the reality that *her* child was still there; *her* child was alive.

It was selfish, but Cass wondered if any parent, thrown into such a bizarre, sickening situation, wouldn't have exactly the same desire.

Cass's wished she had never been the instrument which led this shell-shocked father to the body of his daughter; a sight no man should ever have to endure. Why did she have to be a part of it? Did God give her this ability? Or did some other dark power force this new "gift" upon her? She didn't care that, at the very least, this gruesome discovery had put an end to one family's questions about their missing child. It also put an end to their hope, and marked a beginning of a grief that, Cass was sure, would remain with them throughout their lives.

The police had arrived. Squawking, mechanical voices and rumbling engines filled the chill of the night; whirling blue lights and strobes of white gave a surreal, carnival feel to their discovery.

Lucy Plant's murder no longer dwelled in the realm of the private; it was rapidly becoming public domain. The thought made Cass sick to her stomach. She realized why the police needed to be there. They were only doing their jobs, beginning the relentless hunt for clues that would lead them to the person or people who had done this awful thing. And with that thought, a vision of a platinum-haired woman, her face obscured by the red-blinking light and bulk of a video camera, came chillingly into focus.

Would Cass, in the supermarket, on a walk downtown, or her way to work, recognize the people who had done this to Lucy Plant? And if she did, would anyone believe her when she tried to convince them of their guilt? Would any court accept her visions as evidence?

Cass knew the answer to those questions as she turned to stare out at the shiny blackness of the Ohio River. What good was having this gift if no one believed her?

She turned back to the "crime scene," where spotlights, impossibly bright, were being set up, where yellow crime scene tape roped off a large area around where the body had been discovered, where Lucy Plant, lying lifeless and white, would be invaded by tape measures, the flash of a camera, the stares of the grimly fascinated and the concerned. Why, Cass thought, the scene was almost festive.

It was nauseating.

But what other choice was there? Let the killers go free? And Cass knew, somehow, that there were killers, in the plural; two, not one, a man and a woman. She knew it as surely as she knew her own name.

Cass watched as an older woman with gunmetal gray hair, a man's trench coat, and the orange glow of a cigarette's tip in her fingers, made her way through the uniformed police and others gathered on the scene. The woman looked so familiar. It didn't take Cass long to realize who she was. And once Cass remembered she was the detective she had tried to convince that she knew something about the then-missing girl's disappearance, the woman's name came back to her: Marion Hartley.

Oh, Marion Hartley, would you believe me now?

Why didn't you listen when I came to you before? Why couldn't you open your mind to all the possibilities?

Dejectedly, Cass thought (knew), that when she had spoken to Detective Hartley, it had already been too late. But still...the detective could have listened with less of a scornful look in her eye, with less ridicule brimming at her lips.

For a while, Cass thought of nothing, and watched as Marion Hartley made her rounds, speaking to a uniformed cop here, a black-suited man there, gathering the concrete information she needed to solve this atrocity. No whims or ethereal visions for her, Cass could see that much just watching Marion Hartley. There was nothing tentative in the woman's demeanor. Marion Hartley, it was clear through even cursory observation, was hard, all business. Cass should have known the moment she first encountered her that Marion Hartley would never be the kind of woman who would put any stock in the pronouncements of *psychics*.

Just thinking the word made Cass's stomach leap. *Psychic*. Was that what she was now? Was that how she would become known? And if she was psychic, why hadn't she known that her trip to the police station so recently would have been for nothing?

Why didn't she know, if she had second sight, what she should do now to make things better?

They would want to talk to her. Marion Hartley, others. Hell, they might even suspect her.

"And how did you know exactly where to find the body, Ms. D'Angelo?"

"Where were you when Lucy Plant disappeared?"

"Is there someone who can verify your whereabouts at the time of the girl's disappearance?"

"Maybe you should come along with us."

Cass shook her head, feeling sicker with each passing moment. Why, why, why had she been so *blessed*?

Before she could ponder these fears and questions further, someone approached her. Cass started and turned at a touch of her elbow.

"Hello. I'm sorry to bother you. I'm Dani Westwood, with the *Review*. Do you think I might have a word?"

And both Cass and Ron turned at the same moment to encounter a tired-looking woman, small-statured, wearing jeans and a flannel shirt, with wild salt-and-pepper hair, eyes lost in the reflections of her tiny, round glasses.

Cass didn't know what to say. She hadn't thought yet of the press, of their interest in such a gruesome, and sensational, story. Of course, they would want to talk to her. Talk to the grieving father...so the rest of the world could rest easy, at least it wasn't us...this time.

Ron Plant said nothing. There was a calming fascination for him, it seemed to Cass, in staring at the dark, churning waters of the Ohio River.

"Who did you say you were?" Cass mumbled. The woman waited expectantly, digital camera bag at her hip, mini-tape recorder in her hand. *Just another vulture doing a job*, Cass thought.

The reporter stepped forward and Cass saw her eyes, yellowish and shot through with red, behind the round lenses of her glasses. "Dani Westwood, ma'am. From the *Review*? And you are?"

Cass didn't know what to do. She hadn't prepared for this. Again, she wondered why her second sight didn't ready her for such things, why the gift (or curse) was so selective in what it did, or did not, reveal.

Should she tell the reporter her name? She didn't need ESP to know that giving this woman a bit of her story might thrust her into an unwelcome scrutiny. The public was hungry for such peculiarities, especially when those peculiarities had something to do with something as exciting as murder.

But if she didn't talk to Dani Westwood, the reporter might go after Ron Plant, and one thing the man did not need right now was the prying of reporters.

Or maybe all she needed to do was tell this unhealthy-looking little woman to fuck off.

"Never mind who I am. It's not important. You probably want to talk to the police...and there are plenty of them around. Why don't you go bother one of them?" Cass turned away, hoping the reporter would do the same.

Of course, that wish was not granted. "Please," she heard from behind her. "You're the woman who helped Mr. Plant here find the body, aren't you?"

The woman had certainly done her homework, Cass thought. How could she find so much out so quickly? It was less than an hour ago that they had discovered Lucy's body. Amazing how quickly the discovery set things into motion.

The reporter waited, hands at her sides. "Look. You have no reason to believe me, but I'm not looking to sensationalize this. It's a job I have to do. I don't do it, someone else does. Maybe someone who isn't as ethical as I am. Maybe someone who's just looking for a story that will draw attention to themselves, rather than elicit sympathy or understanding for what's happened here."

"And you're someone I can trust, right?"

Westwood smiled. "I don't know about that. But I'm not some fame-hungry reporter, looking to make a name for herself no matter what. Could you talk to me, please?"

"Promise me one thing."

"What?"

"That...at least for now, you'll leave Mr. Plant here alone. He just lost his daughter."

There was silence, save for the whispering of the trees.

"Thank you, Cass." The voice that emerged from Ron Plant had lost all its confidence. It was a watered-down version of its former self. "You don't have to look out for me."

Cass put her hand on his shoulder, looked up to see the tears standing in his eyes. "Look, why don't you go talk to the police. I'll deal with Ms. Westwood here."

She watched as the man lumbered away toward the lights and activity. Years had been added to his gait in the span of an hour, and all she could think was: *Don't look at Lucy again. Whatever you do, don't look at her again.*

Cass turned back to Dani Westwood. Tiredly. "What is it you want to know?"

Westwood clicked the tape recorder on. "Tell me how you and Mr. Plant happened to find the girl."

Chapter
Thirteen

BY THE TIME Cass returned to her little green-shingled house, the sky in the east was brightening with dull gray light. Fog shrouded her yard, transforming Max's swing set into something dark and geometric: a machine, sinister, its intended purpose vanished under the mist. It had been a night like no other; the darkness more than just an absence of light, but a feeling, a descriptor, a summing up of events that went beyond human comprehension.

She tried to think of nothing. Her eyes burned. Her limbs felt heavy, weighted down. But Cass knew that too much had happened in the past several hours to allow her racing mind the oblivion of sleep. Going to bed right now would be an exercise in futility. It was the old conundrum of being too tired to sleep. She sat down on the stoop, determined to watch the slowly rising sun, an orb of orange in a milky gray sky, as it worked on the fog, burning it away, bringing the day to life.

She didn't want to, but couldn't help replaying the events of the previous night, over and over, a Technicolor nightmare on endless loop. Starting with the horror of the discovery of Lucy Plant's body (the image she most wanted to banish from her mind), and ending with Marion Hartley's cool, incredulous interrogation of her in her office at City Hall, the night was one she wished she could simply permanently excise from her memory.

That interview served only to further impress the memory of Lucy Plant's decomposing and half-buried body on her mind.

MARION HARTLEY HAD remembered Cass from her previous visit. As the two women sat in Hartley's office, Styrofoam cups of coffee on the scarred desk in front of them, a tape recorder bearing silent witness to their talk, the older woman regarded the younger with obvious disdain and suspicion. Cass knew that look: the slightly down-turned mouth, the rheumy eyes that stared at her without sympathy or compassion.

Before they had even begun talking, Cass felt intimidated. She wanted to banish any outward signs of her fear, thinking that those telltale gestures might make Marion Hartley more suspicious of her than she already was. But she crossed and recrossed her legs, folded her arms in front of her, then leaned forward to brace herself against her knees, twirled her hair, wiped at something annoying and absent from her upper lip. And when she realized she was doing any of these things, she would stop, staring out the window at the black night that pressed in against the detective's grimy window like something palpable.

"We've met before," Hartley said, lighting up a cigarette. "I know I'm not supposed to do this." She held the cigarette up. "But it's late. What are they gonna do? Arrest me?" She didn't smile, squinting through the smoke spiraling up in front of her craggy, bespectacled face. Cass was, by turns, repulsed by the smell of the cigarette, its burning stink, and wanting to ask Hartley if she could have one of the Marlboros lying in a box atop her desk.

"Yes. Only a short time ago." Cass looked around the office and thought how little of the personality of its occupant showed: bare white walls, a beige metal credenza with an empty top, a desk piled high with reports, a black telephone, a plain green cup filled with pencils, and nothing else. No photographs. No commendations. Not even a cheap framed print on the wall.

"Remind me what you came in here to talk to me about."

Cass stared at her shoes, noticing how muddy they were, beyond cleaning. Even though she couldn't afford it, she would have to get herself down to Payless Shoe Source and buy herself a new pair. The only thing these shoes were now good for was the garbage. "I, uh, thought I might be able to help you with the disappearance of those girls."

"You mean the disappearance of Lucy Plant?"

"Yes." Cass was about to add, "And Sheryl McKenna," but then thought better of it. She glanced briefly at Hartley, who had leaned forward in her chair, regarding Cass with undisguised distaste.

"Did you know Lucy Plant? Her family?"

"No, not until just recently."

Hartley nodded. "Just recently," she repeated. "And how did you come to make their acquaintance?"

Something small, with razor-sharp teeth, began to gnaw at Cass's gut. What should she say? How could she make this woman, who it seemed had already made up her mind that Cass was a nut case, or worse, a murderer's accomplice, take her seriously? Cass didn't know. She plunged forward. "Ron Plant got in touch with me; he had heard I might know something about his daughter's disappearance and he begged me to help them. They were at their wit's end; they were willing to try anything to help them find out what had happened to Lucy." Cass paused. "Even talking to me."

Hartley nodded her head slowly. "I see. You said that Ron Plant had heard you might know something. Where would he have heard something like that?"

So it would all come out. What did it matter? "I had talked to the McKennas. You know who they are. Their daughter Sheryl is missing. I wanted to tell them that I might be able to help them locate her. Might. I don't know. I just wanted to help." Cass looked up at Hartley, meeting her eyes. "The McKennas told the Plants about me. Warned them, actually. They thought I was nuts—just like you do."

Hartley ignored the comment. "Just so I'm sure I understand: Mr. Plant got in touch with you to see if he could find out what you thought you knew. Having such information might help him find his missing daughter."

"That's right."

"Refresh my memory. How would you happen to know where either of these girls had gone?" Hartley clicked open the tape recorder, ejected the cassette, flipped it over, and pressed Record. "And you certainly seem to have hit the jackpot tonight."

"As I told you when I was in here before, I get visions, if you will. Kind of like waking dreams. Lately I've been seeing things about the girls. I don't know why. They just come to me."

"So, you're like a psychic."

"I don't know what I am." Cass was sure her voice would have been raised, higher-pitched, and edging on hysteria had it not been for her exhaustion. "I was out looking for my son, Max? I got hit on the head. A concussion, a little time in the hospital. When I came to, I seemed to know things. I know it sounds unbelievable, and I really wish it wasn't so, but that's the way things are. Maybe, if there's a God, He gave me a gift for a reason. I have to try and help. I can't keep these things to myself. Obviously, there's some validity to what I see in my head. Don't you think?"

Hartley ignored her question. "And so you saw Lucy Plant's grave, down by the river?"

"Yes. Sort of. I knew something to do with her was down by the river. I knew where it was because I would see the house over in West Virginia and how close the bridge was to where she had been buried."

"And you never knew the girl before?"

"Never. I swear." Cass felt a lump form in her throat, but didn't want to give Hartley the satisfaction of seeing her cry.

THE SUN HAD come up, full, burning the last wisps of fog off Cass's damp lawn. She sat on the back porch stoop, leaning against the house, eyes closed. Marion Hartley had told her that she shouldn't leave town; the police would certainly want to talk to her again.

Cass rose on weighted legs and went inside. The kitchen looked like someone else's, its stack of newspapers on the kitchen cabinet, the little radio, the dishes in the sink and the sunflower place mats on her maple kitchen table all unfamiliar, as if she had stumbled into the house of a stranger.

And maybe she had. Who was Cass D'Angelo? Certainly no one *she* had never met before.

Ah, she was just exhausted beyond reason, traumatized beyond belief. A little sleep, fetching Max from her parents, getting him off to school, cleaning up the house, and going back to her routine at the diner would put things back to normal quickly enough.

Was *normal* a territory to which Cass could ever return? She shook her head, wondering what the future would hold for her. Shouldn't she know that? Isn't that what psychics could do? Read the future? Why was hers so uncertain?

And then she walked into the living room and saw Sheryl McKenna sitting on the couch, waiting for her.

"Oh," Cass mumbled, her hand rising to her forehead. She had a silly thought: imagining herself like some cartoon, closing and re-opening her eyes to test the reality of what lay before her.

But Cass didn't do that. The girl, sitting cross-legged on her living room couch was as real as the tan Berber carpeting beneath her feet. There was no ghostly aura surrounding her. She was just a girl, clad in jeans and a black tank top. Her black hair, straight, shone in the morning light filtering in through Cass's mini-blinds, making slats across the girl's hair and her face, which showed no reaction to Cass's entrance to the room. Sheryl McKenna stared straight ahead, with an intensity that made Cass look to where the girl's gaze was focused. But there was nothing there save for the little cart upon which sat her TV, its screen rolling and static-filled.

And then Cass understood. This wasn't a psychic vision. Sheryl McKenna was alive. Cass didn't understand why the girl would come to her, or how she had gotten into her house, but this was no vision. The girl was as real as Cass herself. Cass was certain that if she sat beside her on the couch, she would feel warmth emanating from her body. If she reached out with her hands, Cass could feel the silk of her hair, the smoothness of her skin.

Sheryl stared at the flickering images of the TV screen. Cass looked to where the girl had focused her gaze. The TV, which usually got pretty good reception, was snowy, little white lines rolled across its surface. It was like a blizzard and almost impossible to make out what was on the screen. Then she saw it: a view of the river. The camera looked down on the flowing muddy waters, as if the shot was taken from a high up, on a hilltop. The camera moved back to reveal a few trees and...a trailer? With all the snow and static, it was hard to make it out, but there it was: a big rectangle. Even through the snow, Cass saw that it was an old trailer, set up on concrete blocks.

The screen went black.

Cass shook her head; the girl remained on her couch, as real as the quivering hand she held in front of her. She had to be real. Somehow, she had made it to Cass's house...

But these thoughts were wiped out in an instant when Sheryl McKenna focused her dead gaze on Cass and said, simply, "Help me."

Cass was left staring at an empty couch. There was no fading away. No puff of ethereal smoke. The girl was just there one moment, gone the next.

Cass ran from the room, whimpering without realizing it, and headed straight for the bathroom, where the scant food she had eaten the day before came up. After, she splashed cold water on her face and looked at her ashen countenance in the medicine cabinet mirror. A wraith stared back at her, thin, hollow-eyed, frightened.

Cass jumped as she heard the thud of the newspaper landing on her front porch. What would the morning edition bring? Would she be front page news? It seemed that even though she had never sought fame, it was suddenly seeking her.

Chapter
Fourteen

MYRA WAS AWAKE first. She lay for a while, listening to Ian's even breathing beside her and wondering what would happen next. She turned, with all the stealth of a thief, to look at Ian.

He looked the same as always. Handsome. His dark face stubbled with black whiskers. The eyelids appeared vulnerable, the thin flesh veined, the quick movements of his eyes underneath the skin apparent. What was he seeing? What grim horrors? Was he dreaming of murder? Suffocation? Watery, moist earth that gave easily under the shovel, digging a shallow grave to bury what he called a sacrifice, hiding the corpse of a girl not much younger than herself? Is that what he was seeing?

And in his dreams, did he justify his killing with the regimentation of a bizarre religion to which only the two of them belonged? Or were his dreams more honest?

Myra turned away from the handsome face, the hairy, muscular chest, and stared at the opposite wall, covered in cheap paneling. Was Ian really obsessed with making sacrifices to some "beast," some "devil"? Did he really believe that making these sacrifices would help them find some sort of power, or peace, or wealth?

Or—and she had to be honest here, alone in the wan light of the morning filtering in through vinyl mini-blinds—did Ian really have a taste, rooted in sex, for snuffing out the lives of young girls?

She recalled how wound up he was after each killing. How the blood pumped into his penis, making it stiff and almost insatiable. She thought of how the only response to his lust after killing was dumb acquiescence. To say no would not be tolerated.

And so she would let him do what he needed to do. Violate her right there on the floor beside the body on the bed. Push into her before she was ready and expel himself into her before she even began to feel the queasy satisfaction of his so-called lovemaking. It was ugly.

Myra sat up, gooseflesh rising on her naked body. She reached over to the chair next to the bed and grabbed her pink chenille bathrobe, a remnant of more innocent times when she was Penny, and not Myra, and quietly shrugged into it.

She went into the kitchen and measured Maxwell House into the receptacle of the Mr. Coffee, added water and waited for the coffee to brew. A mundane start to a morning. She could be anyone. A housewife getting up to make coffee for her husband before he set off for work at the industrial pottery down by the river, where he worked as a caster, or a waxer in the color room.

Did she want such a life?

She did.

While the coffee was hissing and turning out its black sustenance, Myra went to the front door and opened it. More mundane stuff. The daily newspaper lay on the concrete blocks that comprised their front stoop. She bent to pick it up and opened it to the front page.

When she saw what awaited her there, in black and white, Myra would have sworn her heart stopped. Hands trembling, Myra took the newspaper to the kitchen table, where she set it before herself and simply stared at it, waiting. Waiting for the jolt to come into her system that would allow her to begin reading beyond the headline—Missing Girl's Body Discovered—and discover how it could have happened so soon. How they had found Lucy Plant's body already, when Ian assured her that it would be months before anyone would come across the physical evidence of their deeds?

And there was the photograph, a grainy black-and-white testimony that bore witness to their actions. The heaped-up dirt, the blinding lights, the men and women in action around the makeshift grave, the medical examiner, the police in their uniforms, detectives.

The coffee was ready. Perhaps a strong black mug of the stuff would propel her into action, make her able to focus on the smaller type below the headline.

JANET MCKENNA HAD been up all night. Many nights lately, Janet had been unable to sleep. Ever since Sheryl had gone missing.

Rick slept. No problem there. Sometimes Janet wondered if he was glad Sheryl was gone. Glad because now he would have Janet all to himself—to beat her, to fuck her, to make her his slave in a way kept secret from her family and friends.

And when the night grew dark and Summitville silent, no whoosh of passing traffic outside the house, no quick conversations overheard as people passed their little house, Janet wondered if Rick had had anything to do with Sheryl's disappearance.

But she quickly squelched those thoughts. They died before she let her brain give them much sustenance. They were too horrible to contemplate. And so they lingered in the back of her mind, like hulking shadows. Giving them form and shape would have been more than Janet could bear.

And now it was morning. Janet was on good terms with how the darkness of night moved to a washed-out gray and finally to the brightness of day; of how the sounds of activity all around her would grow in intensity.

A thud against the front door made her jump. The newspaper had arrived. She stood on legs that she was always amazed continued to support her and went to the front door.

The paper's front page confronted her like an accusation. "Missing Girl's Body Discovered," the headline shouted, kicking her legs out from under her so that she dropped to her knees, where, weeping, she leaned across the threshold to begin reading.

"Lucy Plant, thirteen, daughter of Mr. and Mrs. Ronald Plant of Summitville, has been discovered in a shallow grave on the banks of the Ohio River."

Janet picked up the paper, walked backward into the kitchen, and kicked the door closed behind her. She sat down and covered her face with one hand. In the other, she held the paper, like something scorched and bad-smelling.

This didn't mean anything. *This did not mean anything.* Janet trembled, unable to even hold the paper still enough to read the printed words. She shoved aside some dishes and pulled an ashtray toward herself, groped behind her on the counter for her Kools and her Bic. She lit up and inhaled a huge lungful of smoke, almost enough to make her choke. Her eyes watered and she smoked the cigarette down to its butt in less than a minute.

She felt better. Her hands had slowed to just a little shakiness, hardly noticeable. She pulled the paper in front of her and read the article, by a reporter named Dani Westwood. There weren't all that many details, just the fact that the girl's father, Ron Plant, and a woman named Cassandra D'Angelo (it didn't immediately register on Janet's foggy brain why that name should be familiar) had discovered the body late last night in a shallow grave on the banks of the Ohio River. She read on, about how the medical examiner had ruled the death a homicide due to ligature marks around the girl's wrists and ankles and burst capillaries in the eyes, indicating suffocation. She read about how Lucy had disappeared a little over a week ago from her front yard in the part of Summitville known as Little England. Janet checked the address and saw that the Plants lived only a couple blocks over, on Etruria Street. That knowledge made her close her eyes, trying to will away the tightness in her chest. She lit up another Kool.

The article had less to say about how the girl was found, keeping the details to a short statement about how investigation into the case was "continuing."

Janet closed the paper and thought about making some coffee. Instead, she went to the freezer, where she kept a bottle of Kirov vodka. She pulled down a glass, filled it halfway up with the viscous alcohol, added a splash of orange juice and sat back down at the kitchen table, where suddenly the light coming in through the window seemed too bright. It felt like the muscles underneath her face were vibrating. Her stomach churned.

"This wasn't Sheryl." She began talking to herself. "This has nothing to do with Sheryl. Sheryl ran away. You know how wild that girl could be." Janet was no stranger to the girl's nocturnal comings and goings, even if her daughter thought different. There was a lot Janet knew about her daughter that was easier to ignore than to confront. Growing pains. She would pass through this phase, just as Janet had, and move on. With her mother beside her, she too would one day find Jesus and see how He could be her personal Lord and Savior.

She just had to wait.

So Sheryl had run off. Pittsburgh's siren call, with its bright lights, tall buildings, and fast pace probably called out to her. Soon enough, she would show up on the back porch, tail between her legs, begging to come home.

"This was not Sheryl. Lucy. Lucy Plant. This was not Sheryl."

Janet downed the orange juice and vodka and stood to make another. Maybe she would skip the orange juice this time.

She pulled the newspaper closer again, letting eyes already getting blurry scan across the columns of type and saw the name Cassandra D'Angelo again.

She sat down hard as it all came back to her. Cassandra. Cass. The weird visit yesterday. Janet replayed it all in her mind, forcing herself into a corner of the kitchen to watch it with bated breath, listening, looking harder at Cass D'Angelo's features: heart-shaped face, green eyes, black hair. Everything contorted, Janet now saw, into a kind of desperate fear. It was obvious now that the girl hadn't wanted to be there in the filthy kitchen, with two hostile people who could only stare at her, cruel words poised on lips drawn into thin lines.

What was it she had said? That she might be able to help them find Sheryl? And then she had gone out and found this Lucy Plant, with her father dragged along.

Janet went cold. Her skin felt clammy; she felt a line of sweat bead up on her forehead and trickle down her face.

How did this woman know where to find Lucy Plant? That's what Janet wanted to know. What had she said? Something about a vision? Visions were the devil's work...and so was murder.

Janet sat stock still in her chair. She was humming something tuneless and didn't even realize it. She didn't want to think anymore. She didn't want to remember the conversation she and Rick had had with the D'Angelo woman, the hateful words, the hurled plate.

She didn't want to wonder if the woman could help them. She didn't want to wonder if she had information that could help them find Sheryl before it was too late. She didn't want to think this woman knew something because she was sick, a twisted creature who preyed on young girls... Maybe she could get away with it because she was just a young girl herself, not that far removed from Sheryl. Who would suspect?

No! No! She couldn't think that way. If she thought that way, it would mean Sheryl was dead. It would mean that she and Rick were part of some devil-inspired game.

But that didn't make any sense. Why would a murderer come to the loved ones and offer to lead them to the body? How stupid was that?

Everyone would be asking the same questions. How did Cass know?

Janet lowered her head to the table and watched as the tears began to drip, hot, onto its greasy surface. She couldn't think anymore, could she?

She downed the second glass of vodka in one swallow and rose to pour another, then jumped when she saw Rick standing in the archway to the kitchen, hair sticking up all over, grimy T-shirt just barely covering his hairy belly. He was grinning. Ignorant bastard.

"Party time? This early? That's my girl." He moved toward her and Janet just stood there, still, as his arms went around her and his stink rose up to engulf her. She reached out blindly with one hand and knocked the newspaper to the floor as she followed her husband back into their bedroom.

MYRA DIDN'T KNOW what to do. She had read the article about Lucy twice because the first time her eyes drifted over the lines of type, her nerves jangling so much that she comprehended none of it. The second time, she sipped half a cup of coffee, forced herself to take several deep breaths, then made herself go slowly. She knew all the details already: the ligature marks, the location of the grave, the identification of the girl. There were no surprises in the news story. From that, she took some solace. There was nothing about the perpetrators; it seemed that if there were any clues to their identities ("*our* identities," she murmured), none had been released. There wasn't even any speculation. The story was all about the bodies being discovered.

But how? Myra searched, during a third reading, for a clue of how the girl's body was found, when she and Ian had so carefully hidden it. Had they been seen by someone in the woods on the banks of the river? Was there some silent observer watching, taking notes as to the exact location—which, Myra admitted, even she would have been hard-pressed to find mere hours after the burial.

She remembered the night they buried the girl. It was hot, muggy, the mosquitoes swarming from the river, diving for their skin and eyes. Little mean pinches and bites that made her gasp. "Over here," Ian had said, motioning her to a place just back from the water's edge, where tall grass and garbage mounded in equal profundity. "This is the place the Beast has chosen."

Myra looked around her, straining to see through the thick pitch of the night, the moon obscured by clouds and no city streetlights penetrating. She stumbled over a rock as she came near him, her nostrils flaring at the fishy smell rising up from the water.

"Are you sure?" she had whispered.

"I don't have to be sure. We can rely on the guidance of the Beast."

Oh please, Myra had wanted to say, casting looks over her shoulder, but there was no one around, the only movement the branches and leaves of the trees that stood like sentinels on the banks, whispering as the wind sloughed through them.

"We need to go back to the car," Ian had said, "for the sacrifice and the tools."

Myra traced the crime scene photograph with a red lacquered nail. It was so prosaic; if she looked closely, it blurred into a bunch of dots, meaningless. She remembered making their way back to the car, which was parked several hundred feet away, where the dirt road leading down to the river abruptly ended in grass and pebbles. Ian had made her carry the shovel and spade they had brought, while he slung the girl's body over his shoulder, expelling a breath as the body draped itself on top of him. She must be heavier now, with all the life sucked out of her. Myra had thought before they left home that they should at least wrap her in a sheet, or fashion some garbage bags around her, but Ian was having none of it. "I trust in the Beast absolutely," he had told her. "He will protect us." Ian panted as he made his way down to the river bank, using one hand to wipe away the sweat from his brow.

She didn't know about trust. What if someone saw them carrying a young girl, obviously dead weight in the most literal sense? What would they say? They would be caught like rats in a trap.

But no one had seen. Or at least, thinking back, it seemed no one had. The woods and riverbank were utterly silent in the moist heat, the rush of the river and wind the only sounds.

But someone must have been there, Myra thought. Someone had to have been hiding and watching. How else would they have known where to find her...and so quickly?

She noted the name of the woman who had been with Ron Plant when he had discovered his daughter's body: Cassandra D'Angelo. Who the hell was that? Was she the one who had guided the man there? The newspaper gave no clues; the story concentrated merely on the body being discovered, no hows or whys. Maybe this D'Angelo woman was out for a walk on the banks high above where they had buried Lucy Plant and had watched them?

But Myra distinctly remembered looking up, searching all through the darkness from every vantage point on both sides of the river, and she had seen nothing, other than the maddening swarms of mosquitoes as they drew near for another attack.

Myra wondered what she should do with this information. Should she keep it from Ian? Stupid idea; this was big news, made bigger by the fact that it had happened in Summitville, where almost nothing ever occurred. Ian would find out, even if she shredded the newspaper and burned it in the rusting can outside their trailer. It would be in other newspapers, on the radio, on the TV news.

No, she would have to let him know. Have to inform him that the Beast, for whatever reason, had failed them. She alone would have to endure what she was sure would be his rage at all his hard work come undone. She flashed on images of his filthy, sweaty face as he dug, his eyes lit up even in the darkness as he glanced over at the body lying in the dirt.

Sleep peacefully, my love, she thought, crossing the short distance from the trailer's kitchen to the bedroom. *Your slumbers will no longer be untainted. Now we have to deal with suspicion and fear.*

Maybe now we will have to run. Myra smiled at the thought; it wasn't such a bad idea. She wrapped herself around thoughts of romance, of being on the lam with her hero. Perhaps they could settle down somewhere warm, and finally Ian would put all of this behind him. They could transform into new identities, ones that didn't involve sacrifices, strangulation, suffocation, and sex.

Perhaps not.

She stood frozen at the bedroom's threshold. Ian was beginning to stir; slowly, his eyes opened to regard her.

"Sweetheart," she said, her voice coming out barely above a squeak. She paused to gather the breath and spit to say the words that would put all the rest in motion. "I have something to show you."

Ian sat up in bed, grumbling. He wiped sleep from his eyes, complaining of the "heaviness" he felt. "I need more sleep."

"But you have to see today's paper." Myra sat gently on the edge of the bed, holding out the newspaper like an offering.

He snatched it from her hands, sighing, and unfolded it so the front page fell open before his sleep-clouded eyes. He scanned the type for a moment, then sat up, spine stiffening. He leaned back against the headboard, scanning the story Myra had just read. His only reaction was a quickening of his breath. After he was finished, he handed the paper back to her. "We have any coffee?"

Myra wanted to scream, "That's all you have to say?" Instead, she hurried to the kitchen, poured a cup of the dark liquid, and brought it back to him the way he liked it: black and steaming. She handed it to him and he gulped, heedless of the heat.

After downing almost half the mug, he patted the bed next to him and Myra sat. Her nerves tingled. She didn't know what to expect. She never knew what to expect.

"How did this happen?"

Myra looked at the wood-paneled walls, as if an answer might be secreted there, in the grains of the paneling. "I..." she began. "Honey, I don't know. We were so careful. Or at least I thought we were."

"I was so careful. The Beast was careful, but I wonder if you let something slip." He took her chin in his hand, roughly, so it hurt, and turned her head toward his face. His beautiful face, eyebrows now scrunched together. "But what did you do? Did you talk to someone about this? Maybe someone in that hoopy family of yours across the river?"

Myra was stunned. Since they had been together, Ian had made certain that Myra had effectively cut off all communications with her "former" family, the ones who knew her as Penny and who, today, might pass her on the street unrecognized.

"No, of course not, sweetheart. You know I don't talk to them anymore."

"Then how did this happen? And so soon?"

Myra's heart began to pound. It was as if Ian expected an answer, as if he believed she must know why their efforts to conceal their crime — sacrifice, he would call it — had failed. She searched her mind for some way she could have given away a clue to the girl's whereabouts, but there was nothing. She had literally talked to no one but him since they had brought Lucy Plant back to the trailer. "I couldn't tell you. For me, there has only been you. I haven't even seen any of my family in months."

Ian flung the sheets off angrily. Normally, Myra would have been excited by this unveiling of his body, so solid and packed with muscle. Ian never wore anything to bed. But now she only felt fear, felt it as an unpleasant sense of dread that made her innards go cold. The fear made a need to flee rise up; she wanted to leap from the bed and hurry outside the trailer.

"Someone must have seen us." He looked down at the newspaper. "Maybe that woman the article mentions. What was her name?"

Myra looked down. "Cassandra D'Angelo." Her voice was barely a whisper.

"Cassandra." He turned to Myra, quickly and unexpectedly, and hit her, the back of his hand connecting hard enough with her cheek to make her head swivel. She raised a hand to her stinging cheek and stared up at him, stunned.

"We have to do something about her. The Beast would want us to do something about her." He stood from the bed, heading toward the bathroom. "Good thing you're already dressed. I'll be ready in a minute and we'll pay a little surveillance call on this woman. Find out just how she knows so much."

"All right." Myra wanted to cry, but held her tears in check. She knew enough to know her tears would do no good. They would only excite him.

Chapter
Fifteen

IT WAS THE second day after the discovery of Lucy Plant's body. The phone had not stopped ringing all morning. Cass sat in the living room, staring straight ahead, and wondered what she had set in motion. Reporters, stringers, and assorted nut cases had all picked up their phones and punched in her listed number, all hoping for a few minutes of her time. Reporters from newspapers in nearby places like Pittsburgh, Steubenville, and Youngstown and as far away as New York City and Orlando (this a tabloid she had often seen as she checked out at the supermarket), all desperate, they said, to help her. "We want to hear your side of the story. We can get that across to the world. Let us be your pipeline. We'll be sympathetic and can act as your spokesperson." Some of them wanted exclusives. Some hadn't bothered to ask.

The phone had begun ringing at 5:00 a.m. The day's newspaper hadn't even been printed yet, but Cass knew word would travel fast. The night before last, she had stood, shell-shocked and dry-eyed next to Ron Plant as the media began to converge shortly after the police and the county medical examiner had arrived. She hadn't thought about it at the time, having been unfamiliar with this world of preying on the lowest, basest news that occurred, but realized now there were whole legions of people with police scanners in their cars, offices, and homes, poised and ready to pounce. She had watched the lights and cameras assemble, like what she would imagine would take place on a movie set, and seen the reporters running restlessly from official to official, looking for comment. It had seemed like something out of the movies to her, but that allusion was always quickly squashed when she thought of the body of the young girl, lying behind her, being measured, prodded, and photographed, no longer a some*one*, but a some*thing*, transported into a realm that only days before she didn't even know existed.

She had managed to fend them off, more out of a protective instinct for Ron Plant than for herself.

When she had to leave the crime scene with Marion Hartley, who "wanted to talk," she felt bad about leaving Ron there alone. But a couple of cops had said they would see him home and there didn't seem to be much more she could do for him. He was like a statue, and her words barely seemed to register on features that were oddly serene and composed. She knew he was just in the early stages of shock. Selfishly, she was glad she wouldn't be around when the real horror hit him. She didn't want to imagine his anguish. But now she was part of his story, and knew that she would have to make at least one more trip to the neatly maintained white house with green trim. To not do so would be heartless.

The phone wasn't ringing now. She had ripped the phone cord from the box on the wall, after someone (not a reporter) had called wanting to know what it felt like to kill Lucy Plant. Had the girl cried at the end and begged for her life, the soft, male voice wanted to know.

That call had sent her over the edge, but she couldn't let herself fall apart; she had responsibilities. So she pulled the blinds shut and roused Max.

"Honey, it's time to get up," she whispered to him, as gently as she could, trying to pull herself together: to dry the tears on her face, to stop herself from trembling.

Max looked up at her, his expression dazed, sleep in the corner of his eyes. It was still dark and the little light on his nightstand gave a glow that was all wrong to his bedroom. He sat up and rubbed his eyes, more alert. Cass could tell from his wary expression he sensed right away something was wrong.

"What's a matter, Mama?"

"Nothing. I just have lots to do today. How would you like to go see Nana and Pap-Pap today?"

Max looked confused.

"Do you have to work? What about school?"

Cass didn't know what to tell the boy; she had completely forgotten he had just returned for second grade. "I just have lots to do," she said, and made it clear with her tone that this pronouncement would be the end of any further questioning. "Nana and Pap-Pap can get you off to school when the time comes."

She slipped out the back door as a grayish light was just beginning to fill the sky and a caul of mist still lay above the dewy grass. There was still a chill in the air. A couple of vans were parked outside and Cass already was learning what it was like to be a celebrity. She wore dark glasses and had thrown on a baseball cap, pulling her dark ponytail through an opening in the back.

"Let's play a game," she whispered to Max, kneeling down just outside the back door. "We're spies and we have to make it to the border, where Nana is, without anyone seeing us."

Max, even at seven, wasn't falling for this. He eyed her with the suspicion of a mental health-care professional and wordlessly followed his mother through the backyard and through the network of other backyards that would lead them to her parents' house, ignoring the barking of dogs and curious eyes glancing out of kitchen windows. At least they were able to make it to their destination without someone running after them, microphone, tape recorder, or notebook in hand.

DANI WESTWOOD WATCHED Cassandra D'Angelo emerge from her back door, a sleepy little tow-headed boy holding her hand, blinking as dawn's pinkish light began to illuminate the day. She kept her eye on them as they headed through their back yard, casting glances behind them, and finally watched as they knelt and then crawled through the bottom of the hedge bordering the southern end of the little yard. Their heads popped up seconds later and the two of them continued running through the yards, a pair of jokers on the lam.

Dani tucked her notebook into her back pocket, not about to pursue a mother and her son obviously trying to make an escape from prying types like her. There would be time enough to talk to Cass. She had a feeling it wouldn't be long before Cass would return to the house alone, after safely depositing her son somewhere out of harm's way.

Was Dani capable of insinuating herself into this woman's life? Could she become one of the vultures she had already seen around town, hungry for a story at any cost? Could she lie, wheedle, and cajole this obviously terrified young woman into giving her a story?

She didn't know. To date, her biggest stories had been sentimental features on the triumphs of local handicapped kids, the scintillating activities of the Summitville city council, and features on topics as world-heavy as the first baby born at City Hospital in the New Year.

But Dani Westwood, for everything she was tired of, for all the failures and upheavals in her life, was not stupid. She knew an opportunity when she saw one, and she knew she might never be handed one like this again. Not here, in this sleepy little river town in a place called Pennsylvania, where she had never expected to be finishing her days, doing work she never thought she'd be doing. If she didn't at least try for this fleeting moment (and for the sake of so many, she prayed it was fleeting), then she didn't see much point in continuing with much of anything.

Dani turned, looked at the TV vans camped outside Cass's house, and walked further down the block, waiting.

THE KNOCK ON the kitchen window startled her. Cass sat, feeling like a trapped animal in her living room, looking up only occasionally through the sheer curtains at the picture window to see the white TV van with its big, rooftop-mounted antenna, sitting in front of her house. A few times, there had been knocks at the front door, but Cass had kept quiet and they stopped after a while.

Finally, she heard the ignition of the van rumble and then fade away, as she assumed its inhabitants moved off to more willing quarry.

She prayed they would leave the Plants alone.

But the knock at the kitchen window set her nerves to jangling all over again. Just when she was starting to think maybe she could go into the kitchen, put on the kettle for some tea and pop some raisin bread into the toaster, that infernal tapping on the glass of her kitchen window had started.

For a moment, Cass had sat frozen, still stuck, as if by glue, to her living room sofa, the light from the TV washing over her. Oprah was on, that much she knew, but who her guest was and what she was giving away today she had no idea.

She stood and walked through the dining room and took a quick peek through the archway that led into her kitchen. What she saw made herself flatten against the wall, gasping.

There was a woman framed by the window, just peering into her kitchen, taking in Max's cereal bowl and juice glass still on the table, Bum's food and water dishes lined up on the linoleum floor. Cass stepped back so quickly, there was no time for details to register about the woman, other than the fact that she was female and white. She didn't even know if this was someone with whom she might have been acquainted.

Her heart began to thud as it came to her. This was the killer. Cass's name was in the paper and listed in the phone book, along with her address. How easy it would be to find her! Cass's mouth went dry and she tried to rein in the fear that was causing her stomach to churn and sweat to form at the nape of her neck and in her armpits.

No, no, she told herself. It's probably just another reporter, or one of those nut cases, hungry for details about the killing.

She stepped out a bit and looked again. The face was still there and soon was accompanied by a hand on the right side, rapping on the glass again. The face looked familiar.

And then it came back to her. She did know this woman. She had met her only a couple of nights ago. She couldn't recall her name, but she had been one of the first reporters on the scene. She had spoken briefly to her and she hadn't seemed as predatory as some of the others who had shown up later. Cass had also seen her around town, and had actually, now that she thought of it, waited on her a couple of times at the diner. Her wild, unruly salt-and-pepper hair, tiny oval glasses, preference for flowing skirts and gauzy Indian-type shirts, and Brit accent made her memorable. It was like she was a refugee from the 1960s.

She rapped again.

Cass had to hand it to her. At least she was trying a novel approach, probably knowing she wouldn't answer her door and knowing the phone was set on endless ring if she had tried that route. She would have had to climb up on the wooden doors that covered the outside stairs down to the basement to reach the window.

She rapped again.

Cass's breathing had returned to normal and she wondered if the reporter would go away quicker if she would just tell her to get lost. She believed she still had the right to call the police to report someone on her property, rental house or not. And that's just what she would do.

Fear replaced by a slow-burning anger, Cass moved to the kitchen and cranked open the little window, having to reach over the stove to do so. In another context, this whole encounter might have had comic overtones.

She closed her eyes as the warm air washed in and the woman smiled. Closed her eyes with a kind of defeat. And disgust. "What do you want?"

"Ms. D'Angelo. Thanks. I'm Dani Westwood; I work for the *Review*? I was wondering if I might have a word."

Cass shook her head. "I have nothing to say."

"I figured you'd feel that way and I can't blame you."

The two stared at one another for a moment. Dani took a breath and said, "Do you think maybe I could swing around to the kitchen door? We could talk through the screen. I'm not sure how much longer this wooden door's going to support my weight." She glanced down. "Damn Krispy Kreme for coming to town." Almost sheepishly, Dani held up a waxed paper bag of glazed donuts. "These are for you."

Cass rolled her eyes and shook her head. "You can come around to the door. But you can keep your donuts and you're not coming inside."

"Thanks."

She listened as Dani clambered down off the cellar door; in a second, her full frame was standing at the screen door to her left. Cass noticed that, in an odd way, the Brit was kind of beautiful, with pale skin and dark, dark eyes the fire of which the tiny glasses could not conceal. Cass wondered if she was Welsh.

Cass reached out to flip the lock on the screen door handle. "As I said at the window, I really don't have anything to say to you. This whole thing has been a nightmare..." Cass caught herself, fearing she was already giving away quotes that could be used in that evening's edition of *The Review*.

Dani Westwood smiled and Cass noticed the yellowing teeth of a smoker. "Cass, I know it's hard. And I know you don't want to be drawn into this. But it's too late; you already are. Now, you can tell me to go away, as you're doing, and I will go. I'm not the kind of woman that gets persistent. But sooner or later, your story will come out. And it can come out one of two ways: with or without your authorization. Do you know what I'm saying?"

Cass considered, soothed by her sensible words, the warmth of her raspy, velvety voice, and her accent which, rather than being foreign and strange, had a calming effect. It seemed like Dani Westwood was in charge and that was something Cass needed right now—someone to take over. Her hand played with the catch on the door's lock. "I don't know," she said, with barely enough breath to make her voice register.

Dani licked her lips. "Look, I'm not from around here, but I've been here more years than I care to mention. I can work with you and make sure what you want to say gets out the right way. Those other reporters from the cities can't make that claim, and if they do, they're liars. They're going to try and make you into something you're not. All I want to do is hear your side of things and report that as accurately as I can."

"I'm not sure I should talk. What about the police? They're already talking to me." Cass's voice broke just a little, but she caught herself, not letting the panic take over.

"There's no law against talking to me. And maybe if you talk to me, it will make things easier when you eventually do have to give the police a formal statement, or whatever they want."

Cass sighed. "You make sense, Ms. Westwood..."

"Dani. Call me Dani. Please."

"Dani. But I'm really torn. All of this happened so fast and I don't even know why I got caught up in it...or how, really. I don't know what's going on." Cass paused, breathing just a little harder. "How do I know I can trust you?"

Dani shrugged. "Trust is the same thing as faith, in a way. You just have to let go and believe. I can give you my word that I won't distort what you have to say. I can give you my word that I will try to be as faithful a mouthpiece as I can for you." She smiled. "I'm sorry I can't offer more proof."

Cass unlocked the door. "All right. I'm probably doing the wrong thing, but come on in." Cass leaned back to let Dani Westwood in. "You can sit down if you want, over there at the table. I was going to make some tea." She laughed. "I bet you like tea."

"Actually, I'm a coffee drinker, but tea is just fine. Are you sure you won't help me eat these donuts?" Dani slid out a chair and sat down, pulling a tape recorder and a notebook from her bag. "Why don't you just start at the beginning? I'm still not sure I understand how you came to help Mr. Plant discover his daughter's body."

Cass's spine went rigid as she stood at the sink, where she was filling the kettle with cold water. She sucked in some air and moved to the stove, listened for the click of the pilot light and watched as the blue flame emerged from the burner. She looked out the window.

Finally, she turned and sat down, thinking she had forgotten to take down the mugs from the cupboard and get out the tea bags.

"It started when we had that storm last week."

Dani clicked on the tape recorder and sat back.

"I was fixing supper and I noticed that Max—that's my son—wasn't in the yard, where he was supposed to be."

DANI COULDN'T BELIEVE what she was hearing. Cass led her through the events of that day last week when a summer storm had gathered in bruised clouds over the hilltops of West Virginia, moving across the river to douse the little town of Summitville with rain that felt like warm hail: big hard drops applauded by thunder and lit up by lightning. Dani wasn't sure of the connection she should make with Cass getting hit in the head with a tree branch and her discovery of the Plant girl's body, but the woman sitting before him seemed to think there was one.

She led her through the visions: the tiny ones (how she knew the evening plans and thoughts of her nurse in the hospital) to the bigger ones that showed her what she now thought was a vision of Lucy Plant's murder (the blinking red light, the whirring ceiling fan) and the location of her shallow grave.

"IT ALL JUST came to me. I didn't ask for it. In fact, I tried to push it away." Cass looked desperately at Dani, searching the lined oval face for understanding. She wasn't sure she found it; the reporter simply stared, implacable, unaffected, waiting for her to continue. She supposed this was part of her reporter's bag of tricks: being silent and letting the subject talk. Well, it was working. Cass felt a curious kind of relief course through her as she unburdened herself of the tale and she hoped that this woman wouldn't see her as nuts. Or worse, as a killer. "I admit, I even drank a little to try and push away the visions. They were so horrible...and so insistent."

As she talked, Cass remembered the visions of the grave, and of Lucy being tortured. They were no longer like visions, but like memories, as if she had been there herself, watching it all, helpless.

"I had to do something. I have a kid myself, you know. If something ever happened to Max, I would be out of my mind with worry. In fact, I was out of my mind with worry the day this whole damned chain of events got started." Cass blew out a big breath. "I had to try to help these people who had lost their children." She bit her lip, still uncertain if she wanted to reveal what she knew about Sheryl McKenna. Maybe she should just keep quiet about the second girl, end all of this right here, as best she could, remove herself from a limelight she had never sought.

She really knew very little about Sheryl McKenna, at least nothing that would be useful. She had felt a painful certainty that the girl was dead, but now wondered if her vision was correct. Was she too buried in a shallow grave down by the river? Were the killers that stupid? Maybe the vision was incomplete. Maybe she was seeing the location where she was killed, not where she was buried. These things she was seeing in her head weren't an exact science. She could be wrong; anyway, if Sheryl McKenna had been buried on the banks of the Ohio

River, wouldn't that have occurred to the authorities? Shouldn't they be searching right now, without any help from her? Maybe some revelation was still in store for her (Cass had a flash of the flickering TV screen with its image of a hilltop trailer and shivered; she had already had a revelation). Cass was torn about being the recipient of such knowledge and wondered what she should do with the information. Put herself out there again, setting herself up for suspicion and ridicule? Or just keep quiet and hope the authorities would find the girl on their own? It was tempting to take the latter route, but again, Cass wasn't sure she could, not when there was at least one grieving parent out there who might be removed from the unendurable torture of not knowing.

Dani Westwood brought her out of her reverie, sounding like she was repeating a question. "So you just saw, like in your mind's eye, where the grave was?"

Cass nodded. She didn't want to do this anymore. She felt sick, and just wanted this woman with her notebook and tape recorder to go away. She blew out a big sigh, realizing the quickest way to get her hope fulfilled would be to simply cooperate.

"I know it sounds crazy, but yes. That's just what it was: my mind's eye. I just saw the area where she was; the river, the bridge. I don't know why it came to me."

"So, are you saying..." Dani Westwood licked her lips. "That your injury might have given you some sort of extra-sensory perception? That you're now psychic?"

Cass shook her head. "That sounds insane to me. I'm not the kind of person that ever put much stock in things like the occult or astrology or even supposed mental abilities like clairvoyance or tele-, tele..." Cass searched for the word.

"Telekinesis? Telepathy?"

"That's right. I never even read Stephen King. Horror movies and thrillers scare me. I like romances and comedies." Cass stirred her tea, gone cold in the mug. "I don't even know what I'm saying here. I don't know if it was a coincidence that I got a bad blow to the head and suddenly could start seeing things or if those things were connected. Even if the blow to my head had nothing to do with things as they are now, I still wish I could go back to before I had visions of those girls." Cass caught herself. She had done what she thought was unwise to do: revealed that she knew something about the other missing girl, Sheryl McKenna.

Dani Westwood looked up from her notebook, where she was jotting something down. "Girls? You said girls. Plural."

Cass laughed. "I know. I meant to say 'girl.' I'm a little frazzled, as you can imagine, with all that's gone on." She laughed again, a high-pitched twittering sound that she knew sounded completely stupid and might as well have been a translation for the sentence, 'I am a liar.'

"Anyway, as I was saying, I'd just like to go back to being what I was:

boring. A waitress in a diner, trying to make ends meet and raise her little boy." She looked at the reporter, eyes wide, hoping Dani wouldn't pursue her earlier slip.

But that was not to be. "You said girls." She bit her lip. "Please don't take this the wrong way, Cassandra, but I'm not sure I'm buying that it was a slip. See, the fact is, there's another girl missing. We even printed something about it in the paper. Her name was..." She began to shuffle around in a fabric briefcase she had with her, looking, Cass supposed, for the name of the missing girl.

She closed her eyes and said, "Her name was Sheryl McKenna." Cass noticed that, without thinking, she had referred to the missing girl in the past tense.

"So you know something about her disappearance?"

Cass gave out another stupid little laugh. "I didn't say that. I get *The Review*. I could have seen her name in the paper."

"Yes, you could have. Or you could have heard it over the radio. But I think there's more than you're saying."

Cass felt jittery and on the verge of tears. She couldn't stand this anymore. And why did she have to? There was no law compelling her to talk to this woman, sympathetic as she seemed. "Well, what you think and reality might be two different things," Cass snapped. "I think I'm ready to call this interview quits. I hope you got enough. Now, if you don't mind, I have a splitting headache and would like to lie down before I have to go pick up my son."

"If you know something, Cass, you should talk about it."

"Please!" Cass screamed, surprising even herself. Dani Westwood's jaw dropped. But the volume and the shrillness had their effect: she was gathering up her things.

"I apologize. If there's anything you want to talk further about, here's my card." She pulled a business card from her briefcase and set it in front of Cass. "It even has my cell phone number, so you can call me anytime." Dani met her eyes. "Any time at all. I mean it."

Cass stared down at the card, not seeing the print on it. Her heart was thudding. She listened to Dani putting away her things, the scrape of her chair along the linoleum, the sound of her taking a few paces. "I'll just see myself out then."

Cass looked up, nodded.

"Thanks very much for your time. Keep the donuts. Maybe your son would like them."

Cass didn't respond.

"Right." And Dani Westwood left her alone.

Chapter
Sixteen

"WE HAVE TO leave."

Myra ran a hand through her hair. She sat at the tiny, scarred kitchen table with Ian, the accusing newspaper spread out on its surface. "We have to leave. They're going to find us out, Ian." Myra's hands were shaking; something ferret-like, with razor sharp teeth, gnawed at her insides.

Ian stared at her. His pale green eyes, which she usually found so seductive and alluring, regarded her with disbelief and a kind of haughtiness best reserved for someone with insufficient intellectual capacities. She hated those eyes and that gaze right now, wished she could just stand, brush the toast crumbs from her lap, go outside, start up the car, and drive herself back to West Virginia. She saw herself returning to her parents' home and heard their questions about her whereabouts, what she had been doing with herself over this blank period when she had disappeared.

Why hadn't they even bothered to come looking for her?

"Are you even thinking about what the Beast wants? I haven't gotten the slightest inkling from him that we need to flee."

"Damn the Beast!" Myra was tired of the game. She assumed all this talk of the Beast, and praying to its evil, was just part of their sex play; she'd always wondered, in the back of her mind, if even Ian believed all the talk, all the mythology about the Beast that she knew was created in his twisted mind. "They've found the first girl. I don't know how, but it seems this woman, this D'Angelo woman, knows something. And that could mean she knows something about the other one. Ian..." Myra tried, and failed, to keep her voice from rising with hysteria. "Ian, if they can find the bodies, maybe they can find a trail back to us. I don't want to go to jail." Myra bit her lip. She knew that if she started crying now, she would end up with her face slapped—or worse. "Can't we just go away, just for a while, until the heat dies down? There's nothing keeping us here. The Beast won't mind. He'll understand." Myra looked wistfully over Ian's shoulder, through the window; a dead-white sky indicated the heat and humidity of the day. In so many ways, Myra felt trapped. Even the air itself closed in on her.

Ian rose and leaned across the table, towering over her. He looked menacing and Myra sharply sucked in her breath, cringing. She put a hand up over her face and he snatched it away.

"How does the likes of you know what the Beast will or will not mind? You don't. I am his conduit and he's telling me we have to remain. So what if they found a body? There's no connection to us."

"How do we know that?" Myra regretted the words as soon as they left her lips. She knew she had no right to speak them. Yet Myra remembered how they had plucked the girl right from *in front of her house...in the same car that sat outside the trailer*. Who was to say that a neighbor hadn't been watching from behind a curtained window as Ian got out of the car and talked to Lucy, luring her into the car? Who was to say that person wasn't down at police headquarters right now, giving a description of the car and the handsome young man who urged the girl to get inside? A child getting into the car of a stranger might put a caring neighbor on the alert, might even make that same neighbor jot down a license plate number. Myra tried to comfort herself with the weak conviction that if someone knew their license plate number, the cops would already be outside, pounding on the door, guns at the ready.

Ian sat thinking for a long time. He smoked a cigarette, wordless. Myra wished she could read him. Suddenly, he was a stranger and she realized she had no entry into his thoughts. His voice startled her.

"The Beast is telling me there's a way out of this. We have to silence this D'Angelo woman, once and for all."

Myra understood what he meant and began to weep softly. "I don't want to kill anyone else." She caught a sob in her throat, thinking of the look on the McKenna girl's face as the life ebbed out of her, how her blue eyes had connected with Myra's, accusing. "I don't think I can do it, Ian." She covered her face to hide the tears and the snot.

Ian pulled her hands away and held on to her wrists so hard it hurt. "I said nothing about killing."

"Then what?"

"The Beast wants us to find out more about her. He says we have to discover what it is this woman holds most dear."

"I don't know what that means."

"You wouldn't. Just trust in me." Ian stood and started toward the bedroom. "I'm going to get dressed. And then we're going for a ride."

Myra sat quivering in her chair, imagining them in a car. Imagining whirling blue lights behind them. She wished she was Penny again—fat, acne-scarred, but safe, safe in her girl's bedroom, writing in her journal, and listening to Shawn Colvin. She feared Penny was as dead as Sheryl McKenna. At least Sheryl McKenna didn't have to live out a nightmare. At least Sheryl McKenna had the comfort of a shallow grave, just outside the door.

CASS SAT AT her parents' kitchen table with Max. He was eating a bowl of *pastina* with butter, egg, and grated Romano cheese. A salad of dandelion greens in oil and vinegar was next the pasta, ignored by Max. "Too bitter." He had twisted his face into an expression of nausea after taking a bite of the greens.

"I need you to stay here with Nana and Pap-Pap for a couple days."

Max kept his head low, the act of eating suddenly requiring intense concentration. Finally, he raised his head. "Why? Why can't I be at home? Who will take care of Bum? You said I was responsible for his food and water."

"I can do it."

"But you said..."

"I know what I said." Cass sighed. She looked out at the Indian summer day. Her skin was moist; strands of hair clung to her forehead and neck. She had endured her mother's questions earlier, when she had decided it might be best to keep Max out of the limelight, what with all the calls (and, unfortunately, visits) she was getting from the media. She had decided that now, since her name was public knowledge, it would be best to shield Max from more than just reporters. The thought sent a chill through her, in spite of the heat outside.

"Listen, honey." Cass took her son's hand in her own, forcing him to look up at her. "I'll come see you every day. And I'm just down the street." She frowned right along with her son. "I know it's hard. But it's just for a short time."

"I still don't understand *why*," Max whined.

What am I supposed to tell him? That he needs to stay away from the house because there are some killers out there who know his mommy's name? That the press might want to interview him about his crazy psychic mommy? There was nothing more to say to the boy appropriate for his level of understanding. Cass stood. "Honey, we can talk more about this later, but I have the afternoon shift at the diner, and if I don't get going, I'm going to be late. And we both know how Mike hates it when I'm late."

Max lowered his head close to the pasta and began shoveling spoonfuls of it into his mouth, refusing to look at her.

She knew she was dismissed and even though it hurt a bit, Cass was relieved. For once, she was glad she had her waitress job to go to. She knew it would be busy, and at least for the hours of her shift, she wouldn't have to think about murders, visions, or why her son was suddenly feeling rejected.

Outside, heat shimmered off the pavement and Cass hoped she would just be left alone. The news vans parked outside her house earlier—she was glad to see—were gone. In their place was the simple to-and-fro traffic on Pennsylvania Avenue: the eighteen-wheelers lumbering by, cars with bad mufflers. In the trees, gypsy moths weaved intricate webs. Cass breathed in, but the air was like smoke, thick and unsatisfying, unable to reach the areas of lung she needed it to reach.

The sun beat down on her head and she longed for the shower, the cool spray of water over her naked body. She could just close her eyes and let it flow over her. Peace...for just ten minutes or so. Was that too much to ask?

And then she felt it. For a moment, everything seized up and Cass was afraid she was going to have another vision of a murdered girl or a shallow grave. But this wasn't the same. Cass slowed her pace, looking out of the corners of her eyes to try to place this feeling of being watched. The traffic on the two-lane road flowed by, the faces behind steering wheels blank.

Yet the hair on her neck rose up and she felt eyes on her. She stopped and turned, a hand to her forehead shielding her eyes from glare, and looked up and down the street. There was a green pickup parked a few yards away and a red Mustang just behind that. Both vehicles appeared empty, though with the glare on their windshields, she couldn't be sure. The street was otherwise empty.

Cass started to walk toward the Mustang, its faded red paint job almost calling to her. She didn't understand why she wanted to draw near. Her breathing came faster as she got closer to the car and saw two people sitting inside.

Cass wanted to scream. Just stand on the quiet street and scream. She had no idea why. But the two silhouettes filled her with horror, with dread. Her feet kept pulling her forward. The rational part of her wondered what she would say to the people in the car once she came abreast of it. The intuitive part was repelled and drawn at the same time. Cass felt sick, and she didn't think it was the heat making her feel that way.

As she neared the car, there was movement and she hurried closer. The engine roared to life, tires squealed, and the red Mustang sped down the street, kicking up pebbles and leaving the smell of exhaust in its wake.

Cass tried to catch her breath, to slow her thundering heart. *It was them.*

"THAT WAS CLOSE." Ian looked into the rearview mirror at the slight figure of the dark-haired young woman standing on the sidewalk, looking frail and afraid.

Myra sat tight-lipped, body rigid, her body language betraying nothing, eyes hidden behind over-sized sunglasses.

Ian slowed the car down as they traveled east. "She almost walked right up to the car! We could have just grabbed her, found out what she knows and then gotten rid of her. But that would have been too easy."

"You said we wouldn't kill anyone else."

"I said nothing of the sort. The Beast decides who dies and who lives. And that includes you, so lighten up." He pulled into a little frozen custard stand. "Ice cream?"

"I'll have a cone."

Ian pulled the keys from the ignition and turned to smile at Myra. "Good work back there."

Myra said nothing.

He put a hand on her shoulder. "You know, with the neighbor? Getting the goods on that D'Angelo woman? What was it you said?"

Myra sighed and looked out the window. "I said I was from the insurance company and that I was trying to track her down because an uncle had left her a small amount of money." Myra continued to stare out the window, her voice dead. "The woman volunteered the stuff about her son, about the grandparents."

"Still, it was a great job; you got her to trust you. I'll be right back with your cone. You deserve sprinkles, and you, my love, shall have them."

CASS WENT INTO the house and slammed the door behind her, leaning up against it. She was as breathless as if she had run a mile. *It was them. It was them. It was them.* She saw the car with Sheryl McKenna in it; could see it in her mind's eye clear as memory.

She hobbled into the living room and collapsed on the sofa. *I need to get ready for work. I can't do this.* She wanted to cry, wanted to pull out hair, wanted to run into the street, screaming and flailing her fists, telling anyone who would listen to chase the red Mustang; it was the car that had taken the girls to their deaths.

But who would listen?

Cass closed her eyes, giving herself a moment to try to compose herself, but it was impossible. Along with the certainty that she had just seen the killers also dawned the knowledge the killers had been parked almost in front of her house and they were watching her.

Thank God Max wasn't with me. Thank God Max is at his grandparents' and not here.

Cass rubbed her forehead, thinking maybe she should just call the police, get that Hartley woman on the phone and lie to her. Tell her to forget about the visions; the truth was she had seen the red Mustang and seen both Lucy Plant and Sheryl McKenna in it. Just look for a beat-up old red Mustang, she could say, and you'll be well on your way to solving these crimes.

Easy enough...if you hadn't already told your "visions" story to practically anyone who would listen. Why were you such a fool? Cass paused, ready to kick herself, to take a slapping hand to her very own face. But then she continued the monologue she was conducting with herself. *How were you to know? How were you to know how to deal with this gift, this curse? You only wanted to help people, and you never wanted to be involved at all.* She sighed. *Get ready for work. You still have a child to support, a living to make.*

And Cass headed for the shower, dropping a trail of clothes as she went.

Chapter
Seventeen

THE CROWD AT the diner was a nightmare — and, in its own way, a blessing. Cass had known that construction on City Hall a few blocks over was going to bring in some workers, but she had no idea how much of an impact the work would have on the diner. Right now, the place was filled with men in dusty work clothes and boots, baseball caps, sunglasses, and toothpicks between their teeth. Each of them thought he was the one who could catch her eye, the "special" one-in-a-million customer whom she would deign to give her phone number, to tell him, suggestively, what time she "got off." They were a noisy bunch, and the small diner was filled with their husky voices, the clatter of their cutlery against Fiestaware dishes, and the smell and sight of blue cigarette smoke rising lazily up toward the ceiling. The few regulars vied for her attention, all of them working her last nerve, and all of them God's blessing. For the past three hours, she had not had a minute to spare to think about missing girls, the danger she was in, the couple in the red Mustang — she was simply a machine, balancing three and four plates up her arm, a glass of iced tea in each hand, scurrying from counter to booth to table, refilling coffee, water, and soft drinks, asking "How is everything? Can I get you anything else right now?" Her body had worked itself into an almost mindless rhythm, and it felt good to be on automatic pilot, to have her brain barely engaged. Maybe, she thought, a lobotomy would be the answer to all her woes.

But there was one thing she couldn't ignore: a vague nausea growing in her gut. It was almost like the morning sickness she had experienced early on in her pregnancy with Max, what her mother used to call a sour stomach. The smell of the grill and the grease splattering in the back as Rosie, the short-order cook, fried up hamburgers and set trays of potatoes into bubbling grease didn't help matters much.

She hoped she wasn't getting sick, but in the back of her mind she knew this queasy feeling wasn't coming from any bug or undigested food, but from fear. As she hurried from table to table, a fake smile plastered permanently on her face, trying to be "good-natured" as the men made wisecracks that she had heard a thousand times before or made grabs at her ass, she tried to quell the notion that she felt sick because she was afraid.

And she didn't want to examine why she was afraid. *Although that might be a very stupid thing to do. Fear usually means pain, or it's a warning.* She thought suddenly of Max. She didn't know why, but it made her gasp. She wanted to drop the plates she had picked up (hot turkey and hot meatloaf sandwiches with mashed potatoes and lots of gravy) and run from the diner. She had even begun lowering them toward the counter when one of the Creche sisters piped up, "Hey, Cass, this coffee ain't gonna refill itself." The woman was smiling to indicate she meant no harm and holding up her mug to indicate she really did want it refilled...*now.*

Cass grabbed the pot and hurried over toward Isabelle Creche. "Sorry, hon. We're just swamped in here today."

"Yeah...too many men."

"You got that right," Cass answered and walked off, laughing, the gaiety belying the fingers of dread continuing to massage her insides. Cass cleared tables, took orders, delivered checks, tried not to let her increasing nervousness show. Faces blurred in her sight until she grew confused. Had she served that four-top yet? What about the back booth, was it cleared?

When Cass saw her, she almost dropped the plates of banana cream pie she was carrying. Instead, she picked up her pace and set the pie down in front of two of the workers, so she could pause for a moment, to try to understand why seeing the woman in the booth at the back made her heart nearly stop and a sheen of clammy goose bumps to break out on her skin.

"Bet you've got a real sweet pie," one of the men whispered.

Ordinarily a comment like that would inspire a less-than-kind response from Cass, maybe even a spill of coffee in the already too-hot lap of the offender, but this time, all Cass did was mumble, "Uh-huh," as she walked away from the table.

She stopped near the counter and pretended to look down at her order pad, keeping her peripheral vision trained on the woman in the booth. Just seeing her sent prickles up and down Cass's spine, ratcheting up the nausea to the point where Cass was afraid she would have to run into the ladies' and throw up the little food she had managed to eat so far today.

Mike bustled by behind her, brushing up against her back. "Customers. Customers," he whispered.

Cass took in a deep breath, trying to slow her heart rate, the rise in her blood pressure, and the awful sickness just seeing this woman engendered.

She didn't know why this woman should bother her so. (And wasn't that more and more the way, ever since her accident?) For one thing, the blonde was barely a woman; she was a young girl, perhaps still in her teens. Never mind the glamour she attempted to project: the platinum bleach job peeking out from under a silky leopard scarf, the oversize tortoiseshell sunglasses, and the sixties-style sleeveless dress Cass's mother would refer to as a "shift." She looked fresh out of high school. The foundation on the face did little to conceal a rash of pimples on her chin.

Cass loaded up on plates and headed to another table, but she couldn't get the image of the girl out of her mind. *Why? She's just sitting there, looking at a menu. Is it because Mike always tells us to kick singles out of booths when we're busy and to tell 'em to sit at the counter? Hardly.* Cass's hands trembled, sloshing coffee into saucers as she set down food and drinks for yet another table of construction workers.

"What time do you get outta here, gorgeous?" one of the men asked.

"Six." Cass wandered away, staring at the girl.

The nausea in the pit of her stomach peaked; Cass felt as though she might faint. She found an empty stool and—even though she knew Mike would give her hell for it—collapsed into it, trying to hold down the bile burning the back of her throat, to stop the room from spinning. She took several deep breaths.

"What's with you?" Brenda Smart leaned close, under the pretense of wiping off the counter. "You're white as a sheet."

Cass managed a weak smile. "Just felt a little weak in the knees is all. Maybe I'm just tired."

"Maybe you're just pregnant. I know the signs." Brenda was the mother of four. She was thirty-one.

"I sincerely doubt that. Not unless this is the Second Coming. Hey, could you get me a glass of water? I need to get back to work or Mike will can my ass." Cass rubbed her head, regarding the girl out of the corner of her eye.

Brenda set a glass of ice water before her. Cass gulped it down and wiped her mouth on the back of her hand. "Thanks." Brenda started to walk away. "Hey. Do you know that girl in the booth at the back?"

Brenda ran a hand through her red hair and squinted. She shook her head. "Nah. Never seen her before. Why?"

Fortunately, Cass was relieved of the responsibility of coming up with an answer because Brenda was called away by an old woman who wondered where the iced tea and the ash tray she had asked for were.

I need to get myself back to normal. A pulse was pounding in Cass's temple; something twitched behind her left eye. She saw the blonde without the scarf, holding a video camera and moving slowly in a circle, keeping the camera trained on something Cass couldn't quite see...but was sure she didn't want to.

Cass hopped from the stool and ran to the restroom, where she threw up. When she came back, the woman was gone.

I have to get out of here. I have to get out of here and get home to Max. Cass felt the imperative with a certainty that went beyond reason. She trembled with the need of it; getting out of here had all the allure of a shot of heroin in the vein of an addict. She'd lose her job over it if she had to. *Something is very wrong.*

Mike Bailey was in his tiny office at the rear of the diner. The room was little more than a closet, with space enough for a battered green metal desk, a chair, a couple shelves, and a cork bulletin board. Mike had a mound of papers before him and his fingers were manipulating a calculator.

Cass stood in the doorway, staring at the sunburned bald spot on the top of her boss's head, took in the stained white shirt and the too-short tie stretched over his paunch. "Mike?"

He looked up at her. There was no sympathy in his eyes; if anything, all his face revealed was a slight trace of irritation. He had never been the kind of man she felt she could turn to with a problem, but now she felt she had no choice. *Something is happening out there. Something I need to stop. They're coming for Max. I have to get out of here. Now!* His face went blank and he returned to looking down at the papers spread out before him.

"What do you want, Cass?"

"I don't feel so good, Mike. I don't think I can finish my shift."

He blew out a big sigh. "I feel for you, Cass, I really do. But have you taken a look at the lunch crowd we have out there today?"

"I know, but..."

Mike held up his hand. "I'd really appreciate it if you could buck up for just another hour, then me and Brenda can prob'ly handle things. Can you do that?"

Cass bit her lip. Swallowing was hard. *No! No, I can't do that. In an hour, it will be too late.* "What will be too late?" Cass blurted out without even thinking. She wasn't psychic, she thought, she was just fucking crazy.

"Huh?"

"Nothing, Mike." *Be strong. If you can't be strong now, it's all over.* Again, Cass wanted to ask, "What?" but caught herself before she spoke the word aloud. "Listen, I gotta go. I'm sorry to leave you like this, but man, I can barely stand up."

Mike threw his hands in the air. "So be it!" He turned his full attention back to his calculator, sighing.

Cass hurried away with Mike calling after her, "Your paycheck's gonna be docked for this."

"Thanks, Mike," Cass whispered, hanging up her apron and grabbing her purse from a shelf in the stock room. "I hope you feel better, too."

MYRA STOOD OUTSIDE the restaurant. Her palms were sweaty and she found it hard to catch her breath. She walked over to the area of the downtown where several streets came together with a little fountain in the middle, called, rather grandly, "the Diamond." She sat down by the fountain, trying to concentrate on the burbling water, to think simple thoughts like how hot it was and how the air was heavy with humidity and car exhaust.

But it didn't take long for her mind to wander back to why she was sitting there in the Diamond, across from a little magazine store called The Smoke Shop, with people hurrying by her to the few stores left in downtown Summitville. Oblivious. All these people and not one of them was aware she was sitting there waiting for her boyfriend to pick her up. Innocuous enough, sure, but not so innocuous when you factored in the awful truth that same boyfriend would have with him a little boy he had just kidnapped.

My God, what am I doing? Murder, kidnapping, rape... How have I sunk so low so fast? Myra had never felt more trapped in her young life. Earlier, she had gotten up the courage to stage a full out-and-out argument with Ian over his plan (a plan that was still sketchy in her mind; she understood why he wanted the boy—to buy the mother's silence—but how long were they expected to keep him? If the ransom was her silence, would they ever give him back?). She had tried to tell him all the good reasons for not doing what he was proposing: they were already in far over their heads, they had already committed enough crime to send them both to prison for the rest of their lives. They could die by lethal injection, or whatever they used; she would have to check and see what the capital punishment laws were in Pennsylvania, she thought, because it might be a future she would be facing very soon. And then there was the whole issue of having this little boy around to take care of, for however long. She didn't think either of them had the ability to take care of themselves, let alone a child. But Ian wouldn't listen. Of course, he invoked the name of the "Beast," saying that He would protect them and that it was out of his own hands. "I am only carrying out orders," he intoned, a glazed look coming into his eyes.

Ian was crazy.

And she was trapped.

Myra had gone to the restaurant not because Ian had wanted her to. He probably would have been furious at her for showing her face. His plan was that she just sit tight downtown while he went to the grandparents'. He would swing by and pick her up once he had the boy, then they could plot their next move. Myra needed to see what Cass D'Angelo looked like. She didn't know why. She *did* know that seeing the woman up close would make things even harder.

Oh shit, Myra...Penny...whatever...come off it! You can be honest with yourself just sitting here on this fine summer day. You went to the restaurant because you wanted to tell Cass D'Angelo that she needed to get home, that she needed to protect her son. You should have told that woman what was going down. By doing so, you could have saved a little boy's life. Because, my dear — don't kid yourself — you know Ian and you know the Beast and you know, sure as anything, that the little boy is going to end up just like the two girls. And you'll be expected to get it all on tape.

Myra swallowed hard, the bile and acid from her stomach splashing up at the back of her throat. She turned on the bench, bit her knuckle hard enough to draw blood, and tried to hold back the sobs. *You're a coward. You could have helped that woman. Thank God she at least left.* Myra had watched from across the street Cass D'Angelo hurry out of the diner, running down the street to a beat-up car, and then watched as the car roared by, muffler chugging and transmission whining. But the car wasn't going so fast that Myra couldn't take in the panic on Cass's face. *You could have run after her. She stopped at a light just a few yards away. You could have made it the short distance and stopped her.*

But you didn't. And hopefully God was watching and winning the battle with the Beast, and Cass D'Angelo would make it home in time to save her son.

"Penny? Penny Landsdale!"

Myra was shocked out of her reverie by a familiar voice. She looked up into the porcine eyes of Tammie Blankenship, former classmate and, once upon a time, one of the few people she called a friend, back in New Hope in a different time, in a different life. She and Tammie had spent many nights at each other's houses, had sneaked their first cigarettes together, had sworn each other to secrecy over what they would be willing to do with certain boys at New Hope High, had played Barbies together when they were far too old for it, experimented with marijuana. She hadn't seen Tammie in ages. It seemed like a different person altogether who had had these experiences with the pudgy dark-haired girl standing before her, pulling down her cropped blouse over a belly that should never have been exposed. But Tammie was like that: she saw someone different in the mirror than everyone else did.

Myra pulled the sunglasses down low, squinting at Tammie, then replaced them. She knew she looked very different from Penny. Different enough to get away with it. "I don't know a Penny Landsdale. You must have me mixed up with someone else." Myra studied her fingernails.

"Oh come on! Girl! You're looking good, but don't play games with your old best friend. I—"

"No, really. My name is *not* Penny...and I wish you'd leave me alone." Myra scanned the street for a red Mustang, thinking this would be exactly the perfect time for Ian to show up, the car screeching to a halt with a screaming kid in the backseat. A perfect witness. Just to get rid of Tammie, Myra added, "I don't even know why you'd think I'd even know someone like you. Why don't you cover up that gut? It's disgusting."

Tammie froze as if Myra had shot a poison dart directly into her heart. Myra could see her swallow, see her face begin to crumple. Tammie hurried away, head down.

Myra sat back against the bench and blew out a big sigh. *Ian, where are you?*

SARAH THWACKED THE veal cutlets with a wooden mallet. It was going to be a good dinner; she would at least see little Max eating some nutritious food for once in his life. She gave the last cutlet one more thwack with the mallet and held it up. "Almost paper thin, good work." Dinner was going to be simple: dredge the veal in a little flour, dip it into some beaten egg, then a pile of bread crumbs seasoned with garlic, parsley, oregano, basil, and thyme. Then the cutlets would go into a pan already searing hot, the olive oil on the surface shimmering, almost smoking. A quick sear, first one side then the other, and...delicious. A squeeze of lemon on top, a few sprigs of parsley, and they would be eating like kings. Accompanied by a side of boiled red potatoes and some Swiss chard sautéed with a little olive oil and garlic, the meal would be the kind of thing, Sarah was sure, Max didn't get to see much of. Hadn't he told her once that Cass fed him cereal sometimes for dinner? Sarah shook her head, shaking the flour off a piece of veal. *I didn't raise her that way. I taught her how to cook just like Mama taught me.*

And now here was Max, coming in the door. "Shoes off! Shoes off! I don't want you tracking dirt on my clean kitchen floor."

"Yes, Nana." Max dropped his schoolbooks in a heap next to him, then unbuckled and removed his sandals (Sandals! Sarah thought, what kind of school lets kids wear sandals?), and placed them near the baseboard. "Where's Bum?"

"Tied up outside, where he belongs. I don't know how you let that smelly animal in the house with you."

"Bum's nice." Max went over to the table and pulled an orange from the fruit bowl in its center. Sarah snatched it out of his hand. "Na-ah! You'll spoil your supper. We'll be eating in about ten minutes. Go upstairs and wash your hands."

"Yes, Nana."

She listened as he shuffled away, heard his quick exchange with Sam in the living room.

"You winnin', Pop?"

"Oh yeah, up to $30,000 now."

Sarah heard the slap of a high five and the theme music from *Jeopardy!* Boys, she thought, sticking a fork into the new potatoes boiling on the stove.

Sarah was just giving the Swiss chard a final shake in the colander when a tap came at the back door. Sarah shook the colander once more, then turned to look through the screen door. She wasn't expecting anyone. She lifted her head a little to peer through the glasses perched on her nose.

A young man stood there. Handsome guy, big, with dark hair and a dark complexion. Maybe he was Italian. He was dressed nicely, not like most of the guys his age you saw around town lately in their uniform of jeans, ball caps, and NASCAR T-shirts. This guy wore a white button-down shirt and nicely pressed black pants. He looked presentable. Sarah wiped her hands on her apron and smiled. The man was holding something behind his back and it made Sarah think, for a moment, that he was bringing flowers to surprise her with. What nonsense!

"Hello?" Sarah came to the screen door, still rubbing her hands on her apron. She reached out to unlock it, then pulled back her hand. These days, you couldn't be too careful. Things weren't like they used to be. But this man looked so nice! So trustworthy. Still, she would keep the screen door locked until she found out what he was doing, standing on her back porch.

"Hi." The young man's voice was deep and warm. He had such an honest face.

"Can I help you?"

"I'm afraid I might have some bad news." He finally pulled his hand out from behind his back and Sarah's eyes widened.

"I think this might be yours?"

"Oh jeez..." Max would be a wreck. The man was holding out Bum's collar and the length of clothesline she had used to tie him up in the backyard. She didn't know how he had done it, but it looked like that dog was some kind of escape artist.

Finally, Sarah unlocked the door. "Come on in. That belongs to my grandson's dog." Sarah shook her head. "Did you see the dog at all?"

"Actually, I did. That's why I stopped. He ran out in front of my car." The man smiled, but there was a bit of sorrow in his eyes. "I just missed hitting him; really had to slam on the brakes."

He moved further into the kitchen, sniffing the air. "Smells like you're a good cook."

Sarah blushed. "A little veal. It's nothin'." Sarah noticed Max had come into the kitchen; well, actually, he was hanging back near the entrance. He regarded the man with wide eyes and Sarah could see his eyes moving from the man's face to the collar and rope.

"That's Bum's."

Sarah looked to the man, then back to Max. "It looks like Bum got away."

Max started shaking his head and his eyes brightened with tears. "*Nooo.*"

"This is..." Sarah cocked her head.

The man gave Max a huge smile. "I'm Ian. I saw your dog running away. He went down First Avenue. I bet he hasn't gotten too far. Maybe you and your grandma could take a walk down there?"

"Nana? Could we? C'mon, we need to move before Bum gets too

far." He tugged at her hand.

Sarah looked over to the stove, where her supper was simmering, bubbling, and sautéing. "I can't leave supper right now, Max."

The man squatted down and put his hand on Max's shoulder. "Want me to help, sport? I saw where he went. With my car, we could probably track him down in a few minutes." He looked up at Sarah and gave her a winning smile. "That is, if it's okay with your grandma, here."

Sarah didn't say anything, rubbing her hands on her apron.

"I know...it's probably not a good idea. These days, you can't be too careful." Ian turned toward the door.

"But Bum!" Max whined. He looked ready to burst into sobs.

"I don't know..." Sarah glanced out the window.

Ian stood and put his hands up. "It's okay. I understand. You don't know me from Adam. Better to be safe these days. I'm sure Bum will come back, tail between his legs and hungry for dinner." He smiled at Max.

"Please, Nana. We'll have a better chance if we can go in the car. Please!"

Sarah swallowed hard. He certainly looked like a trustworthy young man. Why would he have bothered to even go to the trouble of coming to the back door if he wasn't someone who wanted to help, a good Samaritan? He could have just driven on, that's what most folks would have done.

She took in a big breath and let it out quickly. "I guess it's okay. But just for a little bit, Max. Supper's almost ready. If you don't see the dog in—" Sarah glanced at her watch "—ten minutes, I want you to come home. Ian here is probably right; Bum will be back. If you don't find him now, he'll find you. He has a good home with you. Dogs know." Sarah turned back to the stove. "It's okay if you want to run around the block in your car, but please don't spend too much of your time. If you don't see him, I'm sure he'll be back. If not, I'm promising Max right now I'll take him over to the pound first thing in the morning." She looked down at Max. "It'll be all right. Now you better run along, before he gets too far." Sarah smiled. "Or too dirty."

"If you're sure..."

"I think it'll be fine." Sarah sniffed. "Now my food's gonna burn if I don't get back to it."

She watched as the kind young man put his hand gently on the back of Max's head and led him out the door. In a minute, she heard the roar of an engine coming to life. She turned to grab her tongs to take the Swiss chard out of the pan.

She heard the closing theme music from *Jeopardy!* and then Sam's shuffle into the kitchen. He paused in the archway, raising his eyebrows. "Where's Max?"

"Bum got away. Lucky for us someone spotted him before he got too far. A very nice young man who took the time to stop his car and come and tell us."

"That was nice, but where's Max?"

"The young man, Ian he said his name was, is taking Max around the neighborhood in his car so they can find Bum." Sarah turned to the stove and began lifting the veal out with a spatula, transferring it to a platter.

"And you let him go?"

Sarah turned back to her husband. His grizzled face didn't look happy; his heavy eyebrows were pushed together and he was frowning.

She tried to smile, but already she was questioning if she had done the right thing. "He was very nice. I'm sure it's fine."

"For your sake, I hope so." Sam turned and went back into the living room. She heard him call over his shoulder. "For Max's sake, I mean. For Max's sake."

Sarah turned back to her supper. Suddenly nothing looked or smelled so good anymore. *Everything will be fine. He was so nice!*

CASS SPED DOWN Hill Road, toward Pennsylvania Avenue. She could see her parents' green-shingled house in the distance. *Something is not right. Something is not right.*

She almost collided with the car to her left when she saw the red Mustang pull away from the curb. "No!" Cass shrieked and pressed down hard on the accelerator. The sick feeling in her stomach that had begun at the diner was now in full bloom: her stomach churned; there was a thin sheen of sweat covering her face and trickling down her back. She could barely swallow and when she succeeded, the sharp tang of bile came back up. She had to white-knuckle the steering wheel, her hands were shaking so badly.

The car was heading east toward Pittsburgh. Even now, she was talking to herself and trying to rationalize. *It's just a car. It might not even be them. And if it is... Oh God, what if it's them? What about Max? Surely Ma would never let him go with... But what if they just grabbed Max as he played in the yard?*

There was a traffic light up ahead, at the corner of Pennsylvania and Mulberry Street. It was changing from yellow to red and a car was pulling out from Mulberry Street. Cass cried out, "Damn!" and beat her hand on the steering wheel. The red Mustang picked up speed. Cass watched, twitching, as it continued north and then rounded a bend and went out of sight. "No," she whispered.

"Come on, come on." Cass drummed her fingers on the steering wheel, waiting for the world's longest traffic light to cycle through back to green. A voice very much like her mother's began to whisper to her. *Now, Cass, wouldn't it make sense just to stop for a minute at Ma and Pop's? Just see if everything's okay before you go tearing off after some strangers that you might scare half out of their minds? Most likely, Max will be sitting at the kitchen table, playing with one of his X-men figurines and waiting for supper. Ma will be wondering why you're home from work early.*

It wasn't the voice of her mother, Cass thought, burning some rubber as she screeched through the intersection once the light changed, it was her own voice, the one she had before the accident. Before she had begun having the visions and inexplicably knowing things.

She remembered Lucy Plant in her shallow grave down by the river, and she knew Max was in trouble. *That voice – the one telling you something's wrong – is right, Cass, and you know it.* She sped by her parents' house, laying on the horn as someone started to cross the street at First Avenue. She wasn't about to slow down. She would round the bend up ahead and the Mustang would be in view. She would be able to catch up. She had to. She let out a short little cry, not even aware she was making a sound.

They have Max. I don't know what story they gave to Ma. But it wouldn't have been hard. God bless her, she isn't the brightest of souls; it wouldn't have been too hard. Cass let her mind drift and she saw him at her mother's back door, smiling. *Him.* She had seen him in visions before and the thought that he might now have Max made her want to throw up. She pushed the accelerator to the floor, and glanced down to see she was doing almost eighty.

She rounded the bend at Pleasant View Drive, tires squealing and clinging to the steering wheel; she almost lost control. The car felt like it was going to go up on two wheels, but she managed to keep it together. The red Mustang was probably about a mile ahead of her. There was a beat-up Ford pickup, rusted green, and a brand new SUV in a bright metallic blue between them. The Mustang was going pretty fast. Cass swore she could see Max's face peering out of the back window of the Mustang. His arms were extended to her, the way he used to do when he was a baby and wanted to be picked up. He was crying, his little mouth open in a silent howl. Cass knew she was too far away to see any such thing in reality. But still, she knew her vision was right.

What if they get away? Cass's heart thudded in her chest; it felt tight. *Is this what it feels like when you have a heart attack? What if I get stopped at another light and they turn and head up the hill, get lost in the maze of streets? How will I ever find them?* Cass sped up and her front bumper came dangerously close to the back bumper and hitch of the pickup in front of her.

She then had a flash so real it almost caused her to run off the road and right up on to the sidewalk. She struggled to hold on to the steering wheel, as if it had a mind of its own. She burst into sobs and, without warning, found herself wailing.

There was Bum. He was lying somewhere dark. In the gloom, there were things. What were they? Near his head, a jug of something blue...windshield washer fluid maybe? Next to that a jack, the kind you use when you get a flat. Bum was lying in the trunk of a car.

His throat was slit and blood oozed out onto the carpeting: a black pool, growing.

"Oh God," Cass whimpered, and whipped the car out left of the center line in a desperate effort to get around the pickup and the SUV before the light ahead — at Erie Street — changed.

All she could think of was Max. *He's going to die if I don't catch up. He's going to die...* Cass might as well have been dreaming. She didn't even see the little silver Sentra coming toward her, didn't even notice it in fact, until she heard the shriek of its brakes, the bright alarm of its horn, and its grille rising up, huge, in front of her.

She slammed on the brakes, pushing them to the floor, gripping the steering wheel and throwing herself back against the seat for leverage, but it was too late to stop.

Cass didn't even have time to scream as the two cars collided, head on.

Part Two

Chapter
Eighteen

HER SHOULDER HURT. In a few hours, Cass knew, she would have one hell of a bruise. When her car and the Sentra collided, the air bag saved her from any real damage, but she had somehow twisted in her seat upon impact, going up and to her side, slamming into the driver's side window hard enough to crack it. But the only injury was a bruise. The paramedics told her she was lucky as she sat by the side of the road, shaking. The hood of her car pointed toward the sky; steam rose up from the engine compartment. Everywhere, the smell of anti-freeze. A teenage boy had been driving the Sentra and paced nearby, on a cell phone. She tuned out his urgent, fast, and broken-voiced chatter. She couldn't be with him in the panic over this car accident.

Yes, they had told her she was lucky. Both cars had been totaled in the collision, and both vehicles looked like no one should have walked away alive. And perhaps no one would have in the days before air bags. But the collision was head on, and the air bags saved both of them from flying through the windshield or being forced down and into the engine.

Cass didn't feel lucky. As she sat by the side of the road, she began to weep. The red Mustang was, by now, long gone. There was no way she could ever catch up. Max was inside. She knew it now with the same certainty that she knew her own name was Cass and that she was a waitress in a diner in Summitville, Pennsylvania. She saw again Max's terrified face looking out of the back window of the Mustang, the way he seemed to know she was behind him, his despair at her not being able to save him. Every child wants a mother who can rescue him. She had failed as a mother; she had not been able to come to him when he needed her most. And now God only knew what was happening to Max. Cass could only hope that God would watch over him, because she had done a shitty job.

She wondered if the image of Max reaching out to her from the car would be the last she'd ever have of her little boy. A snapshot of despair, burned into her brain for eternity.

She knew — again, with complete certainty — this image was not the hallucination of an over-protective mother, but reality. *Max was in the car, with a person or people who had killed two girls.* Cass could barely work any spit down her throat. She didn't know how long she would have, or even if it was already too late, but she had to find her son. *The only reason they would want him is because they know about me. They know about me because my name was in the paper and in a town this size, it's not so hard to find someone. They know I know something, and Max is their insurance that I don't lead someone to another shallow grave, or worse, to wherever it is they're living.* Cass had a quick flash of a view from a hilltop, a view she had seen many times before, but the image stayed in her mind's eye only long enough to tease her. She wanted to have time to look down from the hilltop, to see how the river curved and what landmarks were on the other side. Already, she was learning how to use this gift, or curse. The knowledge that they had taken Max as some sort of insurance to buy her silence was cold comfort. Who knew how they would treat her baby? Who knew when they would tire of having him around and do to him the same things they had done to those girls, and then move on? Cass balled her fists in impotent rage and looked up to the sky, as if God was looking down and would tell her what to do.

But all she saw were banks of clouds moving in, teasing, threatening—rain.

They had asked her if she had someone to call who could come and pick her up, if she wanted the city to tow her car or if she wanted to call a private company. Cass couldn't think. There was only worry about Max; they could have set the car on fire for all she cared. "Let the city tow it," she had said in a dead voice, barely above a whisper. "I don't care." They had explained the car would be put in the city lot and she would have to make arrangements to get it out. Was she sure she didn't want to call a tow company? Cass just shook her head, feeling shaken and empty. Even the boy whose car she had hit offered her his cell phone. She just waved him away, and ran after the officer who had stopped to write up the details about the accident.

She caught up to him, tapping him on the back. She knew her face must look crazy, a mask of anguish. She didn't know what he'd think about what she was about to say. That she was in shock? She couldn't tell him the truth; she would have to lie.

"Officer! Officer, please! Do you know why I had this accident?"

The officer was young; this might have been his first job out of school. He couldn't have been more than in his early twenties. His dark brown eyes regarded her and she could tell he wanted to be compassionate. She could also tell his guard was up and he was on the alert for the ravings of a crazy woman who had just been in a head-on collision. She didn't know how she knew these things from just a glance at a young and impassive face, but she did.

"You were going too fast?"

Cass nodded. "That's right. I was going too fast. But do you know why?" Cass fought to keep her voice level; she could feel it struggling to go up higher, into the realm of hysteria. "Do you know why?" She moved in close to his face. "Because my son was kidnapped."

The officer cocked his head; his expression changed from one of concern to one of alarm, his dark eyes brightened.

Cass swallowed and nodded. "That's right, officer..." she glanced down at his badge. "Officer Rivera. I was chasing a car—a red Mustang—my son was inside. Someone took him from my parents' house. I was trying to catch up with the car; I could see Max—that's my son—in the backseat. He was reaching out for his mommy. Oh God, we have to find him!" Cass couldn't hold on, she began sobbing uncontrollably, clutching at the officer's arm and chest.

"Calm down, ma'am. Let me take care of this."

A short while later, she found herself sitting in Marion Hartley's office once more. They had gotten her some water and Hartley had been surprisingly sympathetic. Where the older woman had once been cold to the point, Cass thought, of cruelty, she was now suddenly compassionate, her dark eyes filled with concern. She had made sure Cass was comfortable, offered her a drink, and was now sitting back in her chair, a phone receiver to her ear.

Cass watched her. Marion Hartley was calling her mother. Cass had already hiccupped out, between sobs, most of the story, though not saying that the image of Max in the back seat was only a vision and not an actual sight.

"Well, let's just give your parents a call. Maybe they know who he went off with and it's not as sinister as you think."

Cass knew it was probably even more sinister than she could possibly think, but humored the woman; she needed her on her side.

Hartley punched in the number and listened, smiling at Cass. "Don't get too worried just yet. These things often resolve themselves very quickly, often without any problem. We've seen..." Hartley stopped when she made a connection. "Hello? Hello, is this Mrs. Sarah D'Angelo?" Hartley paused. "This is Detective Marion Hartley, from the Summitville Police Department." Hartley stopped and Cass could hear her mother's voice, sounding tinny broadcast through the receiver. She was talking fast, panic making her voice higher. *God, I already know how this is going to go...and it's not going to go well.*

Hartley put up a placating hand, even though Sarah couldn't see it. "Mrs. D'Angelo? Mrs. D'Angelo, could you please calm down for a moment and let me finish? I have a couple of things to tell you and I want you to know up front that your daughter is all right."

A surge of unintelligible words issued out of the receiver again. If the situation weren't so dire, it would have been funny, like some comedy routine. Cass could tell Marion Hartley was trying to keep her cool by the way she drummed her nails on the desk, just waiting for Sarah to say what she needed to say. Cass concentrated on the blunt fingers and square-cut nails, noticing how some of them were stained yellow from tobacco.

"Mrs. D'Angelo? Mrs. D'Angelo...Cass is sitting right here with me. She's been in a car accident." Hartley paused. "No. No, she wasn't on drugs. I just wanted to reassure you that she's okay?" Hartley paused again. "It was on Pennsylvania Avenue, just up from your house."

"C'mon, Mom, let the woman finish," Cass whispered.

"Anyway. Cass is fine, although she'll probably be needing a new vehicle. What I'm calling about is your grandson. Is he, by any chance, there with you right now?" Hartley looked at Cass over the top of her glasses. She looked down at her desk and nodded. "I see." She looked up again and she was frowning. "Did you get the man's name?" Hartley pulled a yellow leg pad over in front of herself and poised a pen above it. "Ian?" She scrawled. "You didn't get a last name? Okay. How long ago was this?"

Cass's heart had begun to thud uncomfortably, feeling like it might break though her chest. She was finding it hard to breathe and the room was beginning to spin. She could barely hear Marion Hartley saying, "And did you get a look at the car they left in?"

Cass felt everything flicker, like the lights going dim in a power surge. She collapsed to the floor.

Chapter
Nineteen

"COME ON, THERE'S nothing to worry about." Myra held out her hand, *again*. But the boy would not get out of the back seat of the car. It was as though he had planted himself there, an immovable force. Myra knew even if she reached in and grabbed him, he would cling to whatever hold he could find in the cramped interior. Even if she could loosen him, he would kick and scream loud enough for people at the bottom of the hill to hear him.

Ian wasn't helping. He stood by, simply watching. *Damn him.* Myra would have liked some help. At least Ian could have used brute force, but he was leaving it all up to her. The more she failed at her task, the angrier he got. She felt like he almost wanted the anger, wanted her to fail, so the rage could build and he could later take it out on her. She knew from past experience what her "punishment" would entail: violation and pain. And Ian could be very creative in delivering those things. She bore the scratches and bruises to prove it.

She wanted to cry herself as she looked at the little boy in the back seat, sobbing, his lower lip out like a comic caricature of a child's despair. Along with his panic and sadness, though, she could see how resolute he was, one hand clinging to the armrest so hard his little knuckles had gone bloodless. He stared at her as if he was challenging her.

Myra sighed. She offered the boy a smile and wondered for the first time if she looked scary, garish with her platinum hair, too much eye make-up, and blood-red lipstick. "Honey, aren't you hungry? Just come into the trailer with us and I'll make you a nice peanut butter sandwich." Myra put a hand to her forehead. "We have cable. We can watch cartoons on the Cartoon Network."

"I want to go home," the boy managed to get out between sobs. "I want my Mom."

"I know you do, honey, and we'll call her a little later."

Ian blew out a harsh sigh. "Get on with it," he whispered between clenched teeth.

She wanted to whirl on him and tell him he wasn't helping. She wanted to ask why he was just standing there anyway. Why didn't he at least go into the house and let her deal with this her way instead of making her feel more pressured and stressed than she already was—which was pretty stressed and pressured. They had, after all, just added kidnapping to the other felonies they had committed this summer. If they were ever caught...

But she couldn't say anything. She knew if she did, the best result she could hope for was to earn herself a bloody nose or lip. Ian lately was quicker and quicker to reach out and harm her in any way he could. She trembled at the thought of it.

Myra ducked her head into the car. "Please, sweetheart." She reached out with her hand and whispered frantically, hoping Ian wouldn't hear. "He'll beat me if you don't get out of the car." She wanted to weep. "He'll really hurt me. And he might hurt you, too. He wouldn't even think twice about it. Is that what you want?"

Max suddenly stopped crying and his face went white. She knew she had scared him and she hated to do it, but this was about survival. She did not want to help dig a grave for this little boy. She didn't want to stand by with a video camera while Ian did unspeakable things to him. "Please." Myra held out her hand, and bit down on her lower lip to hold back her own sobs.

And Max scooted over on the seat, took her hand. Myra breathed a sigh of relief, smiling at the boy. "Thank you," she mouthed.

The pair walked by Ian, who stood silent, arms folded across his chest, watching their progress across the scrabbled weeds they called a front yard, up the two cinder blocks they called a front porch, and inside.

The interior of the trailer was dark and close, as if the heat and humidity outside had made itself a home there, stretching out its heavy, sweaty legs. The little boy held fast to Myra's hand, his own small and clammy. She knew he was having as much trouble seeing as she was; it would take a moment for their eyes to adjust to the darkness inside after the glare outside.

The boy said nothing and neither did Myra. She was waiting. She knew Ian was just outside and wondered why he wasn't immediately behind them. She had left the door open a crack behind them. Quickly, she squatted down in front of Max. "Look, honey, there's a couple of things I want to tell you before my boyfriend Ian comes inside. One is, don't disobey him. Do whatever he asks and do it immediately. There's no gain in backtalk or not obeying. Do you understand?" The little boy stared back at her. Even in the darkness, she could see his eyes were vacant, his skin pale. He had gone, in just a few instants, from terrified to numb. She supposed it was how one coped. She had seen the same thing happen to Sheryl McKenna after Ian... Well, she didn't want to think about that now. That was in the past. And she had the present before her that she needed to deal with—urgently. "The second thing is, you might hear Ian talk about the Beast. The Beast, just so you know, isn't real. It's just Ian and his imagination. So, don't be scared when he

talks about the Beast. The Beast is just like those monster movies you
see on the TV. It's all just made up, just for fun. It's..."

Ian walked in, and it seemed the temperature in the trailer
dropped, like the air had been sucked out of the space. He blocked what
little light was coming in through the crack in the doorway. All the
curtains had been drawn. He stood for a moment, looking down at the
two of them.

Suddenly, Myra felt silly—no, disloyal—crouching before the boy
and she stood and faced Ian. She felt like she was waiting for her orders.

And the orders came. "Tie him up."

Ian went off to light candles, to put on some weird music he had
discovered in a used record store (mostly vinyl; Ian was the only person
Myra knew who owned a turntable). The record was called *Hands of Jack
the Ripper* and was by the British guy who called himself Screaming
Lord Sutch. It was just a lot of screaming, that much was right, horrible
music about death and monsters. Myra didn't like it and was sure it
scared the boy.

"Why are you still standing there?"

Myra jumped when she felt Ian draw close. Shadows danced
around the tiny living room, almost alive, changing with the flicker of
the candle flames. Ian put his face right up to hers. "I told you to do
something. I didn't mean to do it in five minutes, or when you're damn
good and ready. I meant for you to do it immediately."

Myra nodded. She looked down at Max, who stared up with wide
eyes, looking first at her, then at Ian. She could see his lower lip was
trembling, just a tiny bit, and he was trying to hold it in, to be brave. It
made her feel even more protective of him.

"It's not me asking, Myra. The Beast needs it; we have to be able to
control him. Now get busy." He took her face in his hand, squeezing too
hard on her jaw. She gasped. "Or would you prefer I tie him up? I can
do it, but it will be a lot less pleasant for all concerned."

Myra sucked in some air and moved her head very gently and very
slowly to free herself from Ian's painful grasp. She rubbed at her jaw. "I
can do it. But..." She bit on her lower lip, looking up at him. "I can do it,
but do you really think we need to, Ian? I can keep an eye on him, make
sure he doesn't get in any trouble."

"I told you. The Beast commands it. Let's not question Him."

Myra nodded. "It's just that we don't know..." Almost before she
could see it, Ian's hand flew up and slapped her so hard across the face
her head swiveled and she saw stars. "No more chances. Are you going
to do this or not?"

Myra clenched her teeth to keep from weeping. "Yes," she
whimpered.

"Good, because I have a dog in the trunk that needs burying." Myra
closed her eyes. *No.* She opened them to see Ian smiling down at the
boy. "Bum's going to stink up my car if I don't take care of him."

The boy started to cry. Myra listened to his sobs as she went to the kitchenette to find the bungee cords under the sink.

"Not Bum." The boy sniffed. Myra's hand closed around the cords.

She hurried back to the boy, who was sniffling. He was trying not to cry. Squatting down before him, Myra showed him the bungee cords. "Now, you heard what Ian said, right? These won't hurt...and I'm sorry, but we have to do what Ian says."

Myra began wrapping the first cord around the small boy's frame, grateful that he sort of stood there like a dummy, like some sort of mannequin. She didn't know if she had the strength to fight him if he had chosen to be obstinate. "Um, I think your dog was already dead when Ian found him; a heart attack or something." Myra hung her head; it was all so futile.

Ian came back into the trailer, flinging the door open so hard it slammed into the wall behind it. With him came a burst of brilliant light so bright it hurt Myra's eyes. She turned to peer up at his dark figure, a silhouette with a sickly whitish glow surrounding him. Her throat was dry as she fumbled with the second of the bungee cords. "I thought you were going to..."

"The dog can wait. I thought we should have a memento of the occasion. Just hold on."

Myra bowed her head and knelt before the boy, staring at the floor. She wanted to say something to reassure him, but found there were no words left in her head. She felt as numb as the little boy looked, his skin sweaty and ashen, breathing through his mouth. She simply waited. She knew what Ian was up to.

"Got it!" he called from the bedroom.

When he emerged seconds later, he held the video camera in front of him. "Smile for the camera." Even an innocuous comment like this one held a kind of threat in it, a veiled implication of terror. She looked up at him, squinting. "Do we have to?" she whispered.

She wasn't sure Ian heard her. He didn't respond, just began moving the camera up and down the two of them, the lens caressing them, framing them in a forced embrace.

"Get busy, Myra. What do I have you for if you can't even carry out the simplest tasks?"

Myra gritted her teeth and wished she had something, anything — an ice cube, a piece of chewing gum — to alleviate the awful dryness in her mouth and throat. She busied herself with the cords, wrapping them around the boy's limp form, wishing now he *did* have some fight in him. This deadness, this *just standing and waiting* was depressing. It made her want to cry. It was as if the boy had given up already and knew what was in Myra's head: visions of torturous death and a shallow grave.

"It's gonna be all right." Myra tried to put a little breath behind her words. "Would you like to lie down in the bedroom?"

Ian snickered. "What did you have in mind?"

Myra looked up at him, trying to make contact with the eyes behind the camera. "Don't." She shook her head.

Just then, all three of them froze, a weird, almost family-like tableau.

Someone was knocking at the door to the trailer.

Chapter
Twenty

CASS STOOD AT the door to Marion Hartley's office, feeling numb, like if she just shook her head hard enough, all of this would go away and she'd be back at the diner, serving up a big platter of chili cheese fries to a leering trucker.

The visions about the girls were horrible enough. But at least she didn't know them. At least it wasn't personal.

Marion's voice came at her like it was traveling through a tunnel. Cass could imagine how her face looked to the detective: dull, eyes without brightness, mouth partly open, a cow chewing its cud.

"Now you go home and get some rest. Let us get the wheels in motion so we can find your boy. Don't worry; there will be plenty for you to do later. Right now, I need to get on this."

Cass took small comfort in the fact that Hartley was taking Max's disappearance (abduction, really) so seriously. "Before you *do* start to get some rest, though, I need you to go right inside your house and find the best and most recent picture of your boy you can find and give it to the officer to bring back here. We'll take that, scan it, and send it out over the wires, so we can have people looking in the whole tri-state area, instead of just here in Summitville. We can also make up some flyers." Hartley smiled. "Cass, a lot of times, kids come back within the first couple of hours. Try not to worry too much."

Cass let loose a sob. "Try not to worry? Try not to worry? Are you crazy? This isn't a case of some little boy wandering off. He was *taken*. Do I have to remind you? I saw him in a car with someone I don't know." Cass looked down at her watch, its face bleary through her tears, but still clear enough to see that two hours had elapsed since she saw the car speeding away from her, two hours since it had pulled away from in front of her parents' house on Pennsylvania Avenue.

Hartley shook her head. "I'm sorry, Cass. I was just trying to comfort you."

"I don't want comfort! I want my son back!" Cass was trying to rein in her terror, her wildly beating heart; she knew she was just a few inches away from crossing the border into hysteria.

Hartley put a hand on her shoulder. "We're going to plaster this town and all around with that picture of Max you're going to go home

and get right now. Soon, there will be hundreds—no, *thousands* of
people looking for Max. If anyone has seen him, we'll know. Right
away. And we can act on it."

Cass sniffed. "You even believe that?"

Hartley took her face in her large hands and forced Cass to meet
her gaze. "We *have* to believe that, Cass. We can't give up hope already.
Now let the officer take you home, give him that picture and then give
yourself permission to lie down...even if it's only for twenty minutes.
Stress like you're under is draining, and we need you to be strong; we
need your energy so we can find him." She got right up in Cass's face.
"Understand?"

Cass nodded.

"Now go," the detective said gently. "I'll be in constant touch."

Cass followed the detective, a young guy with broad shoulders and
curly dark hair, down a corridor, and into the bright sunshine outside.
Cars passed in front of City Hall, strangers walked along the street,
laughing and talking. An older man with gray hair paused to light a
cigarette.

It was as if nothing had happened. *Don't they know my son has been
kidnapped? I don't even know what's happening to him! What they're doing to
him! And no one even cares!* The bright sunshine of the day was
completely inappropriate. Cass felt sick, like her legs were going to go
out from under her. She sat down suddenly on the concrete steps. The
young officer squatted next to her, his dark eyes alive with concern. "I'll
give you a minute, ma'am."

Cass shook her head, trying to draw in some air. She didn't know if
this faintness, this queasiness, would ever go away. "Never mind." She
grabbed on to his arm and used it to pull herself up. "Let's go. I need to
get you a photograph."

She had given the officer—Justin Garcia—Max's first-grade school
photo. Other than growing a shoe size, he looked essentially the same.
Cass knew from memory what the photograph looked like: Max's
somber expression (she knew there was no way some silly kid
photographer could make *him* smile), the green and blue plaid shirt he
had worn that day, the cowlick sticking up, and the openness in his big
green eyes. Today, she could not bear to look at the photo. She had
simply gotten it from the junk drawer in the kitchen, where it had lain
in a plastic bag for months with others just like it (she had exhorted Max
to trade his photo with classmates, but he insisted the whole idea was
silly. "What do I need to do that for? I see those same old faces every
day anyway.") and handed it—face down—to the officer.

He tried to reassure her. "This is really going to help. Getting his
face out there." He took a quivering breath and Cass suddenly realized
he was almost as scared as she was. She didn't want to think about that.
"I'll get this right down to HQ. Now you listen to what Detective
Hartley said. Get some rest. I'll come back for you in a little while." He

gave her a sickly smile. "Maybe I'll even have Mack with me."

Cass frowned and bit her lower lip. "It's Max."

She closed the door on the officer's apology.

The deadness, the numbness washed over her. *Why am I not having any visions now? Why isn't this thing showing me where my son is?* Cass's mind was as empty as a blank slate. She went into the living room and made herself lie down on the couch, in spite of the sheen of sweat covering her from head to toe and the way her stomach was churning. She forced herself to close her eyes, hoping that blocking out images from the real world before her might make some imagery come.

But there was nothing. This gift—if that's what one could call it— was contrary and stubborn. It called the shots, and it was mostly a bastard. Impulsive. Demanding. Cass felt she no longer had any control over her life.

Yet she kept her eyes closed, hoping that—like a movie—images would begin to appear on the backs of her eyelids, like some sort of screen.

She drifted, thinking of nothing.

Later, she dreamed of awakening groggy. She didn't know how much time had passed. Her head pounded; the couch beneath her was damp with sweat. She swallowed, trying to get some spit going, and swung her legs over the side of the couch, planting her feet on the floor. She was thrilled to see that nausea and dizziness, her constant companions, had not left her side. Outside, it was still light and the sky was a brassy white. The temperature must be in the nineties, but Cass felt cold. *Fall is just around the corner. When's it going to start feeling like it?*

It hurt to stand; her whole lower body felt as if it had been beaten, bruised. *Max is here. While I slept, they brought him back.* The thought just popped into her head as they had a way of doing these days. She smiled a little, but still felt shaky. *It could be a lie. A false impression.*

Cass hobbled to the foot of the stairs. She needed a drink of water. But she would deal with that in a minute. Right now, she had to see if Max was upstairs in his room, as a feeling deep in her bones told her he was. There would be plenty of time for water later.

Holding onto the wall for support, Cass began to mount the creaking staircase up toward Max's room. He had a TV in there and Cass closed her eyes when she heard it on. She let out a little yelp of laughter, relieved. *It's not just an image.* Canned laughter came from the room and Ricky's and Lucy's voices, telling a tale of comic marital discord, wafted out from behind Max's closed door.

Cass paused at the tinny sound of the portable TV. "Thank you," she whispered. "Oh God, thank you."

She managed to get herself down the remainder of the hallway and paused outside his door to listen, hand on doorknob.

"But Ricky, you promised!" Lucy whined.

Cass turned the handle and went inside.

There was no scream. The voice had been stunned out of her.

Max lay on his bed, illuminated by the harsh glare of the sun outside. His bedclothes were covered with soil, as was his naked body. Clumps of dirt littered the bed. He had been opened up from navel to neck with some kind of knife, something that cut jaggedly, leaving pieces of skin and muscle in pieces on his too-white skin. His green eyes were still rimmed by the black lashes her mother used to say were too long ("like a little girl's"), but they stared dully at the ceiling, covered with a milky white substance. His mouth hung open, a trickle of blood seeping from one corner. All of his teeth had been broken and stuck out of his gums, jagged stumps.

And his tongue, ripped or cut from his mouth, lay on the pillow beside his head.

Cass sat up suddenly, the shriek ripped from her throat. She had drenched the couch beneath her in sweat and her heart pounded so fiercely, she was afraid it would stop. She couldn't breathe. "Oh God, oh God. No!"

She hurried into the kitchen. She couldn't stand this. Someone from the police station had to come and get her.

I have to find Max.

Chapter
Twenty-one

ALL THREE PAIRS of eyes went to the door, where the knocking sounded again. It was tentative at first but now it came more forcefully. Ian looked from the door, back to Myra, questioning. She was certain her own expression was one of panic. Max struggled a little in her grip, perhaps seeing an avenue of escape in the knocking on the door. Myra held fast, digging her fingers deeply enough into his arms to make him wince.

"Who is it?" Ian demanded, facial muscles tightening in rage.

Myra shook her head, shrugging, and whispering, "How should I know?"

The knocking continued. A voice came from behind the door. "Hello? Anybody home?"

Myra kept looking quizzically at Ian, as if to say she was as baffled as he was, but there was a queasy knowledge growing in her gut. The voice had the ring of familiarity about it. *Oh God. No.* A few more raps on the shaky metal door and then the next words from the person on the other side confirmed Myra's fear.

"Hello? Penny? Are you in there? Open the door."

Ian's face clouded over. His eyes flashed, as if they had been sparked on flint. "What the fuck?" he mouthed.

Max struggled harder and Ian moved toward them. There was such threat in the simple action that Max froze. Ian roughly shoved Myra away from the boy, so hard she landed on her ass on the floor. Ian snatched the boy up in one arm, clamping his other hand over the boy's mouth, and hurried toward the back of the trailer, toward the bedroom.

"Take care of this," he said over his shoulder. Veins popped out on his forehead and he spoke through clenched teeth.

Myra put a hand to her head, feeling woozy, like she might faint. She braced herself on the floor and forced herself to stand. The pounding continued.

TAMMIE BLANKENSHIP WAS mad. She would say she had a long fuse, but when that fuse finally ignited—watch out. She rapped once more on the cheap imitation-wood trailer door, sweat trickling down her side, knowing she would not be satisfied until she faced that bitch Penny Landsdale and gave her a piece of her mind about what she had said downtown. True, Penny had lost a few pounds, but it gave her no right to talk to Tammie that way, telling her her stomach looked *disgusting* under her crop top. What a thing to say! Worse was when the bitch pretended she didn't even know her. Where did she get the nerve? They had gone to school together, had slumber parties, traded secrets, been *best friends* for Christ's sake. How in the world did Penny expect Tammie to believe she didn't know her?

It was outrageous is what it was.

When Penny had said those awful things and pretended not to know her, Tammie had been so stunned she was literally speechless. She'd walked around the block in a daze, not sure if she wanted to cry or bite someone. As she walked, her rage grew, so that by the time she got back around to the Diamond, she was ready to give that bitch a piece of her mind.

But she was gone. Tammie was shaking with rage. She had to sit down on a bench and light a Virginia Slim to try and calm down. She smoked the skinny cigarette down in about three puffs, scanning the people walking by, hoping Penny would show up again. Tammie wasn't sure if she could keep from slapping her. She almost smiled. *Almost.* Oh, she thought, this could be a scene right out of Jerry Springer.

Reluctantly concluding that Penny would not return, Tammie had gathered herself up, angrily yanking the stretchy black blouse down over her stomach. *I'm not that fat. I've been working out. I look good.* Still, she was furious at Penny for shaking her confidence, for harshing her good feelings about herself. She had started up the street, intending to stop at CVS to see if they had any more of that lip-gloss she liked and then to maybe head home across the river, where she could drown her anger in a nice cold bottle of Michelob.

Lucky for her, and unlucky for Penny, Tammie then had a chance meeting. Up ahead, she saw someone familiar coming out of Clutter's Meat Market, the little butcher shop that had been in downtown Summitville for years, though she didn't know how it stayed in business or why anyone would want to go there when they had the Wal-Mart superstore out by the highway. Penny's mother. Tammie smiled. Perfect. She quickened her pace to catch up with Penny's mom. Talk about fat! That bitch must make the scales twirl around twice. The cotton fabric of Mrs. Landsdale's housedress was soaked with sweat. Her broad back was hunched with the brown paper shopping bags she carried from the butcher's. Probably just bought lunch. Tammie snickered.

"Mrs. Landsdale! Mrs. Landsdale!" Tammie hurried to catch up. Mrs. Landsdale slowly turned around, her features pinched and pink, sweaty. A lock of greying hair fell over her forehead and she blew it out of her eyes. She looked quizzically at Tammie and then Tammie saw recognition dawn. She smiled.

"Is that you, Tammie Blankenship?"

Tammie caught up to her. "In the flesh. I'm glad *you* recognized me."

Mrs. Landsdale cocked her head.

"I just saw your daughter, and do you know she had the nerve to pretend she didn't know who I was?"

The older woman shook her head. "That sounds about right. Our Penny hasn't been the same since she met that man."

"What man?" Tammie took one of the bags from Mrs. Landsdale.

"Oh, I forget his name. She moved out a while back...to go live with him in sin. I've never been so ashamed. How's your mother?"

"Mom and Dad are good. Dad's gonna need a heart transplant, they say. We're just waiting to hear from the VA."

"Oh, I'm sorry to hear that, honey."

"He's gonna be okay. Don't you worry."

The two women regarded each other for a moment. "Did Penny say where she was living?" Tammie tried to act casual.

Mrs. Landsdale's features darkened. "She didn't want us to know. But it's hard to keep a secret around here. You know what I mean?"

"Uh huh."

"A friend of Penny's dad told us just a couple weeks ago they was living in a trailer up on a hill. You don't need to take that; I can handle it." Mrs. Landsdale took the bag back from Tammie. "He was the one rented it to them. I wouldn't have even known that if he hadn't gotten in touch with Frank because they haven't paid any rent in about three months. The man was fit to be tied."

"I can imagine. Whereabouts are they? Maybe I could drop by and let her know she better get that rent paid."

Mrs. Landsdale shook her head. "Oh, I don't know. The girl's not our daughter anymore." Mrs. Landsdale frowned and her eyes brightened with tears just a bit. She took in a big breath. "The trailer's up the Hill Road, all by itself, on a bluff. Me and Frank thought about going over, but we just don't know what to do with her anymore. I'm kind of afraid of her, to be honest. And I'm afraid Frank would wring her neck. He doesn't need that. Not with his heart. He's got a bad ticker, too. Bypass surgery last year, you know."

Tammie nodded. "Well, let me tell you. I'm not going to take my old best friend pretending she don't know me lying down. So I just go up the hill..."

"All the way to the top. The trailer's the only thing up there."

"I think I'll run up there right now."

Mrs. Landsdale grabbed Tammie's hand. "Tell her to come and see her mother, would you?"

"Oh, I'll be sure to tell her that." And a few other things. Tammie started away. "It was nice seeing you again."

"Let me know what she says. Okay, Tammie?"

"Sure thing."

She'd gone directly there. Now, she pounded once more on the door and finally, it opened. Penny peered out at her, just sticking her head around the side of the door. Tammie's anger dissolved. Penny looked terrified.

"What are you doing here?"

MYRA DIDN'T KNOW what to do with Tammie Blankenship. She thought the best course of action would be just to get rid of her, quickly. And pretending she didn't know her was no longer an option. She forced a smile. "I'm sorry about before. I don't know what got into me. Things are a little, um, complicated right now."

Tammie nodded, leaning over to try to look into the dark trailer.

"What's going on, Penny?"

Myra smiled again, hating the sound of her old name, hating the fact that this poor fat girl was putting herself in way more danger than she knew. "Nothing. I just found a boyfriend and, you know how that goes. We're having a few problems."

"Well, I'm glad you're off pretending you don't know your own best friend." Tammie leaned in closer. "You sure you're okay? Why's it look so dark in there?"

"Keeps things cooler. This old trailer gets hot." Myra knew there was an edge to her voice and she struggled to keep her words from coming out sounding shaky. She wanted so desperately to see this girl leave. "Listen, honey, I have a ton of stuff to do. Maybe we could meet up sometime? Have a Coke and catch up?"

"Can I come in? I'll only stay a minute." Tammie moved up and pushed her way right by Myra, before Myra even had a chance to stop her. She stood inside the trailer, looking around at its dirty, weird interior, illuminated by a dozen flickering candles. The video camera still lay on the kitchen counter. Myra saw the place through her eyes: the filth, the skull on the coffee table, the poster of Anton LaVey above the couch.

"Listen, I'm kind of in the middle of something here. Really, I need to get back to it. I'll call you." Myra touched Tammie's flabby arm, urging her back toward the open door.

She could tell Tammie was about to resist, but then she just kind of let go and allowed Myra to lead her to the door. "I saw your mom downtown. She's worried about you."

Myra got her to the threshold. "I'll have to give her a call, too."

Tammie was just about to step back out into the sunshine when there was a loud scream from the back of the trailer. "What was that?"

Tammie's mouth dropped open.

And Myra didn't know what to say. She was too tired to think fast, to come up with a plausible story explaining why the shriek of a young boy had just issued forth from one of the bedrooms.

"Help!" The little boy's voice came out, the "p" ending in a strangled muffling. *Oh God.* What was going to happen now?

Tammie stepped back in. "There's something wrong here." She seemed determined. She started toward the back of the trailer and all Myra could do was watch helplessly as she passed through the living room, into the little hallway, disappearing into the bedroom where she knew Ian was holding the little boy.

She could only imagine what awaited her old friend once she passed into that room.

Chapter
Twenty-two

THERE WAS A pounding at the door. In the bathroom, Cass finished washing her hands and looked at herself in the mirror. It seemed, in one afternoon, she had aged ten years: dark circles under her eyes, a sallowness to her skin, and just an all-around tiredness about her features making the muscles in her face sag. She felt as though she were already turning into an old woman. An old woman alone.

What would she do without Max? What if she never saw him again? The thought caused a short sob to hiccup out of her.

The pounding sounded again and Cass dipped her head, splashing cold water on her face.

She hurried down the stairs to quiet the pounding at the back door, thinking that the officer from the police department must have returned to take her back to the station. Maybe they knew something. Cass shuddered, thinking of her dream. *It was a dream, Cass. A dream. Not a vision. Dreams are symbols and expressions of our fears...* Those things seemed clear enough from what she could remember of the horrific dream images, which, mercifully, were already fading. Cass hoped she was right.

It took her a moment to remember the face at the back door. But when she did, she felt her hackles rising, the anger beginning to buzz inside her like a horde of bees. Her mouth set in a line. She glanced down to make sure the latch on the screen door was secure. She shook her head. "This is *not* a good time. This is *so* not a good time. Would you please just leave? I have nothing to say."

Cass stared out at Dani Westwood, the reporter from the *Review*. Neither of them said anything for what seemed like several minutes. Cass knew she must have taken the woman aback, not giving her even the smallest opening. She was glad.

Finally, Cass cocked her head. "I said..."

Dani put up a hand. "I heard you. I just have a couple things to say and then, if you want, I'll go."

Her cigarette-scarred voice seemed warm and her British accent comfortingly foreign and welcome at the same time. Dani's eyes met hers with a kind of sympathy. *Don't be pulled in, Cass. She's here after her own ends.*

Cass simply stared at her. She was tempted to close the door in her face, but the thought of doing without the hot, humid air coming in through the screen was just too much. At least it was air. That, and she just felt so tired. She almost was willing to risk the nightmares in exchange for going back upstairs and crawling into her bed, where she could pull the covers over her head and sleep, not for hours, but for years. Everything was just too hard.

When she said nothing further, Dani began. "First off, I'm not going to tell you that I'm not here after a story. That would be a lie."

"Please, Ms. Westwood, just go." Cass started to turn away.

"Just allow me to finish. I am after a story; it's my job and as I said before, there are plenty of others out there waiting for the same story...going with someone who lives here in Summitville might help you make sure the story is told right and not sensationalized. I could tell your story."

"I've heard all this already."

"I know. But..." Dani blew out a big sigh. "I think you need a friend. I hope that doesn't sound hokey. Please believe me when I say I'm not here to exploit you. I just want to help. If that leads to some good for both of us, where's the harm?"

Cass looked over Dani's shoulder, hoping to see a blue-and-white police car rolling into the driveway. She needed to be rescued. Even if it was just to go from one nightmare into another. "Listen, I've told you everything I know about the girls. I have other things right now that are more important to me. Please understand. I just can't talk to you now."

"I know about the other things."

Dani pulled a sheet of paper from the battered bag over her shoulder. Cass looked down. Max's somber face stared up at her. She couldn't get past the large type that said "Missing."

"Oh God." Cass felt her knees going weak.

She unlatched the screen door and opened it for Dani Westwood.

Dani followed her in. Cass pulled out a chair and sat down heavily in it. She was glad it was there; she didn't need to faint again. Or maybe that wouldn't be such a bad thing. Blissful ignorance. It was sad, Cass thought, when you found unconsciousness preferable to life. *If something happens to Max, I'll kill myself.* She leaned over, placing her hands over her face and bringing her head down almost to her knees. Trying to breathe. She pulled in some air, sat up, and looked at Dani Westwood, who was sitting down across from her.

"So they're already putting out flyers? Getting the word out?"

"Yes; word has gone out over the wires. The police department is being really great about this, Cass." She reached over as if to grasp her hand, then stopped just short of contact. "A lot of people already know, and that means a lot of people are already on the watch. That's a good thing, don't you think?"

Numbly, Cass nodded. She wondered where someone from the

police force was. Shouldn't they have come back for her by now? "Of course it's a good thing. I'm still not sure why you're here, Ms. Westwood."

"Please, won't you call me Dani?"

DANI WATCHED AS Cass nodded. Her face looked careworn. Dani knew she was only around thirty years old, but if she had said today she was forty-five, Dani wouldn't have doubted it.

She pondered Cass's question. Why *was* she here? The first thought that leapt to mind—and this one very unpleasant—was that she was here to stick with her until her son was found...so she could be on the scene with the mother. A sick feeling inside told her that she would not be reporting on a happy moment. And she felt ghoulish for wanting to be there when a mother found out her son was dead. In fact, wanting to be present at such an event turned her stomach. To want to get a "scoop" like that was just sick and it made her want to throw away her career—if you could call it that—and apply at the McDonalds out by the Wal-Mart.

But she knew there was more to it than that. For one thing, she knew that she could also witness a happy story. She could just as easily be reporting on a mother reuniting with her unharmed child. Happy faces and tears. All recorded in her journalist's words and with her trusty Nikon digital.

She also knew there was even yet another layer to wanting to share with Cass this story, whatever its outcome. When she looked at Cass, something was aroused in her and it wasn't necessarily sexual (although she did find Cass very attractive—and stirrings like these, weak though they were, had not been coming to her for a while now). Cass seemed vulnerable and alone. Dani wanted to protect her, to shield her from the hard times she knew Cass was going through. She hadn't felt this way about any woman since, well since, Sharon, whom she had followed here from England. And Sharon was gone, had been gone for many years. Dani had chased her away, with her demons backing her up, and she would never return. Until recently, Dani had thought she didn't miss Sharon. And she didn't. She had thought she didn't miss what they shared. But since meeting Cass D'Angelo, she wondered if that was true.

She wished she could put aside her reporter's tools—the notebooks, her tape recorder, her camera—but knew she was too much of an old dog working a beat to do that. But she wanted to somehow demonstrate that she was Cass's ally, someone she could count on who would not only not exploit her, but who would be there for support.

She knew that confessing these feelings at the moment would seem insincere. So she was left with trying to be the dutiful reporter with a heart, and hope Cass bought it. She did not want to see her alone.

"I'm here because I want to be with you during this difficult time. Yes, I want to report on it. We get so little news here in Summitville. Unfortunately, willingly or not, you're a star, and people want to know what's going on. But Cass, remember, people care. I know there are people all over town already organizing search parties to help find your son. I stopped at the station on the way over here and believe me, Max is the number one priority. So, it's not just about sensationalism, about wanting to know the worst. People—myself included—are rooting for you. In addition to being a reporter, I'd like to offer my hand and my shoulder for your use right now." Dani smiled, though she knew this was not something she was good at. Her face wasn't used to contorting into the upward motion; the muscles required for smiling had been long out of use, rusty.

IN SPITE OF herself, Cass smiled back at the woman sitting across from her. One thing she had before the "event" as she now thought of it was intuition. She knew immediately when she liked someone or when she didn't. When someone was "real" and when someone was putting on an act. She used to think her feelings of intuition were fallible. But years of experience had shown her they weren't. Time and time again, she was right about people she encountered; initial impressions were always on the mark.

As she felt the smile creep across her features, and the tears brim in her eyes, she knew Dani Westwood was absolutely truthful when she said she was also there as a friend. It wasn't her words that convinced her, it was more the expression in her dark brown eyes. They were eyes, like hers, that were tired and that had seen a lot. But they were also caring eyes. And Cass could see that she wasn't just chasing a story when she said she wanted to help her through this ordeal.

Cass wondered how much people relied on instinct; and wondered further whether people shouldn't trust those instincts more.

"Thanks." She reached out and covered the reporter's hand with her own. "I appreciate it. Now would you mind taking me down to the station? I need to see what they're doing to find my boy. I need to be doing something myself."

Chapter
Twenty-three

MAX COULD HEAR them in the other room. The woman was crying and the man was saying short, angry words to her. He couldn't make out more than a few words (and even those usually meant nothing: words like *what, how,* and *maybe*); but there were others that filtered through that scared him: *please, trouble, kill,* and *stop.*

He shifted on his back, trying to get comfortable, but it was hard here on the floor. The carpeting beneath him was cheap and the hard floor underneath dug into his back. But there wasn't much more he could do to make himself comfortable. She had tied him up, put duct tape over his mouth, and the man had carried him in here to toss him on the floor like a doll. He wished he hadn't screamed out as he had. For one thing, maybe he wouldn't have the tape over his mouth, which made it feel like he was smothering. But the second reason was the one that made it really bad: he had gotten someone else in trouble. If he had just been quiet, she wouldn't be here now.

The fat girl lay across the room from him, also on the floor. Like him, they had tied her up. Unlike him, they had not used bungee cords, but thick rope, like clothesline, first tying her wrists together, then her ankles, and then using rope to pull the two areas together, so her body was bent into what looked like a painful little bow.

The man with the dark hair had done this to her. At first, she hit him and spit at him, but then he beat her, punching her face and hitting her so hard, he started losing his own breath. At first she screamed, but by the time he was done, all she could do was make these little panting, grunting sounds. Max had to rock himself a little, so he could turn over. After the man started punching her, Max didn't want to watch, but there wasn't anything he could do to stop up his ears.

Max had scrunched up his shoulder every time the man's fist made impact with the girl; it was almost like he was the one getting hit. He had felt funny and sick, even though the man hadn't touched him.

The girl was crying on the other side of the room. Max heard her trying to sniff the snot back up in her nose, trying to pull herself together, but there would only be silence for a minute, then she would start crying all over again. Max wished he could tell her to stop because he knew her crying would only make things worse. Her sobbing and sniffling would make the man angrier and then maybe both of them would get hit. The worst had been just before he left the two of them in the room alone. The man had kicked the girl just before he left and she had let out this great big whoosh of air, and then moaned. He slammed the door, but not before he said, "The Beast will be back later."

Max knew from the blonde-haired lady the Beast was just imaginary, like a made-up monster. So his saying that didn't frighten Max too much. What really made him tremble and want to suck his thumb (which would have been so cool, but he had the duct tape over his mouth) was when he had kicked her.

He wished he could scoot over to the girl and comfort her, but he couldn't move. He closed his eyes and hoped the man wouldn't beat her anymore. He also hoped his mother would figure out where he was and save them both.

He swallowed, thirsty, and listened to the sobbing and yelling going on in the other room. What else was there to do?

MYRA CLOSED HER eyes and pulled in a deep breath, forcing herself to exhale slowly. She had to get "a hold of herself" as her mother would have put it, had to stop the hysteria and the crying. Honestly, she could have sworn such behavior only made Ian more aroused; he enjoyed it, she could tell from his eyes, and would do whatever it took, say whatever needed to be said, to keep her upset and crying. Myra knew she might never be able to reason with him, but the only chance she would have to make headway would be if she could do it calmly and rationally.

And she needed to talk some sense into him! She felt like she was living in a house of cards, and one stacked high. It was ready to collapse at any moment. This was a small town they were in; one person had already found them. Another out there (and they had *her* son) already knew they had killed at least one young girl. Myra was smart enough to know the Beast wasn't going to protect them much longer.

She remembered learning one thing back when she attended New Hope High (before she had dropped out after meeting Ian who said he could educate her far better than any school). The knowledge was passed on during psychology class with Mr. Shamus. He had talked about how the mind and the body react to an emergency. She could still see him standing before the bank of windows in their classroom, windows overlooking the tree-covered hills on the other side of the river. She didn't know why she had listened that particular day, when most days she would have been doodling in her notebook or checking and re-checking her cell to see if she had any messages, but right now what he had told them seemed critical. "Human beings, and animals too, usually have two responses to an emergency: fight or flee." He had looked down into the textbook they used, *Beginning Psychology: a Primer for High School Students* and read from it: "Fight or flight is an ancient sympathetic reaction to stress characterized by accelerated heart rate, elevated blood pressure, and an increase in adrenal gland secretions, preparing the animal to either fight or turn tail and run."

Myra knew things had progressed beyond them having any chance of fighting what was certain to come down on them. She knew they needed to flee. Every fiber of her body and mind told her this was the truth.

But convincing Ian was another matter. He really believed the Beast had put some sort of protective force field around them; they were invincible. Myra thought when you believe something like that, it's pretty hard to get you to consider other options. Why should you?

But she had to try. Maybe persistence was the key. She opened her eyes, forced herself to count, in her mind, to ten, and began trying to get through to Ian, to tell him why they should make sure their captives were okay, then load up the car with whatever would fit—whatever they *must* have with them because they were never coming back—and get as far away from Summitville, PA as possible.

She grabbed his hands in hers and looked into his eyes. "Ian? Ian, can you let me talk for just five minutes without interrupting?"

He grinned and leaned his head back, as if shocked at her nerve.

"I'm not kidding, Ian, five minutes. Please."

He sighed and shook his head. "Whatever. Go ahead."

Myra swallowed. Blew out a big breath. "Things are bad, sweetheart. And they're going from bad to worse. I know the Beast has the perfect plan for everything, the ultimate design, as you say, but we have to look at all the facts. We have to look at everything going on around us." Myra scooted closer to him, gratified that he was listening, and that his features were open. Scared as she was, she tried to keep her eyes on his, forcing the contact and not giving him a chance to look away or to begin forming arguments against what she was saying, using flawed logic about the damned mythical Beast. "The facts are...the way I see it, the facts are that, very soon, we're going to get caught. Ian, Tammie Blankenship found me in a matter of an hour or less. That D'Angelo woman somehow knows about us; she has to, she knew exactly where we buried the Plant girl. And after we were so careful! Honey, everything is crumbling around us. I'm telling you it won't be long before the cops are pounding on that door. And then where will we go? Our chance will have gone. And you know as well as I do there's enough right outside this trailer to send us to prison for the rest of our lives...or worse." Myra lowered her head and stared at the floor. The silence seemed to stretch on infinitely. She knew, with a sinking feeling, what Ian was going to say. More bullshit about the Beast protecting them. She felt like a cow being led to slaughter. *You can get out yourself, girl. Nothing stopping you.* Myra thought of how easily Ian had bound the two people lying only a few yards away; he could do the same to her.

She would probably hold up her wrists and ankles to make it easier. Leaving by herself was not an option, even if she had the guts to do it.

She was ready to scream because Ian wasn't saying anything. It was the same way she always felt, waiting for him; like having her eyes closed, shoulders scrunching, bracing herself for a slap or a punch she knew was on its way, and part of the whole deal was wishing he would just get it over with and end the anticipation. But Ian let out a breath and began to talk. His voice had none of the animation it had earlier. It was low, slow, and deep. Resigned.

Myra listened.

"You're right. I know it, too. I didn't want to admit it. I thought the Beast would give us something in exchange for our sacrifices, but so far, we've gotten nothing but into deeper trouble." Ian scanned the dark interior of the trailer, and Myra wondered if he was thinking about the Beast overhearing his disloyal words. She watched as his Adam's apple bobbed. He was just a man. "I know we need to get away from here."

She grabbed his hands; she couldn't resist. "I'm so glad you're finally seeing sense."

His eyes flashed and he frowned; she wished she could take back the words.

"It's not you convincing me, my dear. It's the situation." He looked off into the darkness and Myra could see his face shifting, changing in the candle's flickering light. She'd known it was too good to be true, or she should have. "It's not you convincing me of anything. It's the Beast. He's telling us we have to move on. Because we made those sacrifices, He's going to make sure we have safe passage out of this hole." He smiled. "Where do you want to go, Myra? Someplace warm?"

She hugged him. She didn't care if he was listening to the common sense she was dispensing, or the delusional voice in his head, as long as the end result was the same. They needed to *flee.*

"Yes! I was thinking Florida. We'll be happy, there, Ian, you'll see..."

Ian pondered. "Florida might be good. There are a lot of Satanists there. People like us. Maybe we could work for a while, get our passports, and then get over to England. I would love to see Manchester. And the Moors."

Myra knew nothing about Manchester, England, or why Ian would even want to go there, but the relief coursing through her was enough to block out any doubtful thoughts. She pulled away. "We should go now, Ian. We can throw a few things in bags, just the important stuff, and be on our way." She stood and looked out the window. It was now late afternoon; the sky was bright white, promising a hot, oppressive night. She wished the Mustang had air conditioning, but then she wished for a lot of things she was pretty sure would never be. It was enough that Ian was seeing things her way and they were on their way out of Summitville. Finally. Gone. Without a trace.

"We just need to make sure to call someone once we get on the road and let them know about Tammie and the boy." She chewed on her lower lip, thinking. "No, that won't work. We have to take them with us, Ian; if we let someone know they're here in the trailer, they can connect us to them and then they'll be after us. They'll track us down and we'll be just as trapped as if we'd stayed here." She sat back down on the floor next to him. "What we can do is take them with us. Once we get out of town, we can let them go somewhere...in the woods, somewhere remote, where it will take some time for them to get back." Already Myra could feel herself growing sick, knowing this plan would not work either. Aside from the fact that both Tammie and the boy had seen them, Tammie knew who Myra was and knew the trailer's location. She would need a new identity. Still, didn't people do things like that all the time? Wasn't there a whole market that dealt in phony birth certificates and stuff like that? She didn't know how to tap into it, but she was sure Ian could. He was so smart. They should probably get new identities anyway...

She was so busy with these thoughts she didn't notice, at first, that Ian was glaring at her. She stopped speaking suddenly, as if she had run out of steam. In a way, she had.

"Are you even listening to yourself? To how stupid you sound?"

"I'm sorry, Ian." Myra's voice was tiny.

"The Beast has been talking to me while you prattled on." He took her hands in his and this time, it wasn't gentle, it was a rough grasp that hurt. But this hold didn't scare her as much as the face he showed her, the intensity in his eyes. It was almost like an electric current passing through him and into her. His face was beaded with sweat and he seemed on the brink of a delirious joy.

"The Beast says we can't leave witnesses. The Beast says we must kill the child and the sow and then burn the trailer with them in it."

Myra's eyes grew wide.

"Don't worry. He says we have all night to take care of it. I think it will be particularly fun to take the sow slowly, while you tape it. The boy we can dispense of quickly." He took Myra's chin in his hand, forcing her to look at him. His smile was almost tender. "It will be merciful and quick. I know you'd like that."

Myra tried to swallow, but she had no saliva. She tried to breathe, but there was no air. She just nodded, dumbly.

Chapter
Twenty-four

CASS COULDN'T IMAGINE feeling more exhausted. And yet she couldn't imagine a time when sleep was less likely. "Wait a minute." She put a hand on Dani Westwood's arm after practically stumbling down the front steps of City Hall. If anyone had seen her, they would have assumed she was some lush freshly sprung from the drunk tank. There was a small part of her that would have liked to have escaped into the oblivion that lived in the very bottom of a bottle. But Cass knew no amount of alcohol could quell the terror coursing through her. There were things to do. *What's the quote?* Cass wondered, allowing herself for a moment to go back to her high school English classes at Summitville High. *Miles to go before I sleep?*

"Wait. I just need to sit down...for just a second." She looked up at the reporter, who looked back calmly; she could see Dani was tired, too. But she had stuck by her through everything, even when Marion Hartley objected to a reporter being along for the ride. Cass needed someone beside her. If she had to pay for this luxury with having her name in the paper again, well then, so be it. She didn't think she could survive this alone. And Dani Westwood was there. Nobody else was. "Can we?"

Dani nodded.

In the station, they had helped with the filling out of missing person reports, putting together exact descriptions the department would use to transmit bulletins, and even sitting by while Marion Hartley talked with someone in the Pittsburgh office of the FBI (this was, after all, a kidnapping, and kidnapping was in the purview of the bureau). The department had made sure anyone who might know something about Max, or anyone who had seen him, would know what he looked like and would know how to contact the proper authorities immediately. Cass had washed her face and pulled her dark hair back with a rubber band to face TV cameras from Pittsburgh and Youngstown, and managed to get through an impassioned plea to come forward if anyone knew anything about her boy. She was not going to let people see her cry.

In fact, as she wearily lowered herself onto the curb in front of City Hall, she thought it was curious that she hadn't cried in hours. What was wrong with her? She had cried earlier, sobbed hysterically, and now it was all gone, replaced by a dull numbness, making her feel like she was some sort of robot, just going through the simplest motions of life: movement, speech, respiration...

She looked up at the starless night sky and didn't know how she was going to face other nights like this one alone. *Stop it! You can't give up. Max is alive out there somewhere and you need to find him.* Cass knew that somewhere deep inside, psychic or not, as a mother she would know if Max was dead. She would just know it. She could feel his presence, alive, within her. But she also felt she didn't have much time. And that thought made her feel useless and desperate.

After sitting in silence for a long time, just watching the occasional car roll by, Cass turned to Dani. She had been so patient, not saying a word, not asking questions, just giving her time after all the fuss inside. "What are we going to do?"

Dani shrugged and shook her head. "Maybe we start by going back to your house."

"I suppose that's as good a plan as any." Cass stood and brushed the dirt off the seat of her jeans. "I don't know what we can do there, though."

"We'll think of something." Dani took her hand and led her toward her car. "We can at least stay near the phone, listen to the radio and watch the television. We'll be the first to know if there's any kind of break in the case."

Cass laughed. "Break in the case? You sound like one of those crime shows on TV, *SVU* or something like that." Even though she laughed, the sound escaped her throat dry and hollow.

"You know what I mean." Dani unlocked the doors with a little button on her key chain and then opened the passenger side door of her Civic for Cass.

Cass slid in. She stared out through the windshield at the dark night, which pressed in, almost like a shape, rather than an absence of light. "There ought to be something we can do." She waited for Dani to slide into the seat beside her. Turning to her, she said, "Here I am, supposedly a psychic, and I don't get one tiny little image to help myself or my son when I most need it." She rubbed her eyes. "It's fucking pathetic."

"Just close your eyes now. Try and rest. Let me drive you home." And Dani pulled away from the curb.

AT HER HOUSE, Cass kept her panic at bay by offering Dani a seat in the kitchen, making coffee. The house seemed empty, a shell, without Max and Bum there. It was hard to walk in the kitchen door and not have Bum there to greet her, tail wagging, practically knocking her over to jump on her and cover her face with canine kisses.

Coffee brewed, she set a mug before Dani and sat down across from her. The darkness outside the kitchen window had a different quality than what Cass was used to. It had more of a presence; closing in, like it was alive. *Silly thoughts. Concentrate.* Cass closed her eyes. She took a deep breath, willing an image to come, but there was nothing.

Dani was content to sit across from her, sipping coffee and waiting. Cass liked that she seemed to know just the right way to behave, how to simply be here with her and to let things come. There was no pressure from her. She hadn't seen her open a notebook or flick on a tape recorder for the entire evening. This absence of action on her part made Cass trust Dani even more.

She finally opened her eyes and looked up. "It's funny. Before Ron Plant and I found Lucy down by the river, the images were coming to me without warning. I hated them. I didn't want to see what I was seeing. If someone had offered to cut those images out of my brain, I would have sat back and let them do it.

"Now, I want nothing more than to see those images. I want something to go on."

"What brought the images to you before?"

"What do you mean?"

"I mean, was there anything that triggered you seeing something? Did anything happen just before?"

"No. Not really." Cass thought back and something connected in her tired mind. "Wait a minute. Usually, I would see things when there was some sort of, I don't know, some sort of prompt." Cass thought about the nurse in the hospital, how the touch of her hand had made her see the woman in her backyard, had let her peer into the nurse's desire to get with the young man she was seeing later that night. A pounding started behind her temples. She remembered the first time she had seen anything about Lucy. Cass nodded her head without realizing she was doing it. "When I started seeing Lucy, it happened right after I saw her picture in the paper."

"Did the picture come to life or something?"

Cass gave a mirthless smile. "No, nothing like that. It was like, I looked at the picture and there was a flash...and I was seeing stuff about her. About her death. I kind of knew how she had been killed." Cass took a quick gulp of coffee; it was too hot. "Later, when I met with the Plants at their house, I got a really clear image of Lucy when Ron showed me her school picture. It was so strong, like a jolt of electricity." Cass remembered how she had dropped the framed photo on the floor.

"Did the same thing happen with Sheryl?"

"Kind of. Being in her house, I saw all sorts of things."

Dani scratched her chin. "It seems like you need something from the person to trigger what you see. Or at least an image of that person. I've heard of psychics picking up on stuff from personal items."

"You mean like a bloodhound sniffing some clothes before it sets out to find the person who's missing. Is that what I am? A dog?"

Dani shook her head. "It just makes sense. There's a lot about the mind we haven't yet begun to understand, and I don't claim to know why seeing a picture or touching something the missing person has touched would make a difference, but it has a kind of logic to it."

Cass nodded, and then frowned. "But Max is all around me in this house. Why can't I get anything from him?" She bit her lip, wanting to cry. She was so frustrated.

Dani didn't say anything for a long time. Cass searched her hard, yet warm, features, wondering how old Dani was (forty? Fifty? Too old for her?) and trying to figure out what she was thinking, what connections she was making. She felt she could make the connections herself if she weren't so exhausted and stressed.

Finally, Dani put her hand over Cass's. "Maybe." She stopped and sighed, looked toward the kitchen window above the stove. Cass looked toward it, wondering what she was seeing. But only blackness pressed in, hard enough to break the glass.

"Maybe you saw stuff from the girls because they were already gone."

"You mean..."

Dani stared at the table's surface and raised her head, finally. "I'm sorry. Yes. Dead."

Cass let out a small cry and covered her mouth with her hand. If that was true, she didn't want any images to arrive from Max.

What if the killers took Max? That was the logical explanation, and the one that resonated. *Maybe if we can find Sheryl, we can find Max.* Cass squeezed her eyes together tight; her breathing came faster. She bit her lip hard enough to taste blood.

"I need something of Sheryl's. I'm not sure, but if I could get hold of something of the girl's, it might lead me somewhere. It might lead me to Max." Cass knew there was logic to the plan; she also knew her visions had logic of their own she had not yet figured out, if she ever would. There wasn't always a trigger for seeing something. Sometimes the visions just came, unbidden. But it did seem that the stronger ones came when there was some sort of connection.

All of this is hopeless. But I have to try.

Dani smiled and nodded. "I know nothing about this psychic rot. But it makes sense. How can we get something? Would a newspaper photo do?"

Cass shrugged. She thought a newspaper photo might work, but if she wanted to feel something really strong, it would be better to have something having a more direct connection. She then thought of her visit to the McKennas and remembered how she had been treated. She had practically been thrown out bodily.

"We don't have a lot of time." Cass scratched behind one knee. "We need something of the girl's." She would face them again if necessary;

she would do anything if it would bring her Max back to her. The problem was, would she even be able to speak to them, let alone convince them to part with something like a photo of their daughter or a piece of her clothing? "But I don't know if I can get it."

"Why not?"

"I'm not exactly the McKennas' favorite person." And Cass told Dani about her visit. Everything.

After she finished, Dani said, "I could go. I could get something. I don't have to say I even know you, but what I could say is that I might be able to help publicize the fact their daughter's gone missing. I could tell them the more people who know about Sheryl, the better chance she'd have of being found."

Cass still felt helpless. She remembered the McKenna woman and her horrible husband. Would they be more or less forthcoming or helpful to a reporter, even one who said she wanted to help them find their daughter? Cass had offered the same help, and they had thrown her out of their house.

"I can be very persuasive. Do you want to wait here? Or do you want to come with me?"

Cass just wanted this all to be over. She stood. "I'll come with you. But I'll stay in the car. I can't just be here by myself."

"Then let's go."

"I DON'T THINK you should do any more of that." Janet McKenna had just come out of the bedroom, down the stairs, and into the living room where her husband Rick sat on the couch. A porno was playing on the thirty-two-inch plasma screen. A naked woman (a girl really, Janet wondered if she was even eighteen) with cartoon-sized breasts was on her knees between two men.

Rick looked up at her. His eyes were bloodshot, the pupils so dilated all color was blocked out of his eyes. His nostrils were inflamed. Covered with a sheen of sweat, his naked body looked oily in the flickering light from the TV screen. "What the fuck do you have to say about it?" As if to show her who was boss, Rick lit another cigarette, took a long drag, placed it in an ashtray, then leaned over with a dirty straw to snort up another line of cocaine. Then another. A third. The coffee table was littered with white dust, cigarette ash, beer cans, and a jar of her hand cream.

Janet worried the bottom of her nightgown, wondering where the days had gone when Rick wanted to come to bed with her. Now it was going on ten; they both had to get up early for work. They should both be in bed, whether it was for blissful cuddling or turn-the-shoulder stony silence, she didn't care. She just didn't want him doing this. "I just think you should save some for later." Her voice was small.

"Why? You gonna join me later?"

"No." Janet tried to force her gaze away from the screen. Ever since Sheryl had gone missing, Rick had seen no reason to hide his habit, and evenings like this were becoming way too commonplace. She ran a shaky hand through her hair; it felt like straw. Maybe she should lay off the L'Oreal for a while. "It's just that, honey, you're never going to get to sleep if you keep doing that." She tried to smile and failed. "It looks like you're already pretty wired." She didn't want to look down at his hand, which was pumping and pulling at himself. His penis was small and red, limp. Janet wondered where he was getting the money to buy all the coke; she knew he had sold his Malibu and wondered if the proceeds had already gone up his nose. She wondered how many cash advances would be on their next credit card bill. He was going to kill himself. And then who would she have?

"Go on back to bed." Rick dismissed her, his gaze returning to the screen; a third man had joined the other two. Rick pulled harder. "I'll be up in a little bit. Just give me one more hour." He turned his head. "An hour? Okay? Can you give me that?"

Janet swallowed hard, wondering if she should just give up and sit down next to him, snort a line or two, let it all fall away. She had been a party girl once...before she found Jesus. But where had Jesus gotten her? Stuck with a cokehead drunk and a missing daughter? Oh yeah, her prayers had been answered. *From my mouth to God's ear.*

But she knew how the drug reneged on its promises of euphoria and energy. And she knew, somewhere, that her faith was not just something she had taken up to quell the loneliness of living in a house where she was ignored by the people she loved.

"Okay. I'm going to go back to bed and try to get some sleep. Could you at least turn the TV down? I can hear that moaning all the way upstairs." She didn't wait for Rick to say anything, just turned and started trudging back up the creaking staircase. She also didn't wait for the volume to be lowered. The best she could hope for was that he wouldn't turn it up.

When had her husband started hating her?

Just as she was to the last creaking step and resigned to the lonely bedroom where her only company was a noisy box fan in the window, something happened that made her spine stiffen.

Someone was knocking at the door. *Oh God, no. The cops.* Her breath came a little faster. It was bound to happen sooner or later, what with all the cars pulling up to their house at all hours, and Rick running outside, sitting in the cars for a minute, then running back in. *This is just what we need. What with Sheryl missing... What if they take Rick away?* Janet couldn't stand the thought of being alone, even if she was desperately lonely.

The knocking sounded again, a little more insistent. Janet placed a hand on the wall for support. She was steeling herself for the next sound she expected to hear: "Open up! Police!"

But there were no voices. Other than Rick shouting, "God *damn* it!" The TV went off and she heard him hurrying around the living room. She imagined him sweeping the baggies, straws, credit card, and mirror into the coffee table drawer, hurrying to throw on his jeans and wife beater. "Fuck!" he shouted again as the knocking sounded a third time.

"Who the hell is it?" Rick hollered up the stairs, where Janet stood, frozen.

Janet hurried down the stairs, saw her husband standing, shirtless, in the living room, his grizzled and flushed features bewildered, sniffling, wiping angrily at his nose. There was a little blood on his fingers.

"Just sit down." She made a waving motion to him. "I'll get the door. Just keep quiet. I'll get rid of whoever it is." Janet hurried through the hall. *Unless it's the cops. Then we're fucked. Excuse me, Jesus.*

Janet opened the door, heart pounding, blood beating hard behind her eyes. She worried about fainting.

There was no one in uniform standing on the porch, in the dim light from the sodium vapor lamp on the street. The only person out there was a small woman with wavy, shoulder-length graying hair, John Lennon glasses, jeans, and a gauze Indian shirt. She wore a sheepish grin and looked like she hadn't quite given up on being a flower child. What the hell was she doing at her front door?

DANI WESTWOOD STOOD in the deepening twilight, waiting. She could hear the scurrying around inside, the muffled words. She felt like she was conducting a raid. She watched as a shadowy figure emerged from a room off the front hallway (a yellowing sheer curtain partially blocked this view) then disappeared back into it. Finally, a woman came down the stairs quickly and hurried to the door.

Dani wasn't sure what to say when she opened the door. The only word that came to mind was "slag," the British term for a prostitute, but used more familiarly as a woman who looked as though she'd been rode hard and put away wet. Dani was learning to combine her British and American colloquialisms. She had bleached blonde hair that had seen one too many "beauty" treatments, so it looked like hay. Her face was a network of fine lines spread across a surface of dry, artificially tanned skin; though Dani was sure the woman wasn't even out of her thirties, she looked old. The eyes that peered out from under the platinum fringe were not kind.

She turned her head. Dani knew it was late, but this undisguised hostility was more than she had expected. No wonder Cass was afraid to see this woman again. Rancor and meanness radiated off her just as much as the smell of cigarettes and alcohol. Her thin lips were made even thinner by the way she drew in her mouth. Before Dani had even said a word, this woman was already furious with her.

"What do you want?" The blonde kept the door half closed in front of her. "And this better be good."

Dani attempted a smile and tried to remember the skills she had honed over the years interviewing people who didn't want to talk to the press. She took a quick breath and began. "It's about your daughter."

She saw the woman soften when she spoke that single sentence. Some rigidity went out of her form; her features relaxed, but not in a good way, shifting from hostility to sadness in an instant. Her lower lip trembled and she started to nod. "She's been found, hasn't she?" She shook her head. "I knew this would happen." Her breath started coming faster and Dani was afraid she was going to burst into tears. Belatedly, she realized what she must think—why else would a stranger come to call late at night?

She put up a hand. "Can I come in?"

Though obviously traumatized, the woman took a moment to look behind her, back into the house. She shook her head. "I'll come out." She stepped barefoot onto the porch, shutting the door behind her.

Her face got close enough to Dani's for her to smell the sour smell of cheap vodka on her breath. "You know something about my Sheryl? Tell me."

Dani once again attempted a smile, a winning expression. She again raised her hands in a gesture that said, 'I mean no harm.' "Listen, I don't know anything about your daughter."

The woman's expression was amazing in the speed in which it could shift. The sadness and shock disappeared to be replaced by wariness. Her eyes narrowed. "Then what are you doing here?"

"Let me start at the beginning. I'm Dani Westwood, from the *Review*."

"Oh God! You're a reporter. You've got some nerve, lady, showing up here at all hours when decent people have to get up for work in the morning, when decent people are just trying to get on with their lives when a family member has gone missing." She stuck out her lower lip, her eyes bright, even in the dark, with outraged tears. "I can't believe you people. Can't you just leave us alone?"

Dani put a hand to her forehead. "Listen, we're getting off on the wrong foot. I'm here because I want to help you."

"How can someone like you help? Do you know where I can find my Sheryl? Do you know where she is? Can you tell me what happened to her?" Her gaze was intense; Dani thought it bordered on madness. This might not be as easy as she had originally thought. Originally, this mission had been an abstract. Now, faced with the very real grief and terror of a flesh and blood human being, Dani wasn't sure she could continue. But she had to; Cass was depending on her. And very likely, another young life hung in the balance.

Dani shook her head slowly. "Mrs. McKenna? Is that right? Mrs. McKenna, I really wish I could. I really wish I was here to give you some answers, to lessen your pain. But I think with the *Review* and me on your side, maybe we can get those questions of yours answered sooner rather than later. Now, it's hard to talk out here. Would you let me come inside?"

Again, the woman looked warily behind her. "I don't think so. My husband is ...asleep...on the couch, in the front room. You know? I don't want to wake him up."

Dani nodded, although she didn't understand why she *wouldn't* want her husband to be part of this conversation. Wasn't Sheryl his daughter, too?

"Let's go sit down over here, then." Dani led her over to a couple of plastic laminate chairs opposite them. They sat. Janet McKenna got back up suddenly. "Just a minute."

Bewildered, Dani sat on the porch and waited. In a moment, Janet McKenna returned, a cigarette dangling from her lips and a pack of Marlboro Lights and a disposable lighter in her hand. She sat down, removed the cigarette from her lips, and blew the smoke into the air.

Maybe it will keep bugs away. Dani began her pitch. "There are usually two ways missing people turn up: one is simply that they return on their own. Some have stories to tell, some keep quiet." She looked over at Janet McKenna. At least she was listening. "The other way is through a lot of work by the public. Searching. And that's how I can help you find Sheryl. She's out there, right? And even though there has been some coverage in the paper, on the radio, and even on TV, you can never have too many people looking for a missing person." Dani paused. Janet McKenna smoked silently. She hoped what she was saying was sinking in. "What I'd like to do is this: write a big feature on Sheryl so even more people know she's missing. And with the feature, I'd like lots of pictures of Sheryl."

Janet McKenna nodded. She flicked her cigarette into the yard, which roused an old cur that had been chained up not even fifteen feet away. He howled once, then lay back down. Dani had hardly noticed.

She waited for Janet McKenna to say something. When a couple of minutes had passed in silence, she asked, "Do you think you can get me some pictures of Sheryl? I bet you have lots of them. And I promise to take good care of them and get them back to you straight away." Dani paused, thinking. She had what she thought was a good idea. *There's no harm in asking.* "Maybe you even have some favorite thing of hers, a T-shirt or a stuffed animal. I could take a shot of that down at the *Review* and add it to the pictures." She gave her kindest smile to Janet McKenna — and felt like a ghoul. She had to keep remembering she was doing this for a good cause; she was trying to save the life of a little boy who was out there somewhere right now with people who cared a lot less for his welfare than his mother did. Dani thought of Cass sitting in the car, just out in the shadows of the McKenna's front yard. She was probably watching them right now, wondering what she was saying, hoping she would find success, and wondering if all of this would be in vain.

She had to get Cass something. It suddenly seemed like nothing else mattered.

She put her hand on Janet McKenna's shoulder. The woman didn't flinch and Dani thought that was a good sign. "So, what do you think, Janet? Will you let me help you?"

Chapter
Twenty-five

DANI AND CASS were back in her kitchen. Spread out before Cass were five photographs showing Sheryl McKenna from the ages of twelve to her current age, sixteen. Two of the pictures were school photos, one was of Sheryl and an older boy at a dance, and the last two were snapshots taken at home: Sheryl outside on a tire swing; Sheryl surprised in her bed, hands up in an attempt to shield her face from the camera. Cass shuddered, remembering what she knew about Sheryl's stepfather and wondering if he had been the one who had taken the picture. Dani had also managed to get a charm bracelet and a Pittsburgh Pirates jersey from Janet McKenna. These were set next to the photographs.

Cass stared at them, feeling queasy. She was terrified, not wanting to begin, because beginning could mean failure and she couldn't, didn't, wouldn't accept failure. She had made Dani take the photos and the keepsakes and lay them out on the table. She refused to touch them, had hardly even glanced at them.

What if nothing came to her? What if she touched these things, stared at these photographs, and nothing came? What if her gift/curse was only a temporary thing and the part of her brain that caused her visions had somehow healed? The trauma that caused her to have those experiences was a fleeting thing and now she was just back to being Cass, with nothing special. Just a few hours ago, it would have been a dream come true.

Now, she so desperately wanted the images to come she was afraid to even try. She put her hands over her face, breathing hard. *You have to try. Max. Think of Max. You have no choice. Get busy.*

Dani spoke. "Cass? You need anything?"

She looked over to where she was sitting across the table. "Yeah. I need to be left alone. Can you go outside? I'll come and get you in a little while."

"Sure."

Cass watched as Dani went out through the screen door, listening as it slammed, as her footfalls crunched in the gravel of the driveway, the *thunk* of her car door closing.

"Okay." Cass let out a trembling breath. "It's time." She turned to the photographs, willing herself to just relax, to be open. She had never tried to make this happen before and still doubted she could. She picked up the first photograph, of Sheryl when she was twelve. She smiled. It was summer, and Sheryl was on a rope and tire swing, hung from a big maple tree. Her face was a little obscured in shadow (the sunlight looked blindingly bright), but Cass could see a little girl on the cusp of womanhood. Her tanned legs were long and skinny, sticking out of a pair of too-short terry cloth powder-blue shorts. She wore a tiny white eyelet lace top with spaghetti straps. Her black hair hung to her waist. Cass could make out the little buds on her chest, just beginning to blossom. There was something gazelle-like about the girl. "Why, you're beautiful," Cass whispered. She set the photograph down. Other than a feeling of tenderness, nothing came to her.

She picked up the next photo, an almost thumbnail-sized portrait, Sheryl's school picture most likely taken during the last term. Cass took in the details. Sheryl's hair, still glistening, blue-black, had been cut shorter. She wore too much make-up; the black eyeliner was almost raccoon-like and the bubble-gum pink lip gloss just looked, well, *gross*. She wore large, thin gold hoop earrings and stared out at the camera with her head cocked, a souped-up defiance in her eyes. Cass wondered what had brought the sweet girl from the tire swing to this slutty-looking reject. She knew her thoughts were unkind; she also knew girls abused like Sheryl often ended up acting out in ugly ways. Sheryl was still young enough in this photo to look pretty, in spite of the effort she'd made to mar that beauty, but Cass could see the future, though this vision was born of common sense, not psychic power: Sheryl would continue to use these same tools to adorn herself, continue to be self-destructive, and ten or fifteen years from now, would look as hard and old as her own mother. Cass closed her eyes and shook her head. While it was interesting to have this look into Sheryl McKenna's life, it was not helping her with what she needed to do. It was not helping her find the girl, and then, hopefully, Max. She placed a hand over her face when she realized that Sheryl McKenna would not be seeing the future she had just imagined for her. Sheryl McKenna now lived only in the past and most likely only in the memory of her mother.

She scanned the dance photo and the other school portrait. Both aroused feelings of tenderness in Cass, but both had the same disappointing results: a complete lack of connection. *Where is the switch I need to flip? How do I make it come?* Cass felt a kind of love for Sheryl McKenna. Her heart ached for the girl she knew was dead. That kind of certainty, Cass felt, was part of the power she had gained that day when the tree branch came down on her. With a trembling hand, she picked up the last photograph, though her sight was too blurry to see the image she held. Sheryl was dead. Cass felt it—knew it—and knew, too, that her gift had not left her utterly.

This was the most recent photo of the bunch, Cass guessed. She glanced down at Sheryl's pure and beautiful face on the pillow, sleep in her eyes, her hair a black riot on the pillow behind her. It was plain this photo had been taken without the subject's approval, and Cass was filled with an odd anger. Sheryl did not look like the subject of a joke; the anger on her features was plain. And so was the fear, the violation.

And then it started coming to her. Finally, a vision. *A man stood above the bed, holding on of those Instamatic cameras people had years ago, the kind with the flash built in. The man was smiling and his teeth were stained and dark. His eyes were alive. He giggled like a little boy. "Come on, honey, smile for Daddy." He giggled some more, the laugh finally bottoming into something deep, almost threatening. "This is your wake-up call." Click and flash, blinding.* Cass shook her head, trying to clear the image. She had seen this man before. It was, as she suspected, Sheryl's stepfather, Rick. This wasn't the kind of vision she wanted to have. This was painful. And it led nowhere. She turned the photograph faced down on the table, hoping to block out more of the vision. None of it could help her. *The man taking the picture was naked. Stop. I don't want any more of this.*

Cass picked up the Pirates jersey, suddenly feeling completely exhausted, depleted. Having these visions was like going through a strenuous workout, or running several miles; even though she sat completely still, the process of the visions reached deep down inside her and stole energy. "Please, let there be something." She held the shirt, fingering its nylon weave, lifting it to her nose to sniff — and got nothing. She set the jersey down and reached for the charm bracelet. It made a tinkling sound in her hand and the heft of it surprised Cass, but then, there were a lot of charms on it. Cass went through them all, the bears, the letters, the hearts, the cheap imitation gems, and got nothing. She clutched the bracelet hard in her hand, squeezing it, hoping to wring some essence of Sheryl out of the gold electroplate.

She wanted to cry. "No," she whimpered. She thought of this as her only chance, other than going out and getting in the car with Dani Westwood and blindly combing the countryside, hoping she would see something that would trigger a connection in her mind. That could take days. The police might get there before her, and they might be pulling a body bag, with Max in it, from a shallow grave, or a car trunk.

A car trunk... Something clicked.

And then she saw Bum. *"Come here, boy; come here."* A tall, dark-haired man squatted down in her parents' backyard beside the dog, gesturing with his hand, holding it out like he had something in it. Then things went black. Then a flash, and she saw the trunk open and Bum's limp corpse being loaded into it. He bled from a slit in his neck. Cass frowned; she didn't realize tears were running down her cheeks. "Not Bum," she whispered.

A jolt ran through her. A swirl of red, like blood into oil, swam on her inner eyelids. Cass gripped the bottom of the chair until her knuckles went bloodless. The red Mustang was parked next to a rusting trailer, dingy white and harvest gold. Cass stuffed a fist in her mouth when she saw Max's head pop up in the back window. He looked scared, eyes wide, searching. *He's looking for me. He doesn't understand.* Cass's heart ached. "My baby," she whimpered, feeling helpless and vulnerable.

Another jolt went through her and she shuddered, the nausea in her gut ratcheting up. The man was taking the dog out of the trunk. "Fuck," he whispered, looking down at the crimson stain on his crisp white shirt. He held Bum close. The dog's head lolled; his tongue hung out and his eyes were already filming over, staring up at a milky, cloud-choked sky. The man frowned. "This'll never come out."

Where was Max?

Cass watched as the man—with jerky motions, like a film sped up—dug a shallow grave for the dog behind the trailer. Cass gasped when she saw another mound of dirt beside the hole he was digging for Bum. There were a few old leaves, branches, and rusting tin cans placed strategically over the mound, but it was clear that Bum was becoming part of fast-growing little graveyard.

Sheryl!

Cass wanted to weep, to shut out the images she had encouraged. She wanted to just put her head down on the surface of the table and cover it with snot and tears. Sob for the loss of a young girl, barely into her teens, sob for the loss of a dog that had been a faithful friend to both her and Max. And sob for Max... *Where is Max?*

There's no time for that now. Concentrate. Let yourself go back. Look around. See where you are.

Cass closed her eyes, trembling because she was afraid the vision wouldn't return, or it would come back to a different place. She didn't know how fragile these images were, but she did know how precious they were. Their very value made it easy for Cass to worry they would scatter and leave her with nothing useful. And then what would happen? Would Max end up part of the tiny graveyard on the bluff?

But when she breathed in, it all came to her again: the shovel breaking through the dirt, the rusty skirting around the bottom of the trailer.

Cass realized she could move, just a little, when she concentrated really hard. She couldn't move very much in the vision, but she could turn herself, so she got a clear perspective from both directions on the bluff upon which the trailer sat. First, she could see she was high up on a hill; the Ohio River curved below her, flowing on its muddy journey to the Mississippi. *Think, Cass, think. What do you see? What's at the bottom of the hill? What's across the river?* She narrowed her eyes, both in the kitchen and within her vision. Across the river were two houses, one a red brick ranch and the other a two-story box, sheathed in dingy white aluminum siding, black shutters, a run-down colorless car in the driveway. Down below, she could see the three or four blocks that constituted downtown Summitville. She breathed a sigh of relief. She had her bearings.

She made herself turn and saw, in front of the trailer, a dirt and ash driveway leading out to a pothole-filled two-lane road. The vision was dimming, the images flickering. Cass knew she didn't have much time. *Find something unique. There, a sign along the road, blurred.* Cass squinted, trying to bring the black-and-white marker into clarity. At first, nothing; the sign stayed blurred as if to confound her. She ground her teeth together, unconsciously angling her head one way and then another, squinting, squinting harder.

And she got it! *Route 14.*

Cass stood, heart pounding. She had everything she needed.

She hurried out the kitchen door, running toward Dani Westwood's car. Without a word, the reporter turned the key in the ignition and the engine roared into life.

Cass swung into the passenger seat. "Let's go. I'll navigate."

Chapter
Twenty-six

DANI WESTWOOD WANTED to ask Cass all sorts of questions. When she had rushed out of her house, the screen door slamming behind her like a shot, she was a woman possessed: jubilation, terror, and impatience combined on her dark features like a kaleidoscope, shifting. Her body motions were hopped-up, jerky, trembling. She laughed, smiled, wept a little. Dani wasn't sure whether she should do as she said or drive her to Summitville City Hospital, where they could begin an IV drip of some serious psychotropic drugs.

"I know where he is." Cass stared straight ahead, as though what were outside the windshield was not the night sky and the doors to her little one-car garage, but her son, standing, arms outstretched, waiting for his mother to come get him.

Dani wanted to ask how she knew, what had happened in the kitchen, what she had seen, and how it all worked. But she knew from everything about Cass that there was no time for conversation. There was such urgency in her words, in her body language. Dani felt compelled, under the spell of a force greater than her own will.

She wanted to help Cass, wanted her to be right.

She wondered if care like this portended something larger, something she had thought she was no longer capable of.

Love.

Thoughts like these had to be shelved for now; she could take them out and examine them later. She understood Cass's urgency and her desperation. It was late, after midnight. She had sat by herself in the car, waiting, for almost two hours, wondering if Cass had fallen asleep, but knowing instinctively not to disturb her.

She must have had some sort of breakthrough.

Dani threw the car into gear. "Tell me. Tell me where to go."

Cass breathed out, as if preparing herself for a difficult physical task. "Head for Hill Road. You're going to take that up to Vermont Boulevard and then make a right and then another right at the first road you come to: it will go almost straight up."

Cass shifted in her seat and stopped speaking. There was no more to say.

Dani knew enough to speed. She pushed down on the accelerator and goosed the car up to eighty, checking the gas gauge to make sure fuel was not going to be a problem. Everything was good. They had enough to go for miles and miles, even though Dani already had a sense they weren't going very far.

Excitement surged in her like something electric, pulsing through her veins. Something big was going to happen. Somehow, Dani was going to be able to help this woman for whom a tenderness and protectiveness was growing and blooming within.

She didn't allow herself to think of bad outcomes. *Of a little boy's body...*

Stop. We are not *going to be too late.*

She almost missed the left that would take them on to Hill Road. "Here! Here! Left! Left!" Cass cried and Dani jerked the wheel left, cutting off an oncoming pickup. Amidst the blaring of a horn and the squealing of tires, they began to ascend the road, climbing, climbing, the dark trees reaching branches out above them like ghostly fingers.

"Get ready. Vermont's just ahead."

Dani turned right on Vermont and the little car continued to climb, its headlights and her gaze in synch, searching for the first road on the right. And there it was, almost hidden between sentinels of pine.

Dani took the road up just a little more and then they were on top of the bluff. One side sloped down, and Dani knew the Ohio River was down there, the commercial district of Summitville nestled along its shores. The other side was bordered by woods. The car hit pothole after pothole, the carriage squeaking and whining in protest.

Dani did not slow down.

"Watch for a sign."

"A sign?" Dani thought at first Cass meant some sort of image from God might burst into life on the road before them, or the dark cloudy sky part to reveal a giant hand, pointing to the spot. She stifled a laugh.

"A road sign," Cass said, impatiently. "Route 14. There will be a trailer across from it."

It didn't take long for a scene matching Cass's description to rise up in front of them, as if her words had caused the trailer and the road sign to bloom into reality.

Dani slowed the car and they both craned to look at the trailer, looking forlorn and lonely at the edge of the bluff. It looked like a good wind would knock it right down into the valley.

"Pull over." Cass's voice was hoarse, despair and fear, Dani supposed, stealing all the air from her.

The car crunched on rocks and dirt at the side of the road.

"I don't know if I can do this," Cass whispered. "What if he's..."

"We have to. There's a flashlight in the glove box." Dani glanced over at the trailer. It was all dark, no lights shining from within. She bit her thumbnail, pulling at it. She wasn't sure she wanted to continue either. But she knew she needed to be strong. This was why Cass had brought her along. Cass's motives had nothing to do with providing a story for the *Review.*

Cass flipped open the glove compartment and removed the flashlight. She flicked it on and off, pointing its beam down at the floor, quickly. She whispered, "I think it's better if we keep this off, at least until we really need it."

Dani knew why she wanted to stay in the dark, and shivered. If there were people in there, they were monsters: the kind who killed young girls. The element of surprise was crucial. This encounter could very well be life-or-death. She hadn't yet had time to be afraid, but now the terror hit her like a wave rolling in—sudden, concrete hard, and cold. She felt sweat break out on her back, trickle down her spine and from her armpits. Her heart began to thud.

What waited inside that dark trailer?

CASS GRIPPED THE flashlight so tightly she knew her knuckles were white. She glanced over at the dark, hulking rectangle just feet away from the car. *Is Max in there?* She wasn't getting a sense of anything at the moment. Everything that brought her visions, images, whatever they were, was quiet now. Part of her hoped she was wrong. She didn't want to be inside that awful place.

"Why is it so dark?" she whispered to Dani.

Dani's voice came out with a bit of a quiver, but Cass could tell she was trying to make things a little less menacing. "They're probably asleep." Dani gripped her hand. "Cass, do you think maybe we should phone the police? I have my mobile right here." Dani tapped her pocket.

"And tell them what?" Cass looked into her eyes and licked her lips. "They're not going to come rushing up here because I saw the trailer in a vision. I'm sorry, but we're on our own. You're welcome to stay here in the car if you want, but if my son is in there, I'm getting him out and I'm bringing him home."

"Of course I'm coming with you. What do you think I'm here for?"

"We need to be very quiet. Let's open the doors at the same time and let's not close them. I don't want anyone knowing we're on our way."

"Okay." Dani reached up to switch off the dome light. "One, two, three," she said, and both of them opened their doors at the same time. Both put their feet gingerly on the rock-strewn and weed-choked ground and slipped from the car, leaving its doors open. The two picked their way through the trash and the weeds toward the trailer, both wishing there was more of a moon, and both grateful there was not. Cass hoped the grass didn't contain snakes or rats. She held tightly to Dani's hand.

Cass tried to comfort herself as they crept toward the trailer. *Just think: in a few minutes, you could be seeing Max. You could be holding him in your arms.* The thought made her quicken her pace, helped her to forget what horrors might await them inside. But what if what she held was no longer alive? She realized they had to be purposeful; there was no time for fear or hesitation.

They stopped just outside the trailer. Dani whispered, "Do you think there's a back door? Maybe one of us should go that way and the other go in through here. If we can get in..."

Cass looked around and then noticed something odd. There was no red Mustang parked near the trailer. In fact, there were no cars at all. This trailer was the kind of place where, if you lived here, you needed a car. Her heart sank.

She grabbed Dani's shirt, clutching. "What if they're gone?"

Dani shook her head. "We can't stand here and wonder. Let's not worry about the back door, either. Let's just see if we can get inside."

The trailer's front door was unlocked. Dani went in first and Cass followed.

It smelled bad inside, like rotting meat. The air was close, damp, like being inside a steam room. But a steam room where someone had left pounds of hamburger out to spoil in the heat. Cass covered her mouth and tried not to gag.

"This is an old trick I learned from covering crime scenes." Dani pulled a small blue jar from the pocket of her jeans. In a moment, she placed an oily smear above Cass's upper lip and right away, all Cass could smell was eucalyptus.

Dani did the same for herself.

"Vicks?" Cass asked, not wanting to think why Dani had brought the stuff along; she hoped it was because she had a cold.

Dani nodded.

In spite of the smell, the trailer had an air of emptiness. Cass switched the flashlight on. "Come on." She moved quickly out of the kitchen area and into the living room, where the stubs of dozens of dead candles stood. She took in the sight and shivered.

She moved down the hall, peeking first into a bathroom; filthy, with dark smears on the floor and by the tub, some of the smears still recalling what had made them. In the light of the flashlight, Cass knew what these were: bloody footprints, and they made her feel faint. Gripping the doorway of the bathroom, Cass tried to reach deep down inside herself for courage.

Blood was smeared all around the bathroom. There were handprints, Cass now noticed, on the wall, and splatters and pools of it in the tub.

Cass's mouth was dry. *No. I cannot be sick now.* She backed slowly out of the bathroom, breathing in deep the scent of the Vick's. Dani was silent behind her, never removing her hand from her shoulder. It was a comfort, but it was David-sized comfort in the face of Goliath horror.

She peered into the first bedroom. There was a twin bed with rumpled sheets and a small nightstand. Nothing else. The room was tiny, Cass guessed no more than eight feet by ten. *Did Max stay in here? Is Max in the other bedroom?* Cass didn't know if she wanted to see. She went and sat on the edge of the twin bed. "Will you go look in the other bedroom for me? I can't...I just can't do it." She let out a trembling, choked sob.

Dani knelt before her. "Of course." She pried the flashlight from Cass's fingers. "I'll take a look through the closets, too, if I don't find anything."

Cass didn't like her use of the word "anything." It was like talking already about Max in the past tense. She nodded. Her stomach was churning as she watched Dani leave the room. She flopped back on the bed and shut her eyes tight, afraid of the news she would be getting very shortly.

DANI MADE HER way down the short distance to the next bedroom, at the back of the trailer. She was glad Cass had stayed put; the smell was growing worse, in spite of the Vicks on her upper lip. Sour, sweet, it made her want to retch.

She paused at the dark entrance to the room. The smell hung over the room like a miasma, a fog of stench. The room's interior was dark, and part of Dani hoped her eyes wouldn't adjust to the absence of light. She stood there, frozen, panting, heart pounding, and realized these next few steps would be the hardest steps she had ever taken in her life. She didn't need to be able to see to realize that something horrible waited inside the room.

It crossed her mind that she could simply reach out and grope along the wall until her hand connected with a light switch. But then the room would be flooded with light and she wasn't sure she wanted that much illumination.

For just one moment, she contemplated simply turning around and going back to Cass. She could tell her there was nothing in the room and they should move on. No, she couldn't do that; even without playing the flashlight's beam over the interior of the room, she knew from the heavy smell in the air, something dead awaited her.

But if she was that certain, she thought, why not go back to Cass and tell her there was a body in the room and they should call the police? Why face the horror that surely waited just a few steps away? She didn't know if she could bear it.

Come on now! This woman brought you along because she thought you were strong, thought you could help her. This is not the time to turn tail and run. Dani forced herself to take several deep breaths, then reached down and flicked the flashlight on.

She let the beam play first on the opposite walls, ignoring the bed. There were more blood spatters and bloody hand prints. *Something must be on the bed. Go on...you must.* She lowered the beam of light and couldn't stop herself — she screamed. Forcing herself to look, she fought down the bile rising up. "No, no, no..." she whispered over and over, a litany, not even aware she was speaking. She stood like that, frozen, for minutes, simply staring at the mess on the bed.

Then she turned and went back to rouse Cass from the bed in the other room. She had to tell her what she found. She had to tell her the bad news.

CASS WAS GETTING something, but only snatches, coming rapid-fire, like nightmare slides projected by someone with no patience. A girl she didn't know, her mouth in an O: a silent scream. A bloody butcher's knife raised high. Pale hair in the dark, a face obscured by a video camera. She rocked on the bed, saliva dribbling from the corner of her mouth, not wanting to see, yet unable to stop the parade of gruesome imagery. She was just about to get up and go to Dani, just so she wouldn't be alone, whatever horrors waited in the other room be damned.

And then she heard Dani's scream. Bloodcurdling, it made her want to do the same.

She sat up, squeezing her eyes and opening them rapidly, trying to make herself concentrate on the here and now: the cheap mini-blinds at the tiny window, the room's only view to the outside, the clothes scattered on the floor... She didn't want to the think about Dani's shriek and her mumbled "no-no-no."

She jumped and cried out when she noticed Dani standing in the doorway. The reporter's face, even in the dark, was a mask of fear: eyebrows drawn close, lips pulled low in the deepest of frowns, little breaths escaping.

"What?" Cass asked dully, already beginning to cry.

"I'm afraid I have some very bad news. We need to call the police. *Now.*"

Chapter
Twenty-seven

MAX COULD NOT stop shaking. It wasn't cold in the car, but still he couldn't stop trembling as though it were zero degrees outside and he was dressed just as he was now, in shorts and his Steelers T-shirt. He lay across the small back seat, knees drawn up to his chest, wishing he could suck his thumb, but they hadn't removed the duct tape when they left the trailer. They hadn't even taken off the bungee cords that bound his hands and wrists, even though the lady told the man they could; it would be all right.

The man wouldn't listen. He was very, very mad.

But at least he had let the lady put him into the back seat. And at least she had been gentle about it, almost like when his mom would put him on his bed after he fell asleep downstairs.

She had smiled at him and whispered, "Just don't make any fuss. You don't want to upset him more than he already is." She ran her fingers through his hair and trailed her fingertips along his cheek, smiling. "This will all be over soon."

She had gently rolled him toward the back of the seat and Max tried to calm himself. He was afraid if he got too upset, he would have trouble breathing. He would smother.

The lady had left him alone in the car. Here was his chance! He tried — really hard — to get himself free, but the cords were tight, and he couldn't scream through the duct tape. He heard her running after the man and could hear her voice but not her words. It sounded like she was crying — and begging. Max did hear the word "Don't!" several times.

There was the man's voice, angry. Max heard the "F" word and something about "the Beast" and then the sound of the trailer door slamming. It almost sounded like a gunshot. The lady must have stayed outside, because he could hear her sobbing like her heart was broken.

And then Max heard screaming. Terrible hollering. Wails. The angry voice of the man. Max tried to scrunch his shoulders up to his ears to block out the high-pitched shrieks, but it wasn't possible. There was nothing he could do but listen. He knew the sounds were coming from the other lady, the fat one. And she sounded like she was in horrible pain!

He wished he could stop the man from hurting her.

Max sniffled and tried not to remember what he heard, tried to just concentrate on the steady *thrum* of the road rolling by under the car. It was hard, though. If they would just be quiet, maybe he could calm himself, but every time he tried to go somewhere else in his mind, they would start fighting again. Sometimes, the man would reach over and hit the lady or grab her cheeks and force her to look at him while the words shot out of him, scalding and mean. Those times, the car would swerve all over the road because the man wasn't paying attention.

Max wished they would crash, wished they would hit another car. Then, maybe he'd have a chance. It was funny: having a car accident was better than staying in the car with these two bad people. At least if they crashed, the police would come...and he would be rescued, even if he did get hurt.

Max also wished he had not rolled himself over. He figured the lady put him down facing the back of the seat for a reason. But he had managed to get himself facing the other way, and now he was forced to be a witness to everything in the front seat. Maybe if he didn't have to watch, it would be easier. He had managed to go away in his mind when lots of stuff had been going on: he would imagine himself climbing one of the hills across from his house. He would start by walking down the driveway, then checking to see if the street was clear of traffic to cross, then up to the retaining wall that kept the hill from coming down onto the road. And then he would start climbing, losing himself in the green leaves and golden sunlight of the woods, listening to the crunch of his own footsteps on the dirt and dried leaves, and the birds crying out to one another.

He didn't want to hear them arguing, because they were arguing about him.

MYRA TRIED ONE more time. Common sense was the only tack she could take, and she wasn't even sure that worked anymore with Ian. What he had done to Tammie... She sniffed, thinking of her friend in the trailer. Tammie hadn't deserved to die.

Myra's cheeks stung from Ian's slaps. Soon, he would probably pull over and start punching her. He would pull the car over and pummel her just so she would shut up. He had done it before. A part of Myra told her: *Just shut up and let him do what he wants. It will be easier. One more death won't make any difference.*

But she couldn't. The girls had been bad enough, but this little boy! He was like a little angel with his blond hair, his green eyes ringed by those impossibly long and black eyelashes, even his dirty face — they all made her heart ache. She had wondered at times over the past summer if she even had a heart. Now she knew she did.

She started again, cringing, waiting for Ian's hand to fly out, connect with her face painfully. "Ian, please, honey, just listen to me. Can't we just pull over and put him out by the side of the road? He's just a little kid. When we get to where we're going, we can change our appearances; we'll be no worse off if we let him go. They'll find Tammie; they know we rented the trailer. Ian, honey, they know who we are. All that little boy can do is give them a description. He's little. He won't even be good at that. And by the time he tells them, I'll have black hair and yours will be blonde. We can get you a pair of glasses at the drugstore. I'll start wearing different clothes."

Ian took his eyes from the road to glare at her. "You stupid cunt. Can't you just listen to what the Beast says? Can't you just trust in me? Everything you say is true, yet the Beast says we'll still be safer if we leave a corpse instead of a kid." He smiled, and Myra wondered how a monster could look so handsome. His face was sweet, the stuff of romance novel covers. But underneath, Myra knew, something diseased and monstrous lurked, belying the pretty exterior.

Myra stared at the floor, chewing on her lower lip. "Couldn't you just do this for me? I love you, sweetheart, but I don't think I could bear..."

"I'll take care of it," Ian snapped. "I won't make you record it. You won't even have to watch."

"I don't care about that. He's just so young. It seems a shame." Desperate, Myra thought of another angle. "We could take him with us, make him our kid. Show him the way of the Beast. How would that be?"

Ian was quiet for a long time and she knew he was thinking, imagining what it would be like to have a young impressionable mind at his fingertips to mold, a disciple. She used his contemplation as an opening and she spoke quietly. "We could teach him all about the Beast and he would come to believe." She swallowed. "Just like we do. He'll be the Beast's first real convert, after us. Just imagine bringing him up, like some reverse of Jesus. I'll take care of him, just like a mother...all you have to do is train him in the teachings of the Beast." Myra felt everything she was saying was stupid and groundless; even she didn't believe a word of it.

Yet she could see the wheels turning in Ian's mind. He even had a small smile on his face. She wondered if he saw making Max their son as some sort of beginning. He shook his head. "I don't know."

Myra smiled. 'I don't know' was better than 'We need to kill him. We can't leave any witnesses.'

She decided not to press her advantage. She thought of the Wicked Witch of the West. What was it she said in the movie? "These things must be done delicately." For now, for maybe even the next hour, the boy was safe.

She looked back at him. He lay trembling, almost spasming on the back seat, his green eyes wide. She reached back to touch him, to reassure him, and he flinched at her hand drawing near. She mouthed,

"It's gonna be okay," and smiled. He nodded.

She turned back to Ian. "We can talk more about this when we get to Pittsburgh. Okay?" Myra put a gentle hand on his thigh. "Can you just think about what I said?"

"I am thinking about it, my love. And it seems like a real stupid idea. But it amuses me to listen to your vain efforts at salvation. Who are you really trying to save, though? Him? Or yourself?"

Myra looked out the window at the dark landscape racing by, wishing she could just leap from the car and run into the woods or one of the yellow-lit houses that would come up every so often, a blur.

Chapter
Twenty-eight

THE NIGHT WAS alive with light, squawking voices, people running everywhere. Cass looked dully at all the excitement: a crime scene/death scene/circus. *Why is everyone running? It's too late to do anything for them.* They had just unearthed Sheryl McKenna's body (after they had brought Bum up from out of the earth behind the trailer; when Cass saw him she could no longer watch, so she turned and heaved into the weeds). She only knew they had discovered Sheryl's body because of the calls; she'd heard the policemen and the medical examiner, all of them talking loudly about the "female" and the "victim" as if Sheryl had never had a name in the first place. Cass wanted to close her ears when one of them matter-of-factly said something about the body being pretty far gone in decomposition, "what with the heat." She closed her eyes shut tightly, squeezing out a persistent image of a rotting face, half-eaten by insects.

At the scene's perimeter, Cass found a big old maple and sat down, legs splayed out in front of her, back against the rough bark. She watched everyone scurry and it occurred to her it was like watching a movie, unreal. At least with a movie, she was somewhat involved, if only vicariously. Now she felt only dull, her senses rubbed raw. *What am I doing here?* She looked around, confused, as if she had been transported from her living room to a bluff and had no memory of what brought her here. Touching the ground, the bark of the tree behind her, she tried to get her bearings, to tell herself once again what was going on, what had brought her to this grisly place, in the heat of an Indian summer dawn. She knew she was experiencing shock. The chill and shivers running through her every so often only confirmed the diagnosis.

Thank God Dani had stayed by her side throughout all of this. If it hadn't been for her, Cass thought she probably would lose her mind. Just go—what was the word?—catatonic or something. Maybe it would be a relief.

But Dani had remained with her, doing most of the talking when the police had arrived. She had been the one who walked around the trailer after they had burst from inside, realizing they had stepped into a chamber of horrors. She had been the one who had discovered the shallow graves behind the trailer. Cass didn't know if speech was a faculty she had anymore, but Dani had told the authorities about the dead girl in the bedroom and how someone had tried — and almost — succeeded in severing her head from her body. She didn't know how Dani could describe what she had seen in the bedroom without screaming, but she had managed to keep a level tone and give good directions to whoever had answered the phone at the Summitville Police Department.

And now Cass was having unpleasant memories of the night they found Lucy Plant's body. The area around the trailer — just hours ago quiet, still, dead — was now alive with lights, people, cameras, voices. Dani had set the activity in motion with the simple act of flipping open her cell phone and calling the police. It was only moments before they were hearing sirens in the distance. The *déjà vu* was not welcome as Cass watched, still amazed at how busy everyone seemed. There was a disconnect from the horror of what was actually here and people going about doing their jobs. It was as though they were working on a construction site, putting up a building, or they were in a restaurant, like her, waiting tables. Didn't any of them realize that two young women were dead, their brief lives snuffed out by crazy people? Didn't any of them want to collapse in terror or fight back in rage? Yet they were all taking photos, taking measurements, talking amongst themselves with ghoulish excitement. Didn't any of them feel the concern she felt for her son, who was out there somewhere with the same people who had viciously killed these girls? She let out a long, low sound, something between a moan and a wail. It was the kind of scream that would awaken her from a nightmare. *But this is real. This is really happening.*

Dani squatted down beside her. Before, she had stood, a silent comfort, just holding her hand while she sat on the ground. She touched Cass's face tenderly and forced her to meet her own gaze. Her dark eyes were filled with concern. "Cass?"

Cass shook her head, surprised she had made the noise, and wondered how loud it had been. She looked over Dani's shoulder to see if anyone else had heard, though she wasn't sure she cared. She swallowed hard, a raw lump forming in her throat. She didn't know whether she could talk. She wasn't sure if speech would ever come to her again. She wondered if all she would be able to do from now on would be scream and make guttural sounds.

She grabbed Dani's hands in hers and licked her lips, trying to get her tongue around some words, finally saying hoarsely, "They're all so busy. Hurrying, scurrying..." Her gaze followed all the people, moving from group to group rapidly, never really focusing. She whimpered again, loud, and caught the next one in her throat like a hiccup. "They're all so damn busy with the dead." She began to sob. "And not a one of 'em is out there looking for my boy!"

Dani knelt in the dirt and wrapped her arms around Cass. "Shhh. That's not true. I know for a fact they're working on it." The two of them rocked back and forth while Cass wept, the dam of grief finally burst. Dani stroked her hair, whispering, "Cass, you need to be strong. You can't let yourself collapse, not now. We have to find Max, and you have to be ready to help. Do you understand?"

Cass cried for a long time, cried until her throat felt raw and her eyes burned. Cried for Sheryl, for the girl Dani found inside the trailer, for Bum, but most of all for Max, who was somewhere with these people who took innocence and slaughtered it. She felt so vulnerable and helpless; every minute that ticked by was one more minute without Max, one more minute to worry about what was being done to him, and she, the one who was charged with protecting him, nurturing him, caring for him, could do nothing about it. Her sobs slowed and she shook her head, looking up at Dani. "You've been good to me. Thank you. Thanks for not being a reporter." She managed a wan smile, rubbing at her eyes. "I know. You're right." Cass felt a deep urge—completely inappropriate—to lean into Dani's face and kiss her. And not just a peck, either, but a hungry, devouring, open-mouthed kiss with lots of tongue. She shook her head, trying to free it of the image—and the shame and guilt it induced. *Don't be so hard on yourself. That kind of connection is natural. It's stress. Release.* She looked at Dani and thought that maybe there was a little more than stress at play here. *But there's no time to think of that now.*

Dani brushed the tears off Cass's face and tried to smile. "I care about you, Cass."

Cass was about to say something when there was a flurry of excitement. Cameras flashed and everyone talked all at once, then, almost as if on cue, everyone fell silent as the door of the trailer opened and three paramedics emerged, hoisting a black body bag in their hands. Cass covered her face.

"I don't know how much more of this I can take."

Cass felt there was nothing else to do but remove her hands from her face and watch as the uniformed men loaded the body into the back of an ambulance. Cass thought it looked like they were carrying a piece of cargo, a sack of cement. Was there no respect for the dead here? At least a hush had fallen over them when the door opened and they came out with the girl. At least they did that much, Cass thought. Behind them, there were still bright lights and squawking voices, yells, even laugher as the insanity around the unearthing of Sheryl McKenna continued. Cass wondered how someone could find humor in a scene like this. *Be kind, Cass. Understand: sometimes people laugh at the most horrible times. It's also a release. You want compassion. Show compassion.*

She looked out at the yellow crime scene tape and wooden horses that had been erected on all sides around the trailer. Every minute, the crowd grew larger, as word spread about the horror on the hilltop.

Every minute, someone else made the grim pilgrimage up from the valley of Summitville to witness the biggest news story the area had ever seen. Every minute, as the sky lightened in the east, someone else would push and jockey for position at the crime scene barriers, hoping to get a glimpse of a body or a splash of blood. Cass wondered what drove such morbid curiosity and wondered if she would have been part of the swelling crowd before her if things had been different. She liked to think she wouldn't have, but who knew? Life had a way, especially lately, of being out of control and full of unpleasant surprises.

It made her want to vomit. All the faces! It was as if they were at a carnival. Everyone laughing, talking, pointing, smoking cigarettes. She wanted to stand and scream at them. *Listen! Listen to me, you assholes. Don't any of you have a sense of decency? Who brought you up? Apes? Go home. Let the police do their jobs.* But she said nothing, just continued staring, wide-eyed at the crowd, who seemed ready for a good show.

And then she sucked in a breath. Weaving through the crowd of onlookers, she saw Sheryl McKenna, her long black hair trailing behind her as she moved through the crowd, running, laughing. She glanced over at Cass and their eyes met. Sheryl winked and gave a little wave, then ducked behind a man in a NASCAR baseball cap. Cass put her hands over her face, pressing against her eyes, then looked again. Sheryl was gone.

But then she noticed another familiar face in the crowd, this one desperate to get through the barriers, this one real. The woman's frizzed blonde hair was pulled away from a leathered, overly tanned face. Her eyes were practically bulging with terror or outrage; it was hard to say which. She pushed against the crowd with her hands, thrusting her chest out to get to the front. She started to climb over the wooden barrier and a policeman held her back. She began to wail.

"You let me go, you son of a bitch! That's my daughter over there! That's my daughter!" The woman collapsed into sobs, inconsolable, dropping to her knees in the dirt. She hit her head on the bottom of one of the blue horses stenciled *Summitville PD*. She didn't notice. Scrambling to her feet again, she pushed and clawed at the young officer who was trying to hold her back. "You have to let me see her. That's my baby! That's my baby! Oh God."

People around her were quieting, making room, leaving a wide circle around the hysterical woman. Most just stared. Some whispered behind their hands.

Cass shook her head and remembered being in this woman's kitchen. Janet McKenna. She wouldn't listen to Cass. Cass wondered if it really would have done any good even if she had. Wouldn't the result have been the same? She had thrown Cass out of her house, in fact, calling her visions evil, the product of an association with the devil. Cass recalled a plate smashing against the wall, just missing her.

And yet Cass bore her no ill will. The poor woman was nearly insane with grief. Cass watched as Marion Hartley moved close to the officer attempting to hold Janet McKenna back. She whispered something in his ear and then moved into his place, putting her hands firmly on Janet McKenna's shoulders, leaning in close to talk to her. Janet stopped struggling as the detective spoke, nodding dumbly. Cass didn't know what Detective Hartley was saying, but her words were having an effect. The fight went out of Janet and she shrunk into herself, her head hung low, staring down. Finally, Marion Hartley walked away, leaving Janet to grip the barrier with bloodless knuckles, watching. Someone came over and put an arm around her, whispered to her. A neighbor, maybe? Friend? Relative? Janet nodded dumbly; it was as if all the rage had ebbed out to be replaced by a dull numbness.

Whoever it was, what they had said next obviously brought Janet out of her numbed state. Janet shrugged their hands away and snapped at them. She sunk back into the crowd then and Cass couldn't see where she had gone. Cass looked up at Dani. "Do you know who that was?"

Dani nodded. "Yeah, I just sat on her porch for an hour trying to convince her to give me some of her daughter's things. Poor woman."

Cass couldn't imagine what Janet McKenna must be going through. Well, that wasn't quite true. Maybe a better way to say it would be that Cass *didn't want* to imagine what Janet was going through. She could fear the worst about her son, but as long as Max still hadn't been found, there was still hope. Sustaining hope. Cass knew that was something Janet had had up until a short time ago. Janet could tell herself, over and over, that Sheryl had run away. She was a wild girl, rebellious. Who knew what she could get up to? But all of that, Cass imagined, had been wiped out by a single phone call, or maybe a bulletin on the TV or radio. Every ounce of hope that woman had felt had just been cruelly extinguished with the discovery of her daughter's body in an undignified grave on a hillside. Cass didn't know how she could bear it. She would be ripping her own hair out with grief; she would want to die herself.

Please let Max be all right. Please, please, please...

Cass was just about to ask Dani to go talk to Janet when she noticed her standing off to the side, not three feet away. Cass's muscles tensed. She looked up at Janet and reached to grasp on to Dani's hand. Cass was too raw to weather an encounter with the woman right now; she didn't know if she could stand her rage if it were focused on her. She couldn't fathom how she might respond if the woman started in on Cass's "evil," on the part she had played in Sheryl's death. Maybe Janet knew something the police ought to know? Cass gripped Dani's hand so tightly she was sure it must hurt. But Dani simply bore the pain with grace.

But there was no anger coming from the woman, no harsh words. Janet simply stood close by, staring and wringing her hands.

Finally, she spoke, moving a little closer to Cass, tentative. "I remember you. You were at my house."

"Yes, I... I just wanted to help." Cass looked desperately up at Dani. "I really didn't mean any harm. I just thought I could help you find her."

Janet nodded and moved closer; she stretched her hand out to Cass. "You're just like me. A mama who's lost her baby." The woman's eyes glistened with tears.

Cass didn't know what to say. She stood, so that their faces would be at the same level. She moved closer to Janet McKenna and without even thinking about it, put her hands on her shoulders and placed her forehead on the other woman's forehead, just letting it rest there, letting the simple act of this touch, Cass hoped, be a comfort.

After a minute or two, Cass pulled away. Janet was quietly weeping and Cass realized she was too.

"I shoulda listened to you." Janet's words came out choked, broken. "But Rick..."

"Shhh. It doesn't matter now." Cass touched Janet's cheek, smoothing away the tears. "Now you listen to me. I know you think what I see is the devil's work, but it's not." She leaned in close, so close their noses almost touched and spoke very softly and very quickly. "I have seen Sheryl. Here, tonight. Not her body. But Sheryl. Your girl. The girl you love. I saw her, in the crowd. And Janet—Janet—I want you to know, she was happy. She was okay. For her, the worst of it is over. She's in a good place now." Cass swallowed, wishing she could stop crying. "She's in a good place. Safe. You remember that. Okay?"

Janet McKenna simply nodded, her lower lip quivering. And then she turned and walked away. Cass watched her. She felt Dani come up behind her. She wrapped her arms around her, gathering her close. "That was a good thing you did just now. A very good thing."

Cass looked back at her. "It was too little. Too little, too late."

She pulled away and watched as Janet McKenna turned around and waved. She called, "I hope you find your boy."

Cass nodded and turned back to Dani. "I hope I do too. And not like she found her baby." Cass buried her head in Dani's chest.

She clutched at the gauzy fabric of Dani's shirt and wept. But she didn't get much time with her grief. Suddenly, someone was tapping her on the shoulder.

Cass turned and saw Marion Hartley waiting.

"No," Cass whispered.

The older woman looked tired. Her tough features were marred by fatigue, as though gravity had pulled everything down. Her skin looked gray, her eyes lackluster. Cass remembered their initial encounter in Hartley's office and how the woman had been condescending and skeptical. Now, somewhere in the craggy features and lines of fatigue, she saw real concern in the woman's eyes. Or maybe Cass simply sensed it radiating off the detective like an aura.

The detective held up a hand. "Don't worry, Ms. D'Angelo. I don't have bad news. Unfortunately, I don't have good news either. But I wanted to let you know where we are with the case, where we are with finding your boy. We do have some information..." She paused and glared at Dani. "Do you want her here?"

Cass turned and looked at Dani. She turned back to Hartley. "She's okay. She's my friend."

Hartley gave Dani a long look that said, "Watch yourself." She then turned back to Cass and shrugged. "Whether she listens or not is your choice, but some of this information is sensitive. We can't have this getting out to the general public; it could hamper our work. Is that understood?"

Dani spoke up. "I'll be honest with you: I'm a reporter. But I'm here first for Cass. I would never do anything that would jeopardize her finding her son. I may report on this, but only when you say it's appropriate."

Hartley blew out a big sigh and paused to light one of her Marlboros. "I'm going to trust you, Ms. Westwood, in spite of my better judgment. But I'll go with Ms. D'Angelo's faith in you." Marion Hartley smoked, thinking. "Okay. It's like this. We know who was renting the trailer. We know the car they drive..."

Cass cut in, "An old red Mustang?"

"Right. We have the license plate number. We have their names."

Cass started shaking. "Who are they?"

"The girl is Penny Landsdale, from New Hope. The man is named Ethan Craig and he grew up in Pittsburgh. From a wealthy family. Steel, I think." Hartley leaned close. "He's been in and out of mental institutions since he was a kid. Very bright, though. And very, very dangerous." Hartley shook her head. "I'm sorry. But we've got APBs out all across the tri-state area. State Highway Patrols in Ohio, West Virginia, and here in Pennsylvania are looking for them. They won't get far."

Cass toed the soft dirt, trying not to be negative. She couldn't help herself. "But what if they switched cars? What if they're holed up somewhere?"

"Then we try to find out what happened to the old car; we try to find places where they might go. Cass, we can only do our best. We want to find your boy. We're doing everything we can."

"Right. I know." Cass's voice was barely above a whisper.

"Why don't you head on home and let us look for that red Mustang?"

Chapter
Twenty-nine

PAUL AND VIRGINIA Reese had gotten up early that morning—four a.m.—because Paul liked to get an early start, avoiding "those crazy bastards on the road; they get worse every damn day." They were traveling from their home in Chagrin Falls, Ohio, a suburb of Cleveland, to visit their granddaughter, Emily, on the occasion of her fourth birthday. In the back seat was a stack of presents, all elaborately wrapped and be-ribboned by Virginia, who loved doing it.

Emily lived in Summitville, PA, about a three-hour drive. Virginia had tried to tell her husband that leaving at four o'clock would get them to their daughter and her husband's home at seven. "They might not even be out of bed," Virginia had complained, but Paul wouldn't listen. The older he got, the more he wanted to avoid Cleveland's traffic at busy hours. Virginia was convinced it was because he couldn't see so well anymore and his reflexes weren't what they once were. But would he see a doctor or get anything checked out? No. He would rather crawl along at ten, twenty miles below the speed limit than admit to himself he might be getting too old to drive safely.

Still, Virginia hoped her daughter, Shellie, and her husband Adam would be up and about and happy to see them so early. They were now only about fifteen minutes from Summitville. Maybe if the house still looked asleep, Virginia could convince Paul to take her to McDonalds for breakfast. She loved those Egg McMuffins, even if she knew they set her cholesterol and blood pressure soaring.

"Emily is going to be so thrilled to get that doll," Virginia said, as Paul veered off on yet another back road to avoid traffic. She was glad he still had a good sense of direction and could read a map like nobody's business. "Shellie said she really wanted one, but they couldn't afford it..." Virginia bit her lip, realizing she might be saying too much. Even though Paul was hunched over the steering wheel, eyes intent on the road, she rolled her eyes and attempted to cover up. "How silly! I don't know where my daughter got her cheapskate ways. Must be that husband of hers. The doll wasn't that expensive," Virginia lied, patting her silver upsweep and glancing nervously into the backseat to make sure the doll was still there. The bright red foil-wrapped rectangle lay on the seat, reflecting the sunlight. Virginia smiled.

"What the hell?"

Virginia turned around quickly. Her husband hardly said a word anymore, so just the fact he was speaking made Virginia take notice, even before she registered the annoyance in his tone.

She didn't know what he was talking about as first, then she saw. A young girl with Marilyn Monroe-blonde hair stood by the side of the road, waving both arms over her head, obviously in distress. She practically walked out in front of their moving car!

But Paul just drove on, shaking his head and mumbling to himself.

"Paul!" Virginia punched her husband in the arm. "Aren't you going to stop? That girl was in trouble." Virginia didn't care about the girl as much as taking advantage of an opportunity for delay so they would get to her daughter's house at a more reasonable hour. "How can you just leave her standing there by the side of the road? It's not like we're in Cleveland now. She looked perfectly nice."

"Let someone else help her. Somebody else will be by in a minute. She's a pretty gal; she won't have any trouble getting someone to stop." Paul looked over at his wife, forcing his sagging jowls into a smile. Virginia noticed how the sun glinted off his bald pate.

"What? Out here in the middle of nowhere? It could be an hour before anyone else comes by, and how do we know that person won't be another old meanie like yourself and won't even stop?" Virginia blew out an exasperated sigh. "Now will you please go back and see if we can help that girl?"

"Come on, Ginny. We're almost there."

Virginia looked down at her watch. 6:45. She shook her head. Dully, she said, "I know. Please, Paul, we won't have to spend too much time. Lord knows you know nothing about cars, if hers is broken down. But we can at least give her a lift somewhere. What good is this nice big car if we can't at least do that?" Virginia looked around at the flawless interior of the brand-new Buick Century. Paul spent hours keeping it looking exactly as it had when it rolled off the showroom floor just two months ago.

"You're not gonna shut up until I do what you want, are you?"

Virginia rolled her eyes, but she was smiling. Smugly, she said, "No, sir, I am not." She reached over and patted his knee. "So you might as well turn this boat around and make me happy."

Virginia listened as the car tires crunched on the side of the road as Paul executed a U-turn. In just a couple minutes, she saw the girl still standing by the side of the road. Pretty young thing, almost waifish. How could Paul have wanted to just drive by someone who looked so helpless?

Paul slowed the car to a halt on the opposite of the two-lane road. The girl watched them, smiling, but Virginia could see there was a hint of panic in her features. She didn't see a car nearby and wondered what was wrong.

MYRA WAS ALMOST sorry to see the old couple pull over opposite her. But she knew Ian was waiting just a ways down the dirt road behind her. He had told her they needed another vehicle; the police would be out looking for the Mustang, and it wouldn't take them long to discover to whom the car was registered. Quickly, turning down the dirt road, he had outlined his plan to lure an unsuspecting motorist off the road and then take their car. "How do we do that?" Myra wanted to know, since they had no gun or other weapons they could use to force someone to give up their car. The nausea rose up in her gut; she already knew Ian's intentions, his "leave no witnesses" policy. Ian didn't need a gun or a knife, not when she helped him out by choosing people as old and feeble-looking as the ones across from her and getting ready to get out of their car to "help" her.

She wanted to wave them off, the old couple who looked like they could be someone's grandparents, he pudgy and she with silver hair. But if she waved them off, she would simply have to find someone else. If she failed, God knew what Ian would do to the little boy. She rationalized: *At least they're old. At least they've had some time to enjoy life, to do what they want to do with it. At least they don't have that much longer to live anyway.* She smiled as the older man emerged from the car, looking exasperated. Myra wanted to clutch at her heart when she saw the polyester Sans-a-Belt slacks, the plaid shirt, and loafers. He was real. And so was the woman getting out on the other side. She was smiling and waving and Myra wondered if this was some sort of adventure for her. *If you only knew...*

"What's the problem, honey?" The woman called across the road.

"My car...it's stuck."

The man immediately took on a guarded expression. "I don't see a car."

The old man and his wife crossed the road and Myra did her best to look distressed. "I know, I know. I did a really stupid thing."

The man continued to look around, searching for a car Myra imagined he thought he'd missed earlier. She wondered if Ian was watching them from the bushes. She knew she didn't dare warn them away. What good would it do, anyway? She would only have to flag down the next car and that one might contain a young couple with a new baby, so she continued. "I turned down that road there." Myra turned and pointed to the dirt road just behind her, its entrance almost concealed by leaning maples and pine trees. She laughed, but it came out high and watery, almost panicked—a silly giggle. "I was thinking maybe I could find a short-cut. I was running late, you see, and..." She looked off toward the road, hating herself, just wanting to say, "Get out of here now, while you can." And, "Take me with you." But she couldn't bear the thought of leaving little Max behind with Ian. "So anyway, I start down this dirt road and it's full of bumps and ruts and potholes, and before I knew it, my car slid off into a ditch." Myra lowered her head. "Now, I'm really going to be late."

"Where you headed?" the man asked kindly, peering around Myra to look down the dirt road.

"Summitville."

The woman clapped her hands together and smiled. "That's exactly where we're going, dear. We could give you a lift and you could call a tow truck from town." She looked to her husband. "Couldn't we, Paul?"

"I guess so." He glanced down at his watch. "But I'm not sure anything will be open yet."

"Oh, for heaven's sake! If nothing's open, she can just call from Shellie and Adam's place. It won't be a problem." The old woman smiled at Myra. "I suppose all of this would be much easier if we had a cell phone." She indicated her husband with a jerk of her head. "But this one here is too cheap to get one."

"I don't see what we need more bills for when we have a perfectly decent telephone at home."

The old woman gritted her teeth. "For times like these, dear. What if it had been us who were in this predicament?"

"We've had this conversation before, Virginia. Let's just get a move on." He looked at Myra. "We can take you into town."

"Oh, thank you. I'm ever so grateful." Myra thought it would be so easy to just cross the road and get into their car, speed away. But what would happen to Max? What would happen to *her*? The police had to be onto them by now. They would be waiting in Summitville with handcuffs.

"Listen, I hate to bother you even more when you're being so nice and all, but I have some stuff in the car I need to get and, well, I have a couple boxes that are kinda heavy. You don't suppose we could take them with us? I'm afraid to just leave them in the car. Someone might break in."

Paul rolled his eyes, but Virginia said, "Of course, dear. That's a very smart idea. I hope the boxes aren't too heavy. Paul here has a bad back, but if it's not too much, I'm sure the two of us can manage."

Paul blew out a sigh. Myra wondered if he felt affronted, his masculinity compromised. "I'm just fine, Virginia." He glanced at the dirt road. "How far down did you get?"

"Oh, not too far at all. Are you sure this is okay?"

"Positive," Virginia said brightly.

And the three of them started down the dirt road. Myra hoped they were far enough off the beaten trail that no one would hear their screams.

MAX SAW THE blonde lady coming down the road with an older lady and man. They looked nice and Max felt bad for them. He was still tied up—though Ian had allowed him to sit up—and still had the duct tape over his mouth, so he couldn't cry out a warning...or call for help. But, oh, how he wished he could tell the old people to go back to where they came from! He knew they were in trouble now. Max watched as the old couple suddenly stopped in the road, realizing they must have seen him and Ian sitting in the car. He could hear the man say, "I thought you said you went into a ditch."

The blonde lady laughed like she was embarrassed.

"No, really. I thought you said the car went off the road. That car looks perfectly fine." Max watched as the old lady began to back up. She looked a little afraid. Max thought she should be afraid; they were being led straight into a trap.

Ian opened the car door. Everything happened so fast after that.

Max scrunched down into the seat. Seeing Ian begin to chase the two old people was enough. He didn't want to see what would happen next. The old lady was really scared; Max could see that much in her big eyes and hear it in the little strangled cry she gave before she turned and started to run. When she tripped and fell, Max made himself fall over so all he could see was the back of the red vinyl seat.

The blonde lady slid into the car with him and Max edged up against the back of the seats, into a corner, drawing his knees up to his chest as best he could. Already, there was hollering going on outside. Max didn't want to think about what he had seen the man take with him before he got out of the car: one of those wrenches his mom had used one time when she got a flat tire. She had loosened the bolts with it. Max remembered how hard she had to work to get them free; her sweat. Oh God, he didn't want to hear what was going to happen next...

The blonde lady moved closer to him. Her eyes were bright with tears and her lower lip quivered. She had a big frown on her face and was nodding. Max didn't know why she kept nodding. She reached out with both hands and Max screamed under the duct tape, wriggling himself around within the confines of the cords binding him. She moved closer and grabbed hold of him, but gently. She was crying a little now as she drew him toward her chest, covering his ears with her hands. He could hear the hitting, and the screams, and the dull groans.

The lady pressed harder down on his ears and started singing, "You are my sunshine. My only sunshine..."

A scream, a terrible plea: "Please, no! Don't hit her again!"

The lady sang louder. "You make me happy when skies are gray." Max at last couldn't hear anymore and he was grateful. He leaned against the lady's chest, wishing he could suck his thumb as she continued, at the top of her lungs. "You'll never know, dear, how much I love you. Please don't take my sunshine away."

When she pulled her hands from his ears, all was quiet. The man opened the door and Max wanted to scream. His white shirt was splattered with blood.

The man just stared at the two of them for a moment, panting and

trying to catch his breath. Finally, he said, "C'mon. We just got a brand
new car."

The lady said, "Just a minute." She pulled the scarf from around
her neck, saying, "Honey, this is for the best." She then tied the scarf
around Max's eyes and lifted him gently from the car.

Chapter
Thirty

CASS LAY IN bed, staring at the ceiling. The idea of sleep was absurd, one of those notions you know from the outset is impossible. Every bone, every muscle, every joint felt weighted down with weariness and yet she knew closing her eyes would do nothing; they would only pop back open a second or two later, almost as if on their own accord. Dani had left the cordless on the nightstand by the bed, in case anyone called. Now, it was some cruel thing, taunting her with its refusal to ring. Cass didn't want to look at it, almost as if staring at it would prevent it from ringing. Still, she couldn't help imagining its chirping and her answer, hearing Marion Hartley on the other end, saying two words: "He's safe."

She clutched Sheryl McKenna's charm bracelet in one hand, hoping the contact would cause some sort of psychic fusion and she would get the answers that would lead her, or the police, to Max. With all her heart, she prayed he was alive. But she knew also that if he wasn't, it would be easier to know that. She turned on her side, looking at the dull morning light filtering in through the mini-blinds, and wondered where he was right now, if he was crying out for her, if he was being taken care of. Thoughts like these made her want to vomit. She could see him with the blonde woman and the dark-haired man, imagining him trying to understand why his Mama wasn't there to protect him. Were they hurting him? Did they have hearts that maybe opened just a tiny bit, for a little boy? Was he lying somewhere, covered with dirt and some hurriedly gathered old leaves?

She just needed to know.

She shut her eyes once more, to block out the glare from the window, knowing it was futile to try and sleep. Color swirled on the inside of her eyelids: tones of red, like blood expanding into clear water. Clouds of blood. The red swirled and churned, polluting, growing. Her breath came faster. Sweat trickled from her armpits and down from her hairline. She ground her teeth.

And then she saw Sheryl McKenna again, running through the crowd at the crime scene. She was beautiful, young, healthy, and vibrant. She stopped and turned to Cass. When their eyes met, it was as though all the people around them went into a blurred state, the light dimming; the milling crowd becoming a crowd of shadows, their excited voices dropping to a low murmur. Yet Sheryl stood out, clear and shining. A beacon.

Sheryl stared at Cass and there was kindness in her eyes. Giving Cass a small smile, she held out her hands and Cass moved toward her. This all started to take on an aspect of reality, as if Cass had risen up out of her body and returned to the crime scene. She could feel the heavy heat and humidity outside pressing in on her, hear the whisper of the leaves as the wind rustled through them, high up. In spite of the peculiar sense that she and Sheryl were somehow brighter, more *real* than everyone else, this had all the earmarks of reality. When she placed her hands in Sheryl's, the girl's palms felt warm and alive as she tugged her along.

And then they were moving with alarming speed, feet barely touching the ground, heading down the two-lane road in front of the trailer, then stopping suddenly by a dirt road after going only what seemed like a mile or two. Cass yanked back at Sheryl's hands, wanting to run. She didn't want to see what was around the curve in the road.

But suddenly, they were there. She saw the old woman and the old man, their heads bashed in, their blood soaking into the dirt road like chocolate syrup, eyes staring up at the relentless morning sun.

"No!" Cass screamed. "No," and she turned in her bed, sobbing and clutching at her sheets and pillow.

Dani hurried into the room, sat down on the side of the bed, and gathered Cass up in her arms, holding her close. "Shhh," she whispered. "Shhh. You just had a bad dream."

Cass forced her face into Dani's to make sure she understood. "This was not a dream. We have to call the police." She sat up and reached for the phone. "We have to get hold of Marion Hartley. *Now.*"

Chapter
Thirty-one

MYRA COULD SEE Ian was getting sleepy. It wasn't surprising. When had he last slept? One night ago? Two? He was having trouble keeping his head from nodding. Myra knew the right thing to do would be to take over, but she wasn't up to the task. Here in the back seat with Max, she couldn't stop crying

His head drooped again and Myra screamed when she realized he was headed straight for a big walnut tree on the side of the road. Her scream jolted him awake and Ian threw himself back against the seat for leverage, grinding the brakes down almost through the floorboards. They stopped with a jolt that sent Myra flying into the front seat and Ian hard into the steering wheel. She was surprised the tree was still in front of them and the car hadn't connected with its unyielding wood.

They were stopped horizontally across the road, blocking both lanes. A white Impala came barreling down on them, horn blaring. At the last minute, the car swerved and went up onto the shoulder of the road, sending up a spray of dust into the heavy air. It continued on, laying on its horn, the driver extending his hand out the window, middle finger pointed toward the sky.

Ian was shaking as he put the car in reverse and righted it, returning to the proper lane.

Myra composed herself, crawling over the seat to put the rest of her body into the front, settling into the bucket seat next to Ian. She turned to him. "You need to get some rest. We all do."

She could see he was tempted to argue with her, and knew him well enough to determine what he was going to say — that they needed to put as much distance between themselves and Summitville in as little time as possible. He would probably add something like if she was brighter, she could have figured that out for herself. But he didn't say anything and his handsome face was dulled with exhaustion.

"Ian, are you listening to me? I know we need to get out of here but we can't do it when you're falling asleep at the wheel."

"Shut up, Myra. I know." Ian felt in his pocket, where she had earlier watched him put the old man's wallet. She had seen him look at the array of credit cards inside. So she knew they had the means to stop for rest, and hoped he was thinking the same thing. They could find a quiet motel off the beaten path and settle down for just a few hours. Wouldn't just a few hours' sleep be lovely?

Ian got the car moving. He looked over to Myra. "Poke me if I start nodding off again, okay? I think I'll be all right. Meanwhile, let's keep our eyes peeled for a motel."

The sky was now completely light. They would be safe in this car; no one would find the bodies of the old couple for hours at least. It hadn't looked like anyone had been down that particular dirt road in weeks—quite likely days. They themselves had lay in wait for what seemed like hours, hoping someone would come by.

Ian looked over to Myra and touched her thigh. At least she had managed to stop crying. She smiled at him when he touched her. This was how it always went; she was hungry for his touch, for a kind word from him. Only him.

"We're going to be okay, sweetheart. We'll use their credit cards to buy us a few hours of rest and then we'll use them one last time to buy us some plane tickets out of here, as far away as we can get. By the time they're on to us, we'll have found a way out of this lousy country."

He didn't say anything about the boy. And that frightened Myra. But she didn't want to start that argument with him once more.

Myra sat up straighter and pointed. "Over there." She figured Ian had missed the one-story cinder block motel, it was so unassuming. The neon had gone dark but the dull sign continued to illuminate the words, "The Blue Horizon Motel."

Myra thought the place didn't look like much, just a concrete box with about eight doors in a line; all of the doors were metal, painted white, with some of them rusting. But inside, there would be a bed and welcome darkness. The thoughts of getting Ian in there, watching him fall asleep, were the most glorious thoughts she had ever had. As Ian signaled to turn into the little parking lot, she closed her eyes and smiled, imagining him stretched out on the bed and snoring.

"It isn't the Hilton, is it?" Ian said, situating himself between two yellow lines and looking through the grimy window of the office. "But it will have to do. I can't drive anymore...and I know you aren't going to do it." He looked over at Myra, lips pursed.

She knew she had been insulted, but she gave him a small smile, as if she hadn't caught on. "I'm really beat, too. We'll be a lot better off, a lot more alert, if we catch a few hours of sleep." She glanced into the backseat, where Max was backed up against the upholstery, eyes wide. She winked at him and wished she could tell him not to worry; that everything would be okay soon.

Myra had a thought. "We can't be seen going into the room with the boy like that."

"What are you talking about?"

"What if someone looks out of the office and sees one of us carrying a child all bound up in bungee cords and duct tape across his mouth?

Don't you think it would set off some alarms?" Myra tried to keep the sarcasm out of her voice, suddenly afraid she had insulted Ian. "I mean, it's up to you, but..."

Ian scratched his chin. "I guess you're right."

"I know you knew what's best." Myra was getting better at playing the part of the stupid woman and helpmate. "I can just carry him in." She looked over the seat at Max and smiled, nodding her head to him. "You'll behave, won't you Max?" She winked again, hoping the little boy wasn't too terrified to understand, hoping he was clever enough to realize she wanted to help.

Max nodded once, twice.

Myra turned back to Ian. "See? Why don't you go ahead and get us a room?" Myra looked around the parking lot, empty save for a rusting old pickup truck, its color gone beyond any definition other than blah. "I'll take care of Max."

Ian hesitated and she was afraid for a moment he would make her go instead. She wanted the time to whisper quickly to Max, to tell him of her plan, to calm him. Ian looked toward the office, then back at her, turning around finally to peer at Max. "I guess it will be all right. But you make sure the kid isn't out of your sight for a minute. Not one minute. You hear?"

"You have nothing to worry about, darling. The Beast protects, remember?"

Shakily, Ian responded, "Right." He exited the car and Myra watched as he walked to the office. She got to her knees on the seat and reached over to begin unbinding Max. The cords were off in short order. She paused. "There's no other way to do this, honey. It's gonna hurt, but only for a second." Quickly, she reached up and ripped the duct tape from across the boy's mouth. He let out a little cry and his eyes teared up. Myra immediately felt bad as she saw the red rise up on his soft little face, in the exact shape as the rectangle of tape. "I'm sorry." She got out of the car and hurried to sit in the back seat beside Max.

"We have to make this fast, do you understand?" Myra kept glancing toward the office window, where she could see Ian conversing with a fat woman with dyed red hair. She hoped the police weren't already on to them and the red-haired woman wasn't pressing some silent alarm button under the desk. She put her arm around Max. "Listen, I'm on your side. I want to get us both away from him. But it ain't gonna happen if you don't behave. Understand?"

The boy spoke at last. His voice was tiny and Myra's heart lurched. Somberly, he said, "Uh huh."

"What we're gonna do is go along with whatever Ian wants, okay? Even if it scares you, just go along. Got it?"

Max nodded.

"Once Ian's asleep, you and me, we can sneak out. The office is right there. I'm going to take you over there and leave you outside the door. I can't come in with you, honey. You just tell the lady to call the police. They'll find your mommy for you." Myra paused, hoping she would have time to do all this before Ian awoke. She prayed she could get away in the car before Ian's eyelids began to flutter and he noticed what happened.

And there were a million hopes after that one: that she could get beyond the Pennsylvania state border, that she could find a flight to somewhere far away, that she could start a new life for herself with some other name, a third name...

Ian was coming back out of the office. He had some papers in his hand. He was smiling; Myra knew everything must have gone okay. She reached down and gave Max's chubby thigh a gentle pinch. "Remember what I said. Now, I'm going to carry you inside."

Ian opened the car door. His handsome face was marred by fatigue; his eyelids drooped and his jowls sagged. He had aged by ten years, Myra thought. "Come on, let's get some sleep. You talk to the kid? He knows the score?"

Myra nodded. "Oh, I talked to him all right. We won't be having any trouble from him." She looked deep into Max's eyes. "Will we, Max?"

Max shook his head.

Myra slid from the seat and bent to gather Max up in her arms. "Good boy," she whispered. And Max slid his arms around her neck.

Myra began to see light, freedom, escape. It was so close she could almost touch it.

The three of them made their way to the door of room number seven. Myra hoped it was lucky.

After the morning's glare, the darkness of the room made it almost impossible to see. Myra groped her way to a bureau and found the base of a lamp. She pressed the button and a harsh yellow glow filled the room. The lamp looked like one her mother used to have (made of metal; three stacked geometric diamond shapes, gray on top, tan underneath, topped with a tall thin shade). Myra wondered if the rest of the room was done up in 1960s décor. She looked around and took in the painting over the bed: big mountains against a luridly blue, purple and orange sunset, a threadbare floral-print comforter, a desk and chair in one corner. The carpeting was worn, a burnt orange shag with several bald patches. The room smelled like smoke.

"I hope I don't have to tell you to keep the curtains shut." Ian looked pointedly at her. Even when he was completely exhausted, he could still manage a withering stare. "I'll be right back."

Myra wondered what he was doing. Getting their luggage, perhaps? Just like a real family vacation...

Ian came back before she had time to imagine more scenarios that didn't involve reality. In a way, he did have some luggage: a heavy black bag in one hand, the bungee cords and roll of duct tape in the other.

He shoved the cords and tape at her. "Tie him up."

"Oh, Ian, do you really think we have to? We can put him right between us on the bed." Myra let loose a high-pitched little laugh. "What could go wrong?"

Ian glared at her. "Shall I start making a list, Myra? Besides, I don't want it on the bed with us. It can sleep on the floor."

Myra knelt before Max, trying to communicate warmth with her eyes. She began wrapping the cord around him, wanting to tell him everything was going to be okay. She wanted to ask him if the cords were too tight, but there was, in the end, nothing she could say to comfort him. If Ian suspected her even in the smallest way, she feared, his fatigue would vanish.

She got Max bound—he stood and let her do it without complaint—then she took the scarf she had used earlier as a blindfold and tied it around his face, covering his mouth, hoping Ian wouldn't notice she wasn't using duct tape. Myra could still see red marks where the tape had been; some were even scabbing over and she knew she had really hurt the boy when she ripped the tape from his face.

She grabbed a pillow and blanket from the bed and made a place for him on the floor in the corner and within view of the bed. "Now you just go to sleep," Myra said, trying to make herself sound stern. "No funny business. Understand?" Again, Myra winked at Max, who nodded and let her help him lie down on his back.

When she turned around again, Ian had removed the lamp and the water pitcher and plastic glasses from the bureau and put them on the floor. The lamp was still on. Placed so low, it gave a weird and unearthly glow to the room, making Ian's face look demonic. *Not far from the truth.*

Myra asked, "What are you doing?"

Ian smiled and said nothing. He squatted and began rummaging around in the black bag he had brought in from the car. Soon enough, Myra saw why he had hurried back inside when they were leaving the trailer. Ian pulled out the old skull they'd had on the coffee table and several black candles in holders. He placed them on the bureau, arranging the skull at the head and the three candles at the foot. At the end, he brought out (almost with a flourish, Myra thought) the big chef's knife from the kitchen.

Myra began to tremble. "Oh, Ian, I thought we agreed to make Max our own." She lowered her voice to a whisper. "We can't have another death on our hands." She hoped Max wasn't able to see what was going on. Myra wrung her hands.

Ian just smiled at her. "Your idea, dear one, was stupid. The Beast says we can't leave any witnesses." He gestured toward the bureau. "Like my altar? This is where we'll do the sacrifice, before we leave." Ian giggled. "Won't the cleaning lady be surprised?"

Myra shuddered.

Ian rubbed his hands together, then twisted one in his eyes. "But right now, I'm totally exhausted. I need to get some sleep. Join me?"

Myra took his hand and let him lead her to the bed. She didn't want to get into bed with him, but if this was part of her route to freedom, she would play the part, even if he wasn't *too* exhausted.

Fortunately, Ian wanted nothing more than sleep, and as Myra lay stiffly beside him, regarding the cracked ceiling with cobwebs in its corners, she heard his breathing quickly deepen. She turned softly on her side. Ian's mouth was open and a little line of drool dripped down his chin.

She wanted to jump up immediately from the bed, but knew she should give Ian some time to sink more deeply into sleep. She turned back over, placing her hands across her chest, and waited. She could turn her head and see the little digital clock on the nightstand. She would imagine an hour had passed, would check, and see that it was only five minutes.

At last, Ian began to snore.

It's time, Myra. Get your courage up. You won't have another chance. And yet she remained frozen, unable to move, terror constricting her. Was she capable of betraying Ian this way? *What's wrong with you? He's going to kill that little boy. And it will be ten times worse than with the girls. At least you were jealous of the girls...*

Myra lay there for several more minutes, listening to Ian snore and thinking how worthless she was. *How could I have let it happen? Again and again? Did I ever even love him?* Myra glanced at Ian's face—so handsome and chiseled—and thought how even the most beautiful things can be hideous and rotting underneath.

Get going, girl. You don't have all day. Myra thought of the knife lying on the bureau. It wasn't just about continuing with a cockamamie plan to flee from justice; it was about saving someone's life, someone who had barely begun living his life. She couldn't let anything happen to Max.

Myra wondered why she cared so much, why she was so desperate to save the boy when she had stood by and watched three girls as the Ian stole their lives away. How could she have stood by so emotionlessly, actually videotaping two of the girls as they drew their last breaths in misery and pain? Now sympathetic emotions seemed to be returning, like she was an accident or stroke victim learning to walk again.

Maybe her sympathy had something to do with what had happened when she was thirteen. Her parents had taken her to Youngstown to a girl's home run by the Catholics. It was a hard six months, there with other girls like herself and then again, not. Some of them were so tough, so mean. They made fun of her, asked who would want to fuck a fat thing like her.

The baby had been a boy. They let Myra hold him for just a minute or two after he was born and they had him cleaned up. Soft pink skin, crinkly, and little slits for eyes. But, oh! He had a thick crop of dark black hair on his tiny head and his little fist, even in the delivery room, reached out and gripped her finger.

And then they whisked him away.

Myra had never seen him again. She wondered what he was doing now, if he looked like Max; they would be about the same age.

Don't get all stupid and sentimental. Tick. Tock.

Myra slowly sat up in bed, silently moving her legs to rest on the floor. She didn't make a sound. She didn't even breathe, looking across the room to where Max lay staring wide-eyed at her. Her heart thudded so hard in her chest she worried about it waking Ian. Slowly she turned her head and looked over at him. He was out completely, one arm thrown across his face, his breath alternating between snores, snorts, and deep heavy breathing. She thought she could see his eyes moving back and forth beneath the lids and wondered what horrors he dreamed of.

Very cautiously, being sure not to make the bed move at all, Myra stood. She stayed in one place, taking deep breaths, trying to slow her pulse, the blood thrumming in her ears. Finally, she moved, tiptoeing across the room, grateful for the old shag carpet under her feet. She squatted down beside Max, wincing a little when her knees cracked, and began to untie him. She couldn't say anything to him, couldn't warn him not to speak or make any noise at all; she could only hope he was smart enough to know that absolute quiet was vital. She prayed he understood his life depended on it.

Ian continued to snore as she helped Max to a standing position. She put one finger over her lips and moved her eyes toward Ian on the bed. Max nodded. She took his hand and they began slowly moving toward the door, placing their feet surely and softly.

The door open, Myra was nearly blinded by the bright sunlight. She squinted and paused. There was the office, just across the asphalt. And there was the car, waiting.

Myra closed her eyes. She almost let out a strangled wail of despair. *I don't have the keys! What good is a car without keys?* And with the thought came memory, a clear mental picture of Ian getting out of the car and casually stuffing the ring of keys into his pocket. *The keys are still in his pocket. Shit.*

Myra bit her lip, thinking hard, thinking fast. She looked across the road and saw woods. And the road itself? Well, she had hitchhiked before and could do it again. *But they're probably already out looking for someone who looks like you. There are most likely bulletins on the radio.*

Her reverie, and her inability to come to a decision, were interrupted by a voice behind her. "Going somewhere?"

Before she had a chance to respond to Ian's question, he had taken hold of her hair and yanked her back inside. She screeched, looking up into his rage-filled face, eyes blazing, truly a demon. She let go of Max's hand and screamed, "Run, Max! Run!" She didn't get to see if the little boy did as she told him, if he was running toward the office and safety. Ian pulled her back into the room by her hair and hurtled her against the wall; she slipped and went backward, her head connecting hard with a corner of the bureau. She gasped and shut her eyes, seeing stars. The pain was immediate, intense, and throbbing. There was a trickle of warm wetness at her neck.

But there wasn't time for pain or wondering if she would be all right. Ian was headed out the door. She knew he could take just a few strides and catch up with the boy, swooping him up and bringing him back, where he would not hesitate to plunge the chef's knife right into his heart.

Vision blurry, Myra scrambled to a sitting position and without thinking picked up the lamp on the floor beside her. She yanked its cord from the wall socket and got up on shaky legs. Her stomach heaved; she was afraid she was going to vomit. A voice inside screamed: "No time! No time!"

Myra staggered into the blinding sun and gained on Ian. He was reaching out toward Max, who was only a foot or two out of his grasp. She raised the heavy lamp high and, using all the strength she had, brought it down hard on the back of Ian's head.

He groaned, staggered, and fell, his face slamming into the concrete.

All of this took only seconds. Max stopped to look back, his little head cocked in wonder.

Myra shooed him away. "Go! The office!"

He turned and started toward the glassed-in room, where already the fat redhead was emerging, her eyebrows drawn together in alarm. She held a cordless phone in her hand. "What's going on here?"

Myra didn't answer. She scrambled over to where Ian lay, blood pooling from both his face and the back of his head, and retrieved the keys from his pocket on the very first try.

Bleary-eyed, head pounding, Myra rushed to the car, unlocked it and slid inside, all the while listening to the woman yell, "Listen here, you! What's going on? Don't you go runnin' off!"

With shaking hands, Myra got the key into the ignition, made the engine roar when she pressed down on the gas too hard, threw the car into reverse, then drive, and finally peeled out of the parking lot, glancing into the rearview mirror.

Max stood next to the red-haired woman, both of them looking bewildered; Ian lay on the concrete, inert and bleeding. She hiccupped out a short sob and brought her hand to her mouth.

Gunning the car, she grinned as it picked up speed. Before her, the open road, stretching out to endless possibilities.

She gasped when she looked in the rearview mirror and saw the whirling red and blue lights.

How had they gotten here so fast?

The siren whooped and Myra debated for only a moment whether to try to make a break for it, see if she could outpace the police car. There was no way. No way. She guided the car to the side of the road. Gravel crunched. She placed her head on the steering wheel and, at last, wept.

Chapter
Thirty-two

CASS AWAKENED. SHE hadn't realized when she had fallen asleep, but figured the weariness and the stress must have contributed to such exhaustion that, finally, there was nothing left. Sleep must have come to her like passing out.

She lay in her dim bedroom, sunlight peeking through the slats of the vinyl blinds. Downstairs, she could hear Dani moving about, voices on the radio. Or was it the television? She turned on her side and held her breath. Something was different.

The panic was gone. There was no reason for it to be, but she felt a delicious sense of calm. A voice inside—she wasn't sure it was her own—whispered, "Everything is all right."

She didn't know how she knew, or why, but the peace at her center told her something had changed while she slept. She shot up in bed and cried out, joy infusing her voice, "Max is okay! He's okay!"

She heard the thunder of Dani's footsteps running up the stairs. She paused in the doorway to her room, smiling. "How did you know?"

Cass shook her head, grateful for the intuition and the certainty. She swallowed, nearly shaking with relief and euphoria. "I don't know. Or...I do. I just don't know why. It's over, isn't it?"

Dani nodded and let out a short laugh. She crossed the room and sat down next to her, taking her hands in her own. "Yes. Yes. They've caught them. And Max is okay. Marion Hartley just called. It's all over the news." Dani pulled Cass close, surrounding her in a tight embrace.

Cass wrapped her arms around Dani and squeezed, reveling in the comfort of her solid form. She buried her face in Dani's chest. Dani stroked her hair. "Do you want to hear how it all came about? It's not all pleasant."

Cass moved away. "Not now. I know what's important." She closed her eyes for a moment and an image, almost from nowhere, assailed her: a young blonde woman behind a video camera. She looked into Dani's eyes. "I need to talk to her."

"Who? Marion?" Dani looked bewildered.

"No. The one who took Max."

"I believe she's in hospital, under heavy guard."

Cass stood suddenly, looking around the room for her jeans,

struggling into them and pulling a clean T-shirt over her head. "Come on, we need to go get my son...and then I need to talk to her." She pulled at Dani's hand, impatient. "I have to see her face."

MYRA LAY IN a bed at City Hospital. The back of her head throbbed and the thick wad of bandage there made the pain even more acute. Outside, two uniformed policemen stood guard. They were keeping the press away, but she could hear one or two of them manage to get close and beg for entry.

She had nothing to say to them. She closed her eyes and wished Ian had killed her.

And where *was* Ian?

No one would tell her anything.

A nurse came into the room. She had dark brown hair and the palest of blue eyes. She was pretty and young, like Myra, yet Myra didn't like the distaste she saw on the nurse's face.

"I'm not supposed to do this," the nurse announced, voice quavering. "But I think it's the right thing to do...and I'll take the consequences."

She disappeared, closing the door behind her.

The door reopened a moment later and there she was. Max's mother. Myra was surprised at how small and frail the young mother looked; she remembered her looking stronger in the restaurant, a little bundle of energy. Now her dark hair hung limp and dirty and her eyes simply stared.

Myra bit her lip, trying to force some saliva into her mouth, trying to get her tongue to form around the words, "I'm sorry," but she couldn't say anything.

Cass watched her and didn't, for several minutes, approach the bed.

Myra wondered if she had a weapon concealed somewhere, if this was a set-up and they were going to allow Cass to kill her.

It would be a relief.

Finally, Cass moved toward her. Myra whispered, "I'm a mama, too," and started to cry.

Cass sat down next to her on the bed, smoothed some hair away from Myra's forehead, and looked straight into her eyes.

"Thank you," she whispered. "Thank you."

The End

Also from Rick R. Reed

published by
Quest Books

IM

**The Internet Is the New Meat Market for Gay Men
Now a Killer Is Turning the Meat Market into a Meat Wagon.**

One by one, he's killing them. Lurking in the digital underworld of
Men4HookUpNow.com, he lures, seduces, charms, reaching out through
instant messages to the unwary. He's just another guy.

They invite him over. He's just another trick. Harmless. They're
dead wrong.

When the first bloody body surfaces, openly gay Chicago Police
Department detective Ed Comparetto is called in to investigate.
Sickened by the butchered mess of one of his brothers left on display in
a bathtub, he seeks relief outside where the young man who discovered
the body waits to tell him the story of how he found his friend. But who
is this witness...and did he play a bigger part in the murder than he's
letting on?

For Comparetto, this encounter with a witness is the beginning of a
nightmare. Because this witness did more than just show up at the scene
of the crime; he set the scene. And maybe, he's more than just a
killer...maybe he's dead himself. Comparetto is on a journey to discover
the truth, a truth that he needs to discover before he loses his career, his
boyfriend, his sanity...his life. Because in this killer's world, **IM doesn't
stand for instant message...it stands for instant murder.**

"IM is not for the faint-hearted, but is highly recommended
for all those who enjoy horror a la *Silence of the Lambs*. If you
enjoy a bit of gore, a tense thriller, and well-crafted characters,
you'll be utterly captivated by this book."
~Lori L. Lake, *Midwest Book Review*

ISBN 1-932300-79-6
978-1-932300-79-1

Available at booksellers everywhere.

In the Blood

What Would You Give Up for Immortal Life and Love?

By day, Elise draws and paints, spilling out the horrific visions of her tortured mind. By night, she walks the streets, selling her body to the highest bidder.

And then *they* come into her life: a trio of impossibly beautiful vampires: Terence, Maria, and Edward. When they encounter Elise, they set an explosive triangle in motion. Terence wants to drain her blood. Maria just wants Elise...as lover and partner through eternity. And Edward, the most recently-converted, wants to prevent her from making the same mistake he made as a young abstract expressionist artist in 1950s Greenwich Village: sacrificing his artistic vision for immortal life. He is the only one of them still human enough to realize what an unholy trade this is.

In the Blood is a novel that will grip you in a vise of suspense that won't let go, forcing you to stay up long past midnight, turning page after page, until the very last moment, when a surprising turn of events changes everything and demonstrates, truly, what love and sacrifice are all about.

"In the Blood is a pulsing, vividly pictorial novel of emotions offered in the unique exploration into the lives of vampires...a great read throughout."
~Lea Schizas, Award-winning author of *The Rock of Realm*

ISBN 1-932300-90-2
978-1-932300-90-1

Available at booksellers everywhere.

FORTHCOMING TITLES

published by
Quest Books

Land of Entrapment
by Andi Marquette

K.C. Fontero left Albuquerque for Texas in the wake of a bitter break-up, headed for a teaching and research post-doc at the University of Texas, Austin. With a doctorate in sociology and expertise in American white supremacist groups, she's well on her way to an established academic life. But the past has a way of catching up with you and as K.C. spends a summer helping her grandfather on his central Texas farm, her past shows up in the form of her ex, Melissa Crown, an Albuquerque lawyer who left K.C. for another woman three years earlier.

Melissa's younger sister Megan has gone missing—she's hooked up with a man Melissa suspects is part of an underground white supremacist group and Melissa needs K.C.'s help to find her and hopefully bring her out of the movement. K.C. knows she has the knowledge and contacts to track the group. She knows that in the interests of public service, she'd be helping law enforcement, as well. What she doesn't know is how far into her past she'll have to go in order to find not only Megan, but herself as well.

Working to locate the group without alerting members' suspicions, K.C. finds herself drawn to Megan's friend and neighbor, Sage Crandall, a photographer who challenges K.C.'s attempts to keep her heart ensconced in the safety of research and analysis. Confronted with her growing feelings for Sage while unraveling her complicated past with Melissa, K.C. delves into the racist and apocalyptic beliefs of the mysterious group, but the deeper she goes, the greater the danger she faces.

Available July 2008

OTHER QUEST PUBLICATIONS

About the Author

Rick R. Reed's published novels include *IM, In the Blood, A Face Without a Heart, Penance,* and *Obsessed.* Short fiction has appeared in numerous anthologies, the most horrific of which is collected in *Twisted: Tales of Obsession and Terror.* He lives in Miami with his partner and is at work on another novel. Visit him online at www.rickrreed.com.

VISIT US ONLINE AT
www.regalcrest.biz

At the Regal Crest Website You'll Find

- The latest news about forthcoming titles and new releases

- Our complete backlist of romance, mystery, thriller and adventure titles

- Information about your favorite authors

- Current bestsellers

- Media tearsheets to print and take with you when you shop

Regal Crest titles are available from all progressive booksellers and online at StarCrossed Productions, (www.scp-inc.biz), or at www.amazon.com, www.bamm.com, www.barnesandnoble.com, and many others.